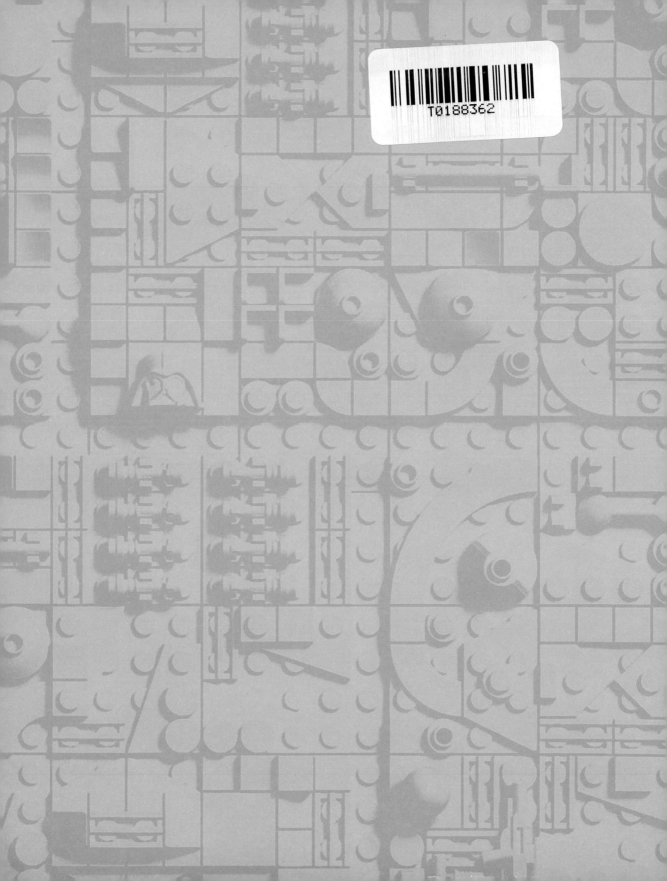

CHARACTER ENCYCLOPEDIA
NEW EDITION

WRITTEN BY ELIZABETH DOWSETT

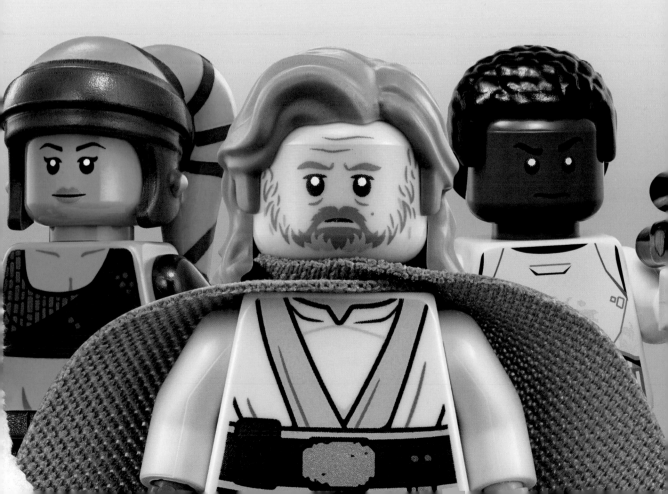

Contents
MEET THE MINIFIGURES

Key to abbreviations in Data Files

I: *Star Wars*™: Episode I: *The Phantom Menace*
II: *Star Wars*: Episode II: *Attack of the Clones*
CW: *Star Wars*: *The Clone Wars*
III: *Star Wars*: Episode III: *Revenge of the Sith*
S: *Solo: A Star Wars Story*
Reb: *Star Wars Rebels*
RO: *Rogue One: A Star Wars Story*
IV: *Star Wars*: Episode IV: *A New Hope*
V: *Star Wars*: Episode V: *The Empire Strikes Back*
VI: *Star Wars*: Episode VI: *Return of the Jedi*

Res: *Star Wars: Resistance*
VII: *Star Wars*: Episode VII: *The Force Awakens*
VIII: *Star Wars*: Episode VIII: *The Last Jedi*
IX: *Star Wars*: Episode IX: *The Rise of Skywalker*
L: *Star Wars* Legends (In this book, "Legends" is classed as anything that falls outside the official *Star Wars* galaxy. This includes original LEGO® creations and anything related to the original *Star Wars* Expanded Universe.)
M: *Star Wars: The Mandalorian*

Maverick Jedi Master Qui-Gon Jinn has appeared in eleven LEGO® *Star Wars*™ sets since 1999. There are seven slightly different Qui-Gon minifigures. Each one appears in his Jedi robes and tunic, ready to undertake a mission for the Jedi Order. Most variants wear a cape and they all have either his distinctive brown hair or a brown hood, which helps him keep a low profile.

STAR VARIANTS

First Qui-Gon
With a yellow head and hands, this Qui-Gon has a cape but no hood. He dates from 1999 and stars in five LEGO *Star Wars* sets.

Submarine hero
This Qui-Gon travels in the 2012 Gungan Sub (set 9499). His head is printed with an aquatic rebreather to travel to the underwater city of Otoh Gunga.

Head Poncho
In 2015, Qui-Gon acquired a poncho over his Jedi robes. Perhaps it helps him evade Darth Maul in Sith Infiltrator (set 75096).

Unique head is printed with brown sideburns, mustache, and beard with gray flecks

Distinctive hair piece was created in 2011 and is unique to Qui-Gon

Qui-Gon Jinn
JEDI MASTER

Torso with Jedi tunic and utility belt was updated in 2011

Qui-Gon is the only minifigure to have brown legs printed with a Jedi tunic

DATA FILE

YEAR: 2017
FIRST SET: 75169
Duel on Naboo
NO. OF SETS: 1
PIECES: 4
ACCESSORIES:
Green lightsaber
APPEARANCES: 1

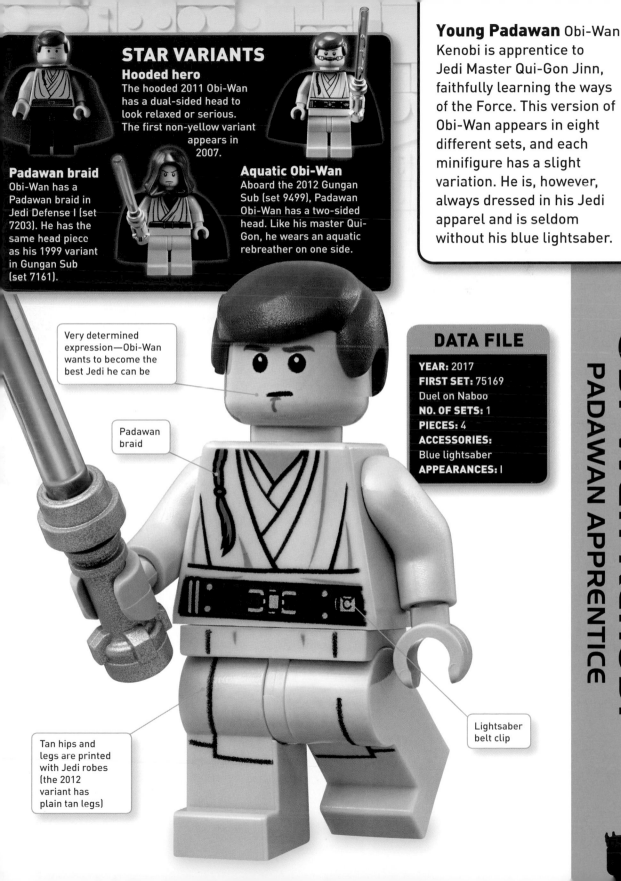

Hooded hero
The hooded 2011 Obi-Wan has a dual-sided head to look relaxed or serious. The first non-yellow variant appears in 2007.

Padawan braid
Obi-Wan has a Padawan braid in Jedi Defense I (set 7203). He has the same head piece as his 1999 variant in Gungan Sub (set 7161).

Aquatic Obi-Wan
Aboard the 2012 Gungan Sub (set 9499), Padawan Obi-Wan has a two-sided head. Like his master Qui-Gon, he wears an aquatic rebreather on one side.

Young Padawan Obi-Wan Kenobi is apprentice to Jedi Master Qui-Gon Jinn, faithfully learning the ways of the Force. This version of Obi-Wan appears in eight different sets, and each minifigure has a slight variation. He is, however, always dressed in his Jedi apparel and is seldom without his blue lightsaber.

Very determined expression—Obi-Wan wants to become the best Jedi he can be

Padawan braid

Tan hips and legs are printed with Jedi robes (the 2012 variant has plain tan legs)

DATA FILE
YEAR: 2017
FIRST SET: 75169
Duel on Naboo
NO. OF SETS: 1
PIECES: 4
ACCESSORIES:
Blue lightsaber
APPEARANCES: I

Lightsaber belt clip

Obi-Wan Kenobi
PADAWAN APPRENTICE

Protocol droids are among the smartest droids in the LEGO *Star Wars* galaxy. They assist their masters with everything from general secretarial duties to complex tactical planning and spy detection. Many protocol droids prove invaluable to their masters— K-3PO, for example, was promoted to lieutenant in the rebel army for his exceptional work.

Chrome coating on LEGO elements is very rare, particularly on minifigures

Female droid
Most protocol droids are programmed to be male. TC-14 is an exception. She works for the Trade Federation Viceroy Nute Gunray. She distracts Qui-Gon Jinn and Obi-Wan Kenobi, who are disguised as Republic ambassadors, while Gunray tries to gas them.

Protocol Droids
HUMANOID HELPERS

DATA FILE
NAME: TC-14
YEAR: 2012
FIRST SET: 5000063 TC-14
NO. OF SETS: 1
PIECES: 3
ACCESSORIES: None
APPEARANCES: I

Red coloring matches the robes of TC-4's master, Chancellor Palpatine

Chrome silver leg piece is found only on one other minifigure— a silver stormtrooper

Mechanical elements and wires extend to the back of the torso

Unique leg printing shows metal plating

DATA FILE
NAME: TC-4
YEAR: 2014
FIRST SET: 5002122 TC-4
NO. OF SETS: 1
PIECES: 3
ACCESSORIES: None
APPEARANCES: I

R-3PO performs his spying duties by closely observing others with his photoreceptors

Distinctive red protocol droid armor

Face and torso pieces have much more detailed printing than K-3PO's previous minifigure from 2007. It appears in Hoth Rebel Base (set 7666)

Plate pattern

Two red dots identify K-3PO as a rebel lieutenant

Gunmetal gray minifigure pieces

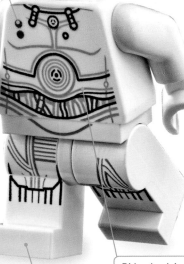

Ridged pelvic armor plate

K-3PO's armor is all-white—perfect camouflage on the icy planet of Hoth

Protocol Droids
HUMANOID HELPERS

Bumbling Gungan Jar Jar Binks broke the LEGO mold as the first minifigure ever to have a personalized head sculpt. He found his way into five Episode I sets in 1999–2000. Then in 2011, he made a comeback with printing added to his head-mold to give him a new look, which was included in three more sets.

STAR VARIANT
Early Jar Jar
The first LEGO Jar Jar Binks has a very similar head-mold to the 2011 design except for one thing: his eye stalks are split to depict his eyes. On the 2011 design, Jar Jar's eye stalks are flat and he has printed eyes.

Protruding eyes are molded and printed

Mottled skin is good for camouflage

Amphibious ears
Jar Jar's distinctive floppy ears (called haillus) are integrated into his head-mold and have a mottled pattern.

Jar Jar is an outcast from his people and lives alone in the swamps, so his clothing is dirty and ragged

Torso design was new for 2011. The pattern continues on Jar Jar's back

2011 Jar Jar's arms and hands have peach flesh tones, while the original has lighter tan arms and hands

DATA FILE

YEAR: 2011
FIRST SET: 7929
The Battle of Naboo
NO. OF SETS: 3
PIECES: 3
ACCESSORIES: Cesta, shield/harpoon
APPEARANCES: I, II, CW, III

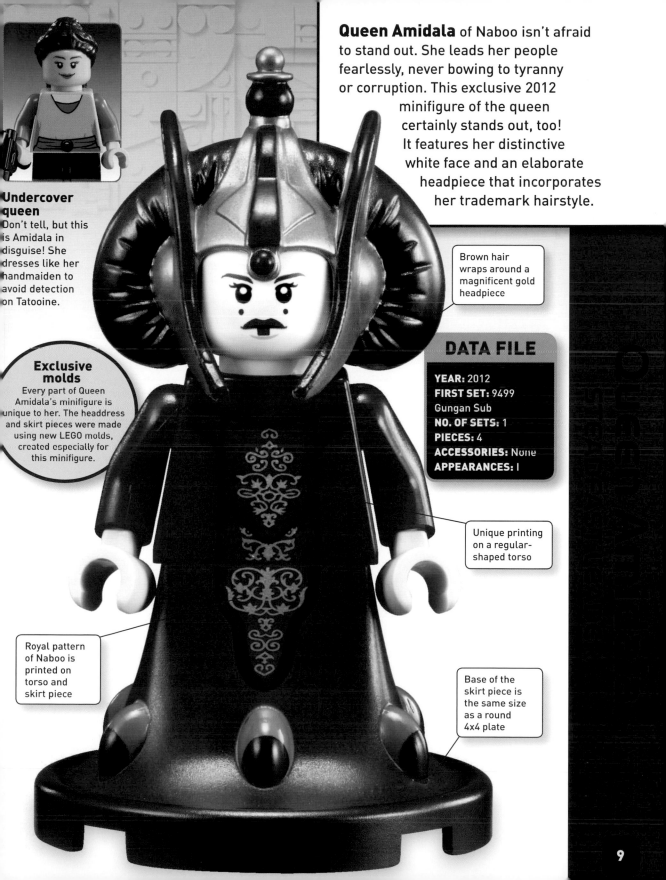

Queen Amidala of Naboo isn't afraid to stand out. She leads her people fearlessly, never bowing to tyranny or corruption. This exclusive 2012 minifigure of the queen certainly stands out, too! It features her distinctive white face and an elaborate headpiece that incorporates her trademark hairstyle.

Undercover queen
Don't tell, but this is Amidala in disguise! She dresses like her handmaiden to avoid detection on Tatooine.

Exclusive molds
Every part of Queen Amidala's minifigure is unique to her. The headdress and skirt pieces were made using new LEGO molds, created especially for this minifigure.

Brown hair wraps around a magnificent gold headpiece

DATA FILE
YEAR: 2012
FIRST SET: 9499 Gungan Sub
NO. OF SETS: 1
PIECES: 4
ACCESSORIES: None
APPEARANCES: 1

Unique printing on a regular-shaped torso

Royal pattern of Naboo is printed on torso and skirt piece

Base of the skirt piece is the same size as a round 4x4 plate

Young Anakin Skywalker may be just a boy, but he can handle a podracer like no one else! This minifigure made his podracing debut in 1999 and has since sped into 12 sets with seven versions. He changes from ordinary boy to a podracing supremo or unexpected Naboo starfighter pilot.

Anakin's Podracer—20th Anniversary Edition (set 75258)

To mark 20 years since the beginning of the LEGO *Star Wars* theme, Anakin races in the Boonta Eve Classic podrace in a special reissue of Anakin's Podracer (set 7131).

The original Anakin minifigure in 1999 wore a dark-gray helmet with light-gray goggles

DATA FILE

YEAR: 2019
FIRST SET: 75223
Naboo Starfighter Microfighter
NO. OF SETS: 2
PIECES: 5
ACCESSORIES: Wrench
APPEARANCES: I

STAR VARIANT

Short stuff

The young Anakin minifigure was one of the first to try out shorter legs. The first variant seen with them is in Naboo N-1 Starfighter with Vulture Droid (set 7660) in 2007.

Rare racer

This early variant is exclusive to Naboo Fighter (set 7141) from 1999. A similar variant with a gray helmet appears in three 1999–2000 sets.

Necklace given to Anakin by his mother

Anakin wears a simple tunic with a brown belt on Tatooine. His clothing can be seen on the back of his torso, too

The shorter LEGO legs do not have a movable hip joint like regular legs

Podrace face

One side of Anakin's 2011 face has goggles and a determined look. He's ready to podrace!

Anakin Skywalker PODRACER

STAR VARIANT

The original
The star of 14 sets from 1999 to 2008, the first R2-D2 has a white head with printing just around the top.

Barge2-D2
R2-D2 is forced to serve drinks from a tray in two sets both called Jabba's Sail Barge (sets 6210 and 75020).

Bogged down
In 2018, R2-D2 is spattered with mud from Dagobah's swamps in Yoda's Hut (set 75208).

Festive astromech
In the 2012 Advent Calender (set 9509) R2-D2 turns into a snowman. In 2015 (set 75097) he wears reindeer antlers on his head.

Brave astromech droid R2-D2 has ventured into 47 sets to date, making him the figure with the most appearances in LEGO *Star Wars* history! Excluding novelties, R2-D2 has had six head pieces and three bodies, used in different combinations. In 2009 he got a cartoon-style design for *Star Wars: The Clone Wars* with a simpler body and more elongated head print.

This latest head features a red light instead of a lavender one

Holoprojector transmits holographic images and acts as a spotlight

This gray head piece is from 2016. Others were released in 1999, 2008, 2009, and 2014

This torso with dark-blue ink is from 2014. The 1999 variant and the 2009 Clone Wars variant both have bright blue

DATA FILE

YEAR: 2016
FIRST SET: 75136 Droid Escape Pod
NO. OF SETS: 10
PIECES: 4
ACCESSORIES: None
APPEARANCES: I, II, CW, III, Reb, RO, IV, V, VI, VII, VIII, IX

LEGO® Technic pins join legs to his body

All R2-D2 variants have the same white leg pieces with wide treads

As **Grand Master** of the Jedi Order, Yoda is the most respected Jedi in the LEGO *Star Wars* galaxy, despite his small size. Though Yoda's minifigure is dressed in the traditional tan robes of a Jedi, he is easily recognizable by his short legs, unique head sculpt, and sand-green or olive-green skin.

STAR VARIANT
Christmas, it is
This exclusive Santa Yoda minifigure appears behind the final door of the 2011 LEGO *Star Wars* Advent Calendar (set 7958). He carries a backpack full of presents and a stick and has a candy cane tucked into his belt.

Standard size LEGO lightsaber even though Yoda is smaller than most Jedi

Yoda's head is made of rubber instead of the harder plastic usually used for LEGO pieces

Going white
Three of Yoda's Clone Wars heads feature a clumpy cloud of hair. Two are white; one is gray.

Torso shows glimpse of green skin at the neck

Yoda's unique torso piece has detailed folds as well as a Jedi hood printed on the back

DATA FILE
YEAR: 2016
FIRST SET: 75142
Homing Spider Droid
NO. OF SETS: 3
PIECES: 3
ACCESSORIES:
Green lightsaber
APPEARANCES: I, II, CW, III, V, VI, VIII

Yoda was the first LEGO minifigure to have short, unposable legs

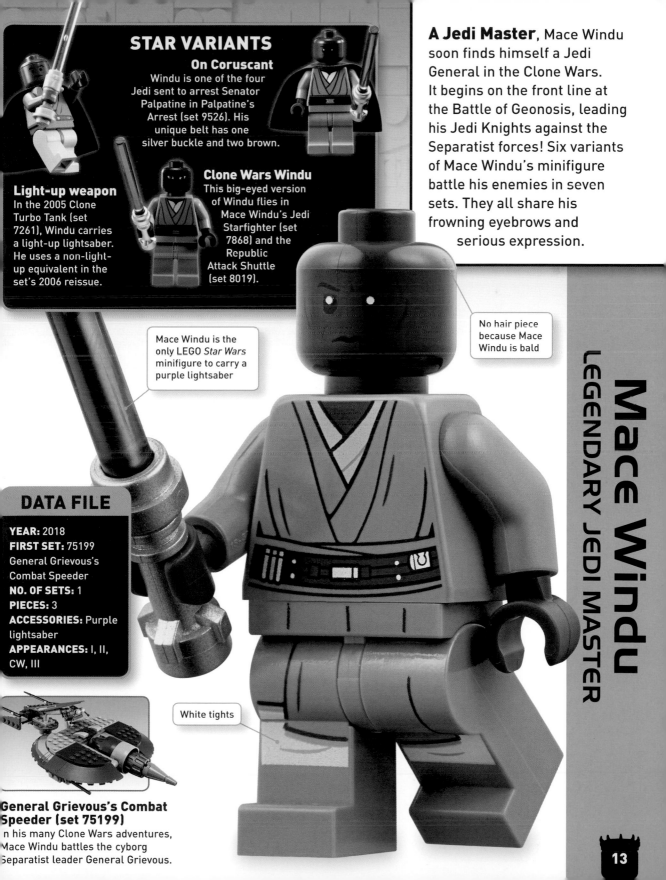

On Coruscant
Windu is one of the four Jedi sent to arrest Senator Palpatine in Palpatine's Arrest (set 9526). His unique belt has one silver buckle and two brown.

Light-up weapon
In the 2005 Clone Turbo Tank (set 7261), Windu carries a light-up lightsaber. He uses a non-light-up equivalent in the set's 2006 reissue.

Clone Wars Windu
This big-eyed version of Windu flies in Mace Windu's Jedi Starfighter (set 7868) and the Republic Attack Shuttle (set 8019).

A Jedi Master, Mace Windu soon finds himself a Jedi General in the Clone Wars. It begins on the front line at the Battle of Geonosis, leading his Jedi Knights against the Separatist forces! Six variants of Mace Windu's minifigure battle his enemies in seven sets. They all share his frowning eyebrows and serious expression.

No hair piece because Mace Windu is bald

Mace Windu is the only LEGO *Star Wars* minifigure to carry a purple lightsaber

DATA FILE

YEAR: 2018
FIRST SET: 75199 General Grievous's Combat Speeder
NO. OF SETS: 1
PIECES: 3
ACCESSORIES: Purple lightsaber
APPEARANCES: I, II, CW, III

White tights

General Grievous's Combat Speeder (set 75199)
In his many Clone Wars adventures, Mace Windu battles the cyborg Separatist leader General Grievous.

Mace Windu
LEGENDARY JEDI MASTER

Although all battle droids are structurally identical and made from the same LEGO pieces, specialist battle droids are fitted with a colored torso to identify their function. Super Battle Droids are stronger versions with their own special pieces. All of these droids are found in select LEGO sets where their specific skills are required.

DATA FILE

NAME: Battle droid
YEAR: 2007
FIRST SET: 7662 Trade Federation MTT
NO. OF SETS: 26
PIECES: 5
ACCESSORIES: Blaster
APPEARANCES: I, II, CW, III, Reb

Specially molded head-and-body piece

Regular infantry battle droids have plain tan torsos

Blaster

DATA FILE

NAME: Super battle droid
YEAR: 2007
FIRST SET: 7654 Droids Battle Pack
NO. OF SETS: 12
PIECES: 4
ACCESSORIES: None
APPEARANCES: II, CW

Leg piece is unique to LEGO *Star Wars*. It is also found on the MagnaGuard, the TX-20 tactical droid, and the commando droid

DATA FILE

NAME: Battle droid commander
YEAR: 2008
FIRST SET: 7670 Hailfire Droid & Spider Droid
NO. OF SETS: 2
PIECES: 5
ACCESSORIES: Blaster
APPEARANCES: I, II, CW, III, Reb

Yellow coloring is used on three variants of the clone commander

Into battle
Yellow coloring on the chest signifies that this droid is a battle droid commander. One commander, OOM-9, was responsible for leading the entire battle droid army at the Battle of the Great Grass Plains.

Head and neck are a single piece that clips into the torso

Battle colors
Specialist battle droids have had varying amounts of color on their torsos since their first release in 2000. The earliest variants have mostly tan torsos with only small patches of color, while others have full-color torsos.

DATA FILE

NAME: Security battle droid
YEAR: 2014
FIRST SET: 75044 Droid Tri-Fighter
NO. OF SETS: 1
PIECES: 5
ACCESSORIES: Blaster
APPEARANCES: I, CW, III

Red markings feature on all four variants of the security battle droid

Molded head piece is found only in LEGO *Star Wars* sets

DATA FILE

NAME: Battle droid pilot
YEAR: 2011
FIRST SET: 7958 LEGO *Star Wars* Advent Calendar (2011)
NO. OF SETS: 6
PIECES: 5
ACCESSORIES: Blaster
APPEARANCES: I, II, CW, III

Green markings for camouflage on Kashyyyk

Blue markings identify the battle droid pilot

One hand is at right angles; the other is straight

DATA FILE

NAME: Kashyyyk battle droid
YEAR: 2019
FIRST SET: 75233 Droid Gunship
NO. OF SETS: 2
PIECES: 5
ACCESSORIES: Blaster
APPEARANCES: CW

Made to match
All these battle droids are designed to look like their Geonosian creators—with elongated limbs and faces. LEGO *Star Wars* battle droids resemble their movie counterparts by putting extra emphasis on these features.

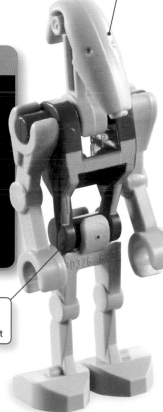

Battle Droids
METAL SOLDIERS

Darth Maul is the Sith apprentice of Darth Sidious. He lurks in the shadows, waiting for his chance to attack the Jedi! Maul's minifigures appear in 12 LEGO *Star Wars* sets. His horned Zabrak head mold is a ring-shaped piece created in 2011. It is worn by all of Maul's minifigures apart from those with a hood.

Surprise Maul
Maul was thought dead, but he reappears with mechanical legs. He gets a LEGO pair in Mandalorian Speeder (set 75022).

STAR VARIANTS

The eyes have it
Early Maul minifigures have regular LEGO heads printed with Nightbrother tattoos and yellow eyes. This 1999 variant from Sith Infiltrator (set 7663) has black pupils and different face patterns.

Merry Sithmas
The 2012 LEGO *Star Wars* Advent Calendar came with a Santa Maul. He wears a red cape with a fur-lined hood, and has a candy cane printed on the back of his torso.

Darth Maul is a Nightbrother from Dathomir. His eyes have turned yellow from studying the dark side

Double-bladed lightsaber

Black Sith robes

Darth Maul
SITH APPRENTICE

DATA FILE
YEAR: 2017
FIRST SET: 75169 Duel on Naboo
NO. OF SETS: 2
PIECES: 4
ACCESSORIES: Double-bladed red lightsaber
APPEARANCES: I, CW

STAR VARIANT
Headsetted hero
Two yellow-faced Jedi Knight Obi-Wan minifigures were released in 2002. He wears a headset to pilot the Jedi Starfighter (set 7143), but is without one in Bounty Hunter Pursuit (set 7133).

A skilled Jedi Knight, Obi-Wan Kenobi is focused and controlled at a time of turmoil in the LEGO *Star Wars* galaxy. Four variants of his minifigure star in sets where he must pursue dangerous bounty hunters—Jango Fett and Zam Wesell. The third Jedi Knight Obi-Wan faces super battle droids on Geonosis in the Republic Gunship (set 75021) in 2013.

Most Jedi Knights wear their hair long

Dual-sided head with a headset for flying (the other side looks more alarmed)

Jedi Starfighter with hyperdrive (set 75191)
The fourth variant of Obi-Wan's Jedi Knight minifigure can jump into hyperspace in his Jedi Starfighter when it docks into its separate hyperdrive ring.

Obi-Wan wears three layers of Jedi robes

Utility belt for Jedi essentials

DATA FILE
YEAR: 2017
FIRST SET: 75191 Jedi Starfighter with Hyperdrive
NO. OF SETS: 1
PIECES: 4
ACCESSORIES: Blue lightsaber
APPEARANCES: 11

Shared hair
Obi-Wan Kenobi's long Jedi Knight hair is a standard LEGO hair piece for both male and female minifigures. It is used in eight different colors, including Obi-Wan's dark orange.

17

Headstrong Padawan Anakin Skywalker is training under his more cautious mentor Obi-Wan Kenobi. The minifigure has broken away from Jedi tradition by wearing a torso piece with dark Jedi robes. Also, Anakin's expression is hard to read. These things could suggest a darkness within him that he cannot control.

Anakin Skywalker
JEDI PADAWAN

Dual-sided head has printed cheekbones on both sides—the reverse side has a grimace

Fire power
Exclusive to Republic Gunship (set 75021), Padawan Anakin sits inside the cockpit of one of the starship's four ball gun turrets. Now all he has to do is aim and fire!

Brown Jedi robes worn with a utility belt—the printing continues on the back

Green lightsaber with chrome hilt was given to Anakin in the Petranaki Arena

DATA FILE

YEAR: 2013
FIRST SET: 75021 Republic Gunship
NO. OF SETS: 2
PIECES: 4
ACCESSORIES: Green lightsaber/blue lightsaber
APPEARANCES: 11

STAR VARIANTS

Original Jango
The 2002 Jango has a black head. One side has a face print that can be worn with a hair piece. His jetpack and helmet are a single piece.

Santa's bounty
Jango wears red for his Santa variant in the 2013 LEGO *Star Wars* Advent Calendar (set 75023). He has presents tucked into his belt and holly on his chest.

Bounty hunter Jango Fett keeps a low profile in the LEGO *Star Wars* galaxy, being in just four sets since 2002. He had a redesign in 2013 and got new print details in 2017. Although his Mandalorian armor inspired the clone armor, his minifigure is made up of many unique LEGO pieces that make him as legendary as the man himself.

Silver helmet with antenna, first used in 2013, has a printed T-visor. (The 2002 variant is open at the front)

Angry hunter
Between 2013 and 2017, Jango's mood and temper deteriorate. His previously smiling face now snarls.

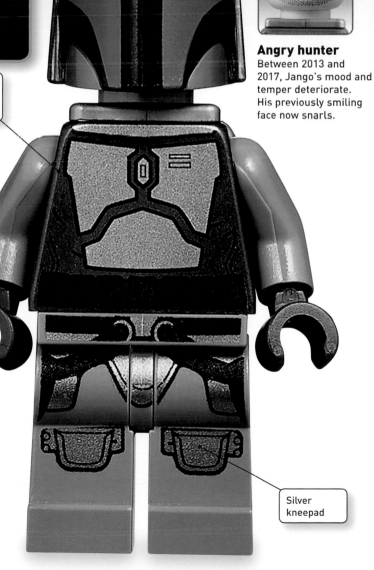

Torso piece with silver Mandalorian armor plates

DATA FILE

YEAR: 2017
FIRST SET: 75191 Jedi Starfighter with Hyperdrive
NO. OF SETS: 1
PIECES: 6
ACCESSORIES: Twin blasters, jetpack
APPEARANCES: II

ocket power
ango's silver JT-12C jetpack
ith a built-in missile launcher)
so comes in the 2013 LEGO
ar Wars Advent Calendar, but
anta Jango does not wear it. It
ves a boost to a sleigh instead.

Silver kneepad

This determined young clone will one day become a great bounty hunter, but for now he is learning combat skills under the guardianship of his father, Jango. Three young Boba minifigures appear alongside Jango, all with short LEGO legs. He first arrived in 2002. He had a remake for the 2013 LEGO *Star Wars* Advent Calendar (set 75023), and he returned in 2017 with a new design.

STAR VARIANT
Boy Boba
Exclusive to Jango Fett's *Slave I* (set 7153) in 2002, the first young Boba has a yellow face with a serious look. His printed torso piece is unique to this variant.

Boba Fett
YOUNG CLONE

Boba shares this hair piece with Ezra Bridger, Kylo Ren, and Baze Malbus, but he had it first

Boba's malicious smile is drawn in the cartoon-style used for many *Star Wars: The Clone Wars* minifigures

This uniform is worn by all young clones studying on Kamino

DATA FILE

YEAR: 2017
FIRST SET: 75191
Jedi Starfighter with Hyperdrive
NO. OF SETS: 1
PIECES: 4
ACCESSORIES: None
APPEARANCES: II, CW

Half-size legs and torso are paler than on the bright blue 2013 variant

This fearsome Tusken Raider is part of a fierce nomadic species native to Tatooine. The mysterious minifigure can move almost invisibly through dusty desert dunes dressed in his beige sandshroud. His unique LEGO head and torso pieces are adapted to help him survive in Tatooine's intense heat.

STAR VARIANT

Color change

Exclusive to Tusken Raider Encounter (set 7113), released in 2002, this variant has unique head and torso pieces. Some Tusken Raiders were released with tan hips, but most have these gray hips.

Gaffi stick is a traditional weapon favored by Tusken Raiders and is made from salvaged scrap

Leg printing depicts the Tusken Raider's flowing robes

Eye goggles offer protection from the harsh desert sun

Bandages keep the Tusken Raider cool

LEGO torso, with a moisture trap around the neck, was created in 2015 and reused in 2017 and 2018

This variant features tan hand pieces rather than the original gray ones

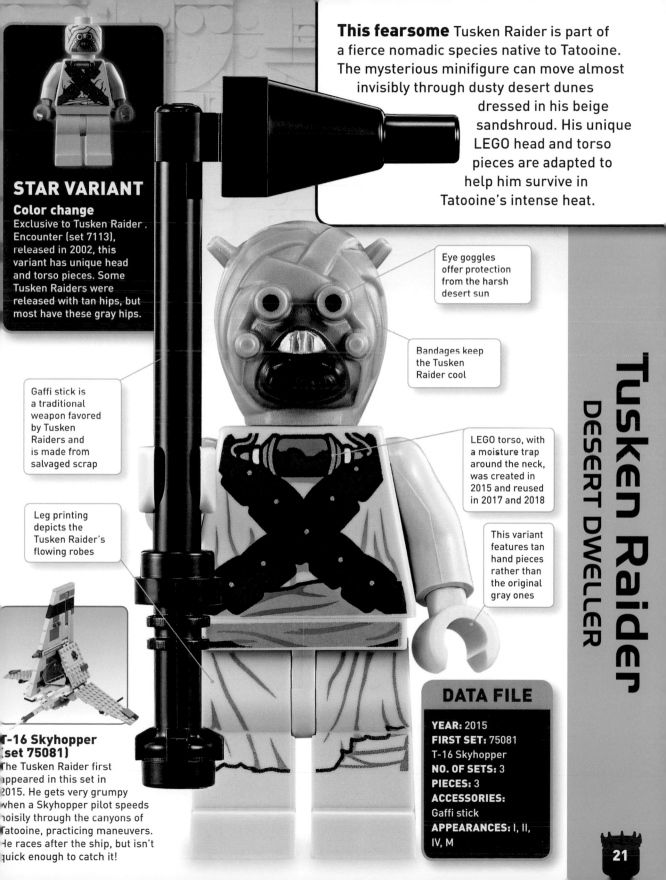

T-16 Skyhopper (set 75081)

The Tusken Raider first appeared in this set in 2015. He gets very grumpy when a Skyhopper pilot speeds noisily through the canyons of Tatooine, practicing maneuvers. He races after the ship, but isn't quick enough to catch it!

Tusken Raider
DESERT DWELLER

DATA FILE

YEAR: 2015
FIRST SET: 75081
T-16 Skyhopper
NO. OF SETS: 3
PIECES: 3
ACCESSORIES:
Gaffi stick
APPEARANCES: I, II, IV, M

21

Accustomed to a life of privilege on Naboo, Padmé swiftly adapts to a life of action when she sides with the Jedi and finds herself on the run from the Trade Federation. With her hair in a bun and her top ripped, this version of Padmé is dressed as she was when she came face to face with the nexu beast in the Geonosian arena. There are six Padmé variants, including this Tatooine version and one in full royal regalia.

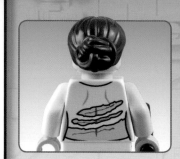

Battle scars
Padmé's back is printed with scratch marks from her run-in with the nexu. The vicious catlike beast is used in an attempt to assassinate Padmé in the Geonosian Arena. She escapes its clutches, but not without a few wounds!

Rescued by reinforcements
This Padmé minifigure appears with Jedi Knight Obi-Wan Kenobi and Padawan Anakin in the third LEGO *Star Wars* version of the Republic Gunship (set 75021), released in 2013.

Padmé Amidala
ROYAL ON THE RUN

Dual-sided head with two beauty spots

One of Padmé's sleeves has been torn off in battle

Padmé comes armed with a blaster, based on the BlasTech E-11 rifle

Top torn by the nexu beast

DATA FILE
YEAR: 2013
FIRST SET: 75021 Republic Gunship
NO. OF SETS: 1
PIECES: 4
ACCESSORIES: Blaster
APPEARANCES: 11

STAR VARIANT

Brainy battler

Ki-Adi-Mundi enters the fray in 2011. He has plain brown pants, fewer clothes ruffles, and a *Clone Wars*-style face print.

Ki-Adi-Mundi is a Jedi from the planet Cerea. Highly intelligent, he is a member of the Jedi Council and a top Jedi General. He has a specially designed additional head piece to house his extremely large Cerean brain. His first minifigure fought a Geonosian Starfighter (set 7959) and his second returned for more battles in 2018.

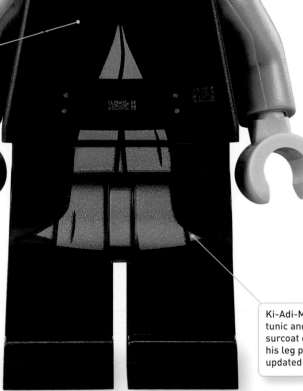

Cerean head

Ki-Adi-Mundi's Cerean head is topped with a white ponytail. Each of his minifigures has a binary brain piece with creases down the back. They continue as printed lines on the head piece.

Ki-Adi-Mundi's large binary brain makes him logical and a skilled tactician. (He has a second heart just to support his big brain)

Long vest is styled on ancient Cerean clothing

Ki-Adi-Mundi's tan tunic and dark surcoat continue on his leg piece in this updated variant

Ki-Adi-Mundi
JEDI TACTICIAN

DATA FILE

YEAR: 2018
FIRST SET: 75206
Jedi and Clone Trooper Battle Pack
NO. OF SETS: 1
PIECES: 4
ACCESSORIES:
Blue lightsaber
APPEARANCES: II, CW, III

23

This experienced Jedi is a wise negotiator, but he can be masterful with a lightsaber when needed. Released as part of the 2013 AT-TE (set 75019), the minifigure has a unique head mold on a new Jedi body. There have been many Jedi minifigures before, but this is the first Coleman Trebor.

AT-TE (set 75019)
There are five minifigures in this 2013 set. As well as Coleman himself, there is fellow Jedi Master Mace Windu, a clone commander, and two battle droids.

Rubbery head with a large crest and printed eyes

Vurk
Jedi Trebor is a Vurk from the oceanic planet of Sembla. He is the only Vurk to appear as a minifigure. His head, with its distinctive reptilian crest, is a dark bluish-gray color.

This is the only Jedi torso to have dark bluish-gray skin

Reddish-brown belt carries food and energy capsules

These tan Jedi robe legs also appear on four Obi-Wan Kenobi minifigures

DATA FILE

YEAR: 2013
FIRST SET: 75019 AT-TE
NO. OF SETS: 1
PIECES: 3
ACCESSORIES: Green lightsaber
APPEARANCES: II

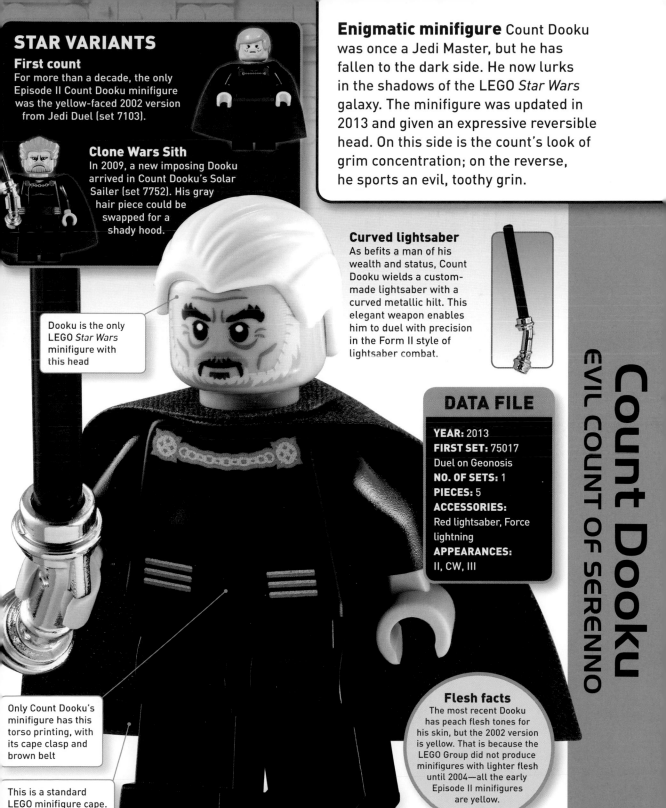

STAR VARIANTS

First count

For more than a decade, the only Episode II Count Dooku minifigure was the yellow-faced 2002 version from Jedi Duel (set 7103).

Clone Wars Sith

In 2009, a new imposing Dooku arrived in Count Dooku's Solar Sailer (set 7752). His gray hair piece could be swapped for a shady hood.

Enigmatic minifigure Count Dooku was once a Jedi Master, but he has fallen to the dark side. He now lurks in the shadows of the LEGO *Star Wars* galaxy. The minifigure was updated in 2013 and given an expressive reversible head. On this side is the count's look of grim concentration; on the reverse, he sports an evil, toothy grin.

Dooku is the only LEGO *Star Wars* minifigure with this head

Curved lightsaber

As befits a man of his wealth and status, Count Dooku wields a custom-made lightsaber with a curved metallic hilt. This elegant weapon enables him to duel with precision in the Form II style of lightsaber combat.

DATA FILE

YEAR: 2013
FIRST SET: 75017
Duel on Geonosis
NO. OF SETS: 1
PIECES: 5
ACCESSORIES:
Red lightsaber, Force lightning
APPEARANCES:
II, CW, III

Only Count Dooku's minifigure has this torso printing, with its cape clasp and brown belt

This is a standard LEGO minifigure cape. It acts as a symbol of Dooku's prestige as Count of Serenno

Flesh facts

The most recent Dooku has peach flesh tones for his skin, but the 2002 version is yellow. That is because the LEGO Group did not produce minifigures with lighter flesh until 2004—all the early Episode II minifigures are yellow.

Archduke of Geonosis and one of the leading members of the Separatist Council, Poggle the Lesser makes for an imposing minifigure. Although he resembles previous Geonosian minifigures, Poggle's head piece and elaborate printing make him stand out from the rest. He appears in just one LEGO set, carrying his staff and a hologram of the Death Star plans.

Duel on Geonosis (set 75017)
Poggle is found only in this 2013 LEGO set. While Count Dooku battles Yoda in his secret Geonosis hangar, cowardly Poggle lurks in the background.

Poggle the Lesser
ARCHDUKE OF GEONOSIS

DATA FILE

YEAR: 2013
FIRST SET: 75017
Duel on Geonosis
NO. OF SETS: 1
PIECES: 4
ACCESSORIES:
Death Star hologram
APPEARANCES:
II, CW, III

Crownlike head crest is a sign of high status

Long wattles are a sign of Poggle's age and status

A single transparent, printed wing piece sits between the head and torso

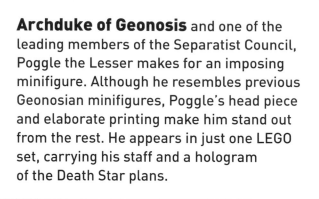

Secret plans
Poggle's minifigure holds an orange hologram of the Geonosian-designed Death Star.

Geonosian exoskeleton printing continues on lower back of torso

Intricate gold and black details are symbols of royalty

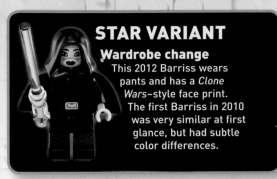
Young Barriss Offee learns all she can from her experienced Jedi mentor, Luminara Unduli. Barriss wears her own Mirialan robes instead of regular Jedi attire, and she has a unique face, with blue lips and tattoos. There have been three Barriss minifigures in three sets, and they all wield a blue lightsaber.

Jedi hood in blue—not the usual brown

Mirialan tattoos are a sign of high achievement

Mirialan skin tone

Barriss Offee and her Jedi Master, Luminara Unduli, are from the planet Mirial. To reflect their origins, their minifigures' heads and hands are differentiated by a distinctive skin color, which has a greenish hue.

This variant wears a skirt for the first time. It is a new LEGO piece for 2018—more curved than previous LEGO skirts

Barriss Offee
LOYAL PADAWAN

DATA FILE

YEAR: 2018
FIRST SET: 75206 Jedi and Clone Trooper Battle Pack
NO. OF SETS: 1
PIECES: 5
ACCESSORIES: Blue lightsaber
APPEARANCES: II, CW

These clone troopers carry out specialist missions for the Republic in the *The Clone Wars* and original trilogy sets. They all wear Phase I LEGO armor and have identical pale-peach clone trooper head pieces beneath their helmets. Specialist troopers have unique armor markings, and all possess equipment that is crucial for their specific tasks and specialty missions.

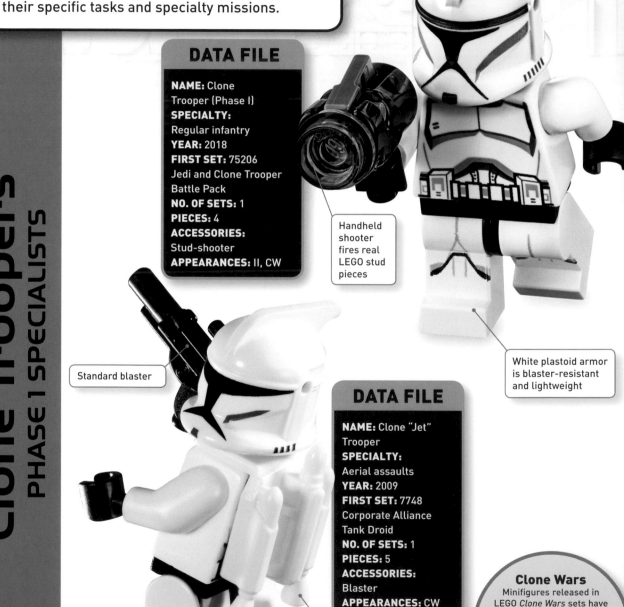

DATA FILE

NAME: Clone Trooper (Phase I)
SPECIALTY: Regular infantry
YEAR: 2018
FIRST SET: 75206 Jedi and Clone Trooper Battle Pack
NO. OF SETS: 1
PIECES: 4
ACCESSORIES: Stud-shooter
APPEARANCES: II, CW

Handheld shooter fires real LEGO stud pieces

White plastoid armor is blaster-resistant and lightweight

Standard blaster

DATA FILE

NAME: Clone "Jet" Trooper
SPECIALTY: Aerial assaults
YEAR: 2009
FIRST SET: 7748 Corporate Alliance Tank Droid
NO. OF SETS: 1
PIECES: 5
ACCESSORIES: Blaster
APPEARANCES: CW

LEGO jetpack piece is a white version of the one used for the Mandalorian and Boba Fett minifigures

Clone Wars
Minifigures released in LEGO *Clone Wars* sets have been designed with a "cartoon" feel. The Clone Wars troopers have stylized torso patterns and brighter, bolder coloring than the classic LEGO *Star Wars* troopers.

Blaster rifle keeps the bomb squad trooper safe during a mission

Orange helmet is extra sturdy to protect against bomb blasts

DATA FILE

NAME: Bomb Squad Trooper
SPECIALTY: Disarming bombs and explosive devices
YEAR: 2011
FIRST SET: 7913 Clone Trooper Battle Pack
NO. OF SETS: 1
PIECES: 4
ACCESSORIES: Blaster rifle
APPEARANCES: CW

Orange markings denote bomb squad affiliation

DATA FILE

NAME: Clone Pilot
SPECIALTY: Piloting
YEAR: 2015
FIRST SET: 75076 Republic Gunship
NO. OF SETS: 1
PIECES: 4
ACCESSORIES: Blaster pistol
APPEARANCES: II, CW

DATA FILE

NAME: Clone Trooper Gunner
SPECIALTY: Heavy artillery
YEAR: 2017
FIRST SET: 75182 Republic Fighter Tank
NO. OF SETS: 1
PIECES: 4
ACCESSORIES: Modified blaster
APPEARANCES: CW

Unlike the previous helmet, this 2017 variant does not have Imperial symbols

Blaster offers protection if landing on a battlefield

2015 variant is the first of four clone pilots to feature leg printing

Ahsoka Tano is Anakin Skywalker's enthusiastic Padawan. Her two *Clone Wars* minifigures have fought for the Republic in nine sets since 2008. As a Togruta, Ahsoka's minifigure has brightly colored skin and striped head-tails. She wears an unusual Jedi costume and, in her second variant, wields two lightsabers.

STAR VARIANT
All grown up
A third Ahsoka minifigure was created for the *Rebels* theme in 2016. Now an adult, Ahsoka has mature head-tails and an older face and she wears armor in Rebel Combat Frigate (set 75158).

Lekku
Ahsoka's hair piece is not hair at all! It is a unique mold of the blue-and-white lekku (head-tails) that grow from the heads of all Togrutas.

Ahsoka Tano
PLUCKY PADAWAN

Ahsoka's head-tails aren't yet full-length because she is still young

DATA FILE
YEAR: 2013
FIRST SET: 75013 Umbaran MHC (Mobile Heavy Cannon)
NO. OF SETS: 2
PIECES: 4
ACCESSORIES: Two green lightsabers
APPEARANCES: CW

Unique double-printed head piece has two expressions: contented smile and angry frown

Torso is printed with Ahsoka's orange skin and distinctive Jedi costume

LEGO Togrutas
For a while, Ahsoka was the only Togruta character available in minifigure form. In 2011, however, Jedi Master Shaak Ti's red-skinned minifigure was released, with fully grown, adult-length head-tails.

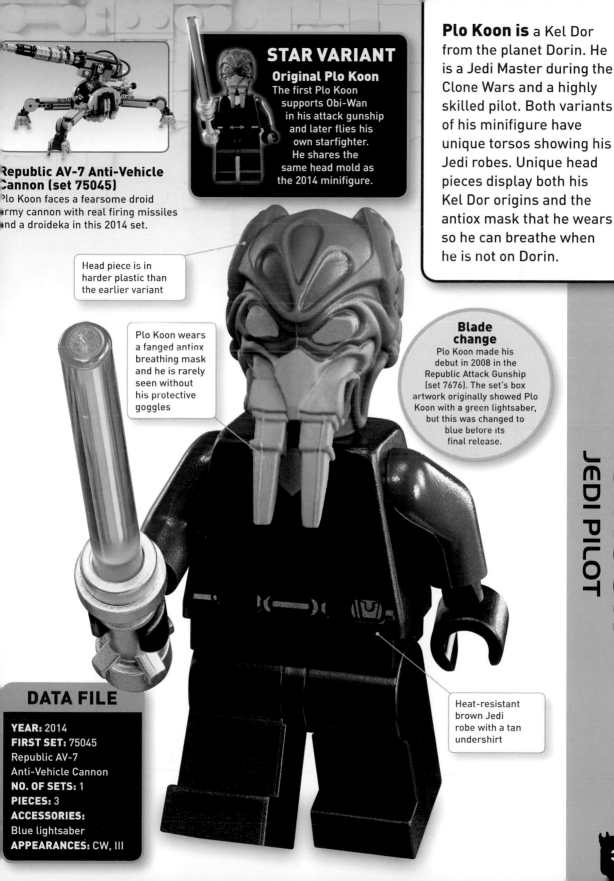

Republic AV-7 Anti-Vehicle Cannon (set 75045)

Plo Koon faces a fearsome droid army cannon with real firing missiles and a droideka in this 2014 set.

Plo Koon is a Kel Dor from the planet Dorin. He is a Jedi Master during the Clone Wars and a highly skilled pilot. Both variants of his minifigure have unique torsos showing his Jedi robes. Unique head pieces display both his Kel Dor origins and the antiox mask that he wears so he can breathe when he is not on Dorin.

Head piece is in harder plastic than the earlier variant

Plo Koon wears a fanged antiox breathing mask and he is rarely seen without his protective goggles

Blade change
Plo Koon made his debut in 2008 in the Republic Attack Gunship (set 7676). The set's box artwork originally showed Plo Koon with a green lightsaber, but this was changed to blue before its final release.

Heat-resistant brown Jedi robe with a tan undershirt

Plo Koon
JEDI PILOT

DATA FILE

YEAR: 2014
FIRST SET: 75045 Republic AV-7 Anti-Vehicle Cannon
NO. OF SETS: 1
PIECES: 3
ACCESSORIES: Blue lightsaber
APPEARANCES: CW, III

This band of brothers all have highly specialized roles and their own task-specific weaponry and equipment. Whether scouting enemy territory or tackling elite missions on the home front, they put themselves in the line of fire every day against the menace of the Separatists and their droid forces.

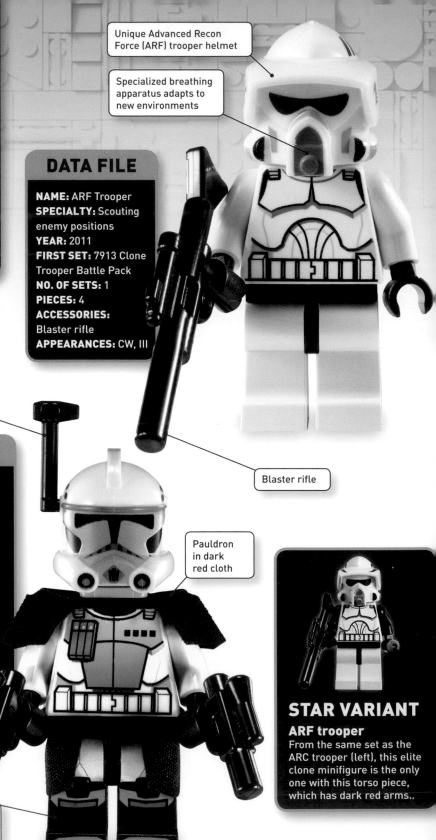

Unique Advanced Recon Force (ARF) trooper helmet

Specialized breathing apparatus adapts to new environments

DATA FILE

NAME: ARF Trooper
SPECIALTY: Scouting enemy positions
YEAR: 2011
FIRST SET: 7913 Clone Trooper Battle Pack
NO. OF SETS: 1
PIECES: 4
ACCESSORIES: Blaster rifle
APPEARANCES: CW, III

Helmet rangefinder makes sure this specialist never misses his target

Blaster rifle

DATA FILE

NAME: ARC Trooper
SPECIALTY: Advanced combat
YEAR: 2012
FIRST SET: 9488 Elite Clone Trooper & Commando Droid Battle Pack
NO. OF SETS: 7
PIECES: 8
ACCESSORIES: Twin blaster pistols, backpack
APPEARANCES: CW

Pauldron in dark red cloth

Red legs with blue-and-white armor printing is unique to this ARC trooper

STAR VARIANT

ARF trooper
From the same set as the ARC trooper (left), this elite clone minifigure is the only one with this torso piece, which has dark red arms..

The striking red color is used on all gear connected with the Coruscant high command

Markings show the trooper is part of the elite Coruscant guard

STAR VARIANT

Shock trooper

From the 2007 Clone Troopers Battle Pack (set 7655), this shock trooper has a more rounded helmet with a plain black head piece underneath. His arms and legs are plain white.

Legs with red markings are unique to this shock trooper

Helmet is the same mold used for ARF Troopers, but in black with a silver printed visor

Mysterious minifigure

The Shadow ARF trooper of 2011 is truly intriguing. He only appears in the LEGO *Star Wars* galaxy!

The shadow ARF trooper was given away as part of the "May the Fourth" promotion in 2011

Standard armor pattern is printed in gray on a black torso

Performing daring raids and rescue missions across the LEGO *Star Wars* galaxy, these elite clone troopers will follow their Jedi commanders into any peril. They all wear Phase II clone trooper armor, which is identifiable by the shape of their helmet and its breathing filters. Their armor is customized—its color, symbols, and decoration reveal each wearer's unit affiliation.

Clone Troopers
UNBEATABLE UNITS

Blaster rifle

DATA FILE

NAME: 212th clone trooper
SPECIALTY: Frontline troops
YEAR: 2013
FIRST SET: 75013 Umbaran MHC (Mobile Heavy Cannon)
NO. OF SETS: 1
PIECES: 4
ACCESSORIES: Blaster rifle
APPEARANCES: CW, III

Unique legs with orange 212th battalion markings

Blue markings indicate that this trooper is a member of the 501st legion

This minifigure appears in two 2013 sets: AT-RT (set 75002) and Z-95 Headhunter (set 75004)

DATA FILE

NAME: 501st Legion Clone Trooper
SPECIALTY: Frontline troops
YEAR: 2013
FIRST SET: 75002 AT-RT
NO. OF SETS: 2
PIECES: 4
ACCESSORIES: Blaster
APPEARANCES: CW, III

Torrent force
The 501st is famous for including the renowned Torrent company, led by Captain Rex under the command of Jedi General Skywalker. It fights at the Battles of Christophsis and Teth, among many others.

Unique blue printing on legs

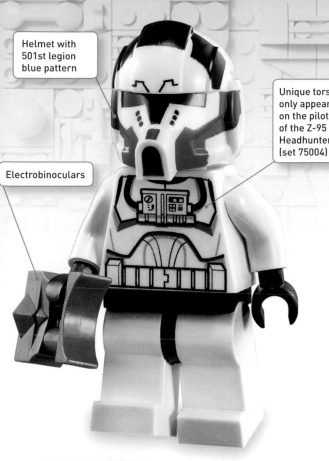

Helmet with 501st legion blue pattern

Unique torso only appears on the pilot of the Z-95 Headhunter (set 75004)

Electrobinoculars

Clone Troopers
UNBEATABLE UNITS

DATA FILE

NAME: 501st clone pilot
SPECIALTY: Aerial combat
YEAR: 2013
FIRST SET: 75004 Z-95 Headhunter
NO. OF SETS: 1
PIECES: 4
ACCESSORIES: Electrobinoculars
APPEARANCES: CW

Headhunter
Wearing an exclusive helmet, this 501st clone pilot minifigure flies the 2013 Z-95 Headhunter (set 75004). His electrobinoculars can be stored in the plane's rear compartment weapon rack.

Blulsh-gray markings of the Wolfpack unit

Wolf insignia on Phase II helmet

DATA FILE

NAME: Wolfpack clone trooper
SPECIALTY: Rescue missions
YEAR: 2014
FIRST SET: 75045 Republic AV-7 Anti-Vehicle Cannon
NO. OF SETS: 1
PIECES: 4
ACCESSORIES: Blaster
APPEARANCES: CW

STAR VARIANT

Wolfpack clone trooper
The Phase I variant of the Wolfpack clone trooper has light blue arms and legs. He appears in the 2011 Republic Frigate (set 7964) and comes equipped with a jetpack that has twin nozzles.

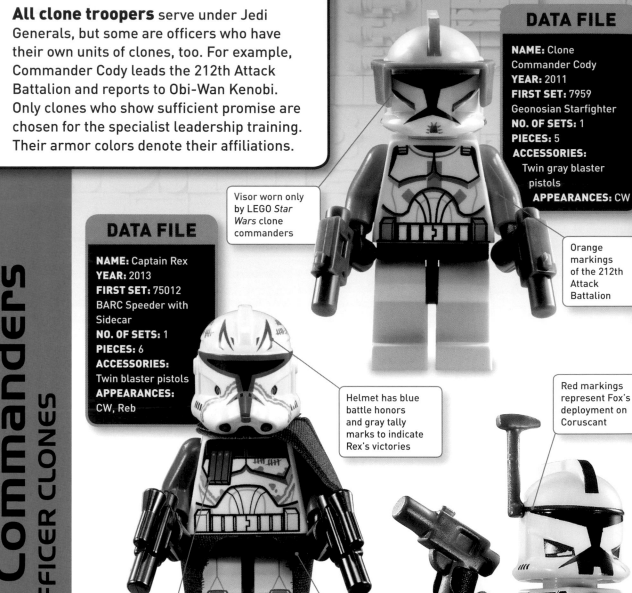

All clone troopers serve under Jedi Generals, but some are officers who have their own units of clones, too. For example, Commander Cody leads the 212th Attack Battalion and reports to Obi-Wan Kenobi. Only clones who show sufficient promise are chosen for the specialist leadership training. Their armor colors denote their affiliations.

DATA FILE

NAME: Clone Commander Cody
YEAR: 2011
FIRST SET: 7959 Geonosian Starfighter
NO. OF SETS: 1
PIECES: 5
ACCESSORIES: Twin gray blaster pistols
APPEARANCES: CW

Visor worn only by LEGO *Star Wars* clone commanders

Orange markings of the 212th Attack Battalion

DATA FILE

NAME: Captain Rex
YEAR: 2013
FIRST SET: 75012 BARC Speeder with Sidecar
NO. OF SETS: 1
PIECES: 6
ACCESSORIES: Twin blaster pistols
APPEARANCES: CW, Reb

Helmet has blue battle honors and gray tally marks to indicate Rex's victories

Red markings represent Fox's deployment on Coruscant

Unique printing, which continues onto the back torso, includes three cartridges

Cloth kama (anti-blast leg armor)

Red ranking stripes

Helmets
Commanders wear a mix of Phase I and Phase II helmets. The first LEGO Phase I helmet from 2002 has a cut-out visor over a black head. This was revised in 2008 and 2013. The first Phase II helmet, from 2005, was updated in 2008.

DATA FILE

NAME: Clone Commander Fox
YEAR: 2008
FIRST SET: 7681 Separatist Spider Droid
NO. OF SETS: 1
PIECES: 7
ACCESSORIES: Twin gray blaster pistols
APPEARANCES: CW

Rangefinder feeds to a computer and a display screen in Wolffe's visor

DATA FILE

NAME: Clone Commander Wolffe
YEAR: 2011
FIRST SET: 7964 Republic Frigate
NO. OF SETS: 1
PIECES: 6
ACCESSORIES: Twin blaster pistols
APPEARANCES: CW, Reb

Wolfpack armor is the same as regular clone trooper armor, but with sand-blue markings and sleeves

DATA FILE

NAME: Clone Commander Neyo
YEAR: 2014
FIRST SET: 75037 Battle on Saleucami
NO. OF SETS: 1
PIECES: 4
ACCESSORIES: Blaster
APPEARANCES: CW

Kama is plastic rather than cloth

Gray-and-green helmets are worn by two Gree minifigures; the first Gree from 2012 has a white-and-green one

Straps are worn by some troopers who ride BARC speeders

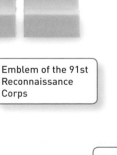

Emblem of the 91st Reconnaissance Corps

DATA FILE

NAME: Clone Commander Gree
YEAR: 2019
FIRST SET: 75234 AT-AP Walker
NO. OF SETS: 1
PIECES: 4
ACCESSORIES: Blaster
APPEARANCES: CW, III

Green markings for camouflage on Kashyyyk

Clone Commanders
OFFICER CLONES

Asajj Ventress is a deadly assassin who works for the Sith Lord Count Dooku. Her fearsome minifigure has a new head and torso and wields twin red-bladed lightsabers. Asajj has dark side powers and a fiery temper—and she is on a mission to cause trouble in three *Clone Wars* sets.

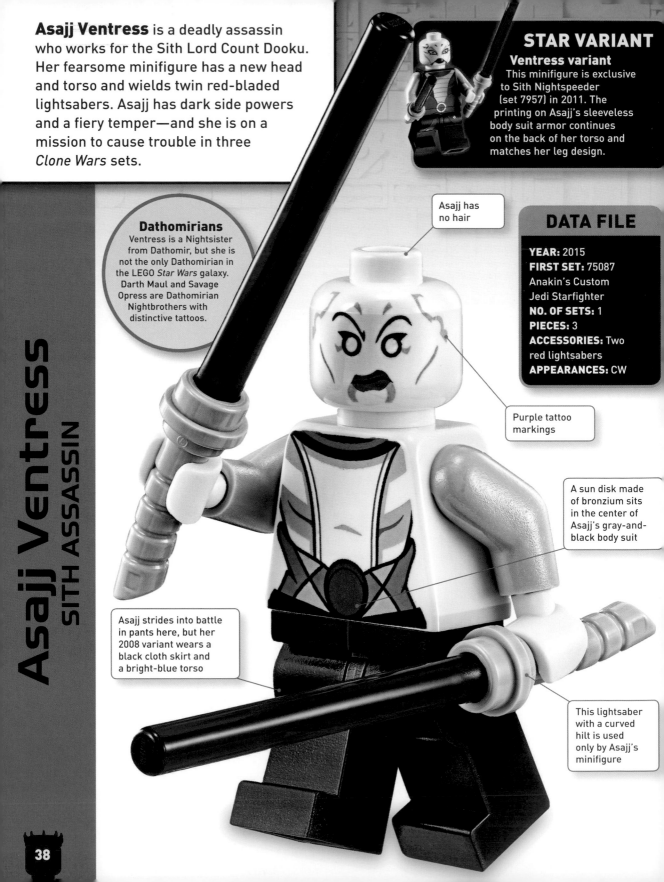

STAR VARIANT

Ventress variant
This minifigure is exclusive to Sith Nightspeeder (set 7957) in 2011. The printing on Asajj's sleeveless body suit armor continues on the back of her torso and matches her leg design.

Dathomirians
Ventress is a Nightsister from Dathomir, but she is not the only Dathomirian in the LEGO *Star Wars* galaxy. Darth Maul and Savage Opress are Dathomirian Nightbrothers with distinctive tattoos.

Asajj has no hair

DATA FILE

YEAR: 2015
FIRST SET: 75087 Anakin's Custom Jedi Starfighter
NO. OF SETS: 1
PIECES: 3
ACCESSORIES: Two red lightsabers
APPEARANCES: CW

Purple tattoo markings

A sun disk made of bronzium sits in the center of Asajj's gray-and-black body suit

Asajj strides into battle in pants here, but her 2008 variant wears a black cloth skirt and a bright-blue torso

This lightsaber with a curved hilt is used only by Asajj's minifigure

Asajj Ventress
SITH ASSASSIN

STAR VARIANTS

Plain evil
There are two all-white Grievous figures. The 2005 version wears a cape, but this 2007 version does not as he flies in his starfighter.

Clone Wars cyborg
General Grievous's figure was updated in 2010. Despite his top-to-toe figure makeover in tan, he is still the same old cyborg with a deep hatred of the Jedi.

This nasty cyborg might look like a LEGO droid, but don't tell him that! He will react savagely, as his many victims will attest. General Grievous is Supreme Commander of the Droid Armies. His figure wields four lightsabers—two blue and two green—to fill his four hands, making him a match for any Jedi.

Grievous's head piece resembles the mask he wore as a Kaleesh warlord

Grievous's four arms have hinged joints so they can be positioned in many ways

Grievous collects the lightsabers of his Jedi victims

Not a droid
Grievous hates being called a droid. He is a cyborg: part flesh, part metal. Grievous's first figure is built from some droid parts, but his two later figures are built with custom-made pieces. Grievous would probably approve!

DATA FILE

YEAR: 2014
FIRST SET: 75040 General Grievous's Wheel Bike
NO. OF SETS: 2
PIECES: 8
ACCESSORIES: Two blue and two green lightsabers
APPEARANCES: CW, III

A passionate voice in the Senate, Amidala can handle herself in a crisis. There are many Padmé minifigures, but this *Clone Wars* one from 2012 is the only one of her as a senator. Her hair is swept back in a low ponytail and she wears a practical suit for traveling on dangerous Senate business.

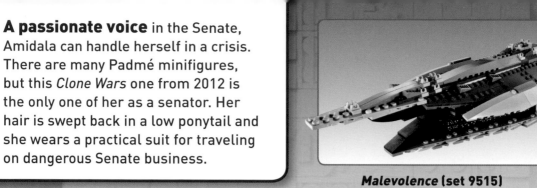

Malevolence (set 9515)

Padmé's senator minifigure is exclusive to this 2012 set. Padmé boards General Grievous's deadly ship in a bid to destroy it. The set comes with five minifigures, one of which is Anakin. He comes to the rescue when Grievous holds Padmé captive.

Padmé Amidala
DEDICATED SENATOR

Ponytailed hair piece is also used in the *Pirates of the Caribbean*™ theme

Tiny brown beauty spot

New torso piece includes dark red vest with diplomatic insignia

2011 version of a blaster pistol

DATA FILE

YEAR: 2012
FIRST SET: 9515
Malevolence
NO. OF SETS: 1
PIECES: 4
ACCESSORIES: Blaster pistol
APPEARANCES: CW

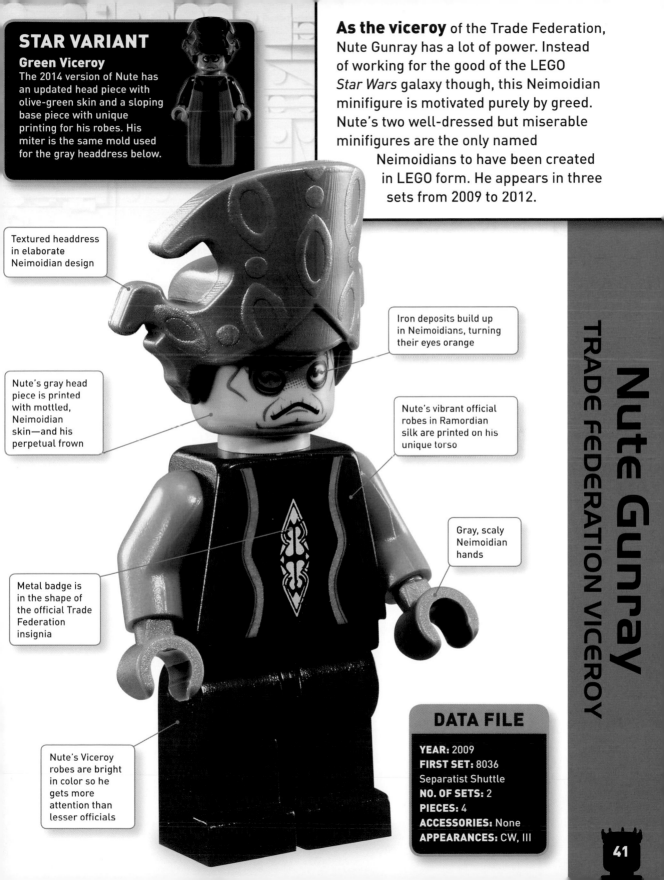

Green Viceroy
The 2014 version of Nute has an updated head piece with olive-green skin and a sloping base piece with unique printing for his robes. His miter is the same mold used for the gray headdress below.

As the viceroy of the Trade Federation, Nute Gunray has a lot of power. Instead of working for the good of the LEGO *Star Wars* galaxy though, this Neimoidian minifigure is motivated purely by greed. Nute's two well-dressed but miserable minifigures are the only named Neimoidians to have been created in LEGO form. He appears in three sets from 2009 to 2012.

Textured headdress in elaborate Neimoidian design

Iron deposits build up in Neimoidians, turning their eyes orange

Nute's gray head piece is printed with mottled, Neimoidian skin—and his perpetual frown

Nute's vibrant official robes in Ramordian silk are printed on his unique torso

Gray, scaly Neimoidian hands

Metal badge is in the shape of the official Trade Federation insignia

Nute's Viceroy robes are bright in color so he gets more attention than lesser officials

Nute Gunray
TRADE FEDERATION VICEROY

DATA FILE

YEAR: 2009
FIRST SET: 8036 Separatist Shuttle
NO. OF SETS: 2
PIECES: 4
ACCESSORIES: None
APPEARANCES: CW, III

Jedi Shaak Ti is a powerful Clone Wars general. She also trains new clone cadets. Shaak is renowned for her skill and intellect, even though she appears in only one LEGO set. Her minifigure has red Togruta skin and a unique detachable piece with blue-and-white head-tails that clips onto her head.

Head-tails

This unique piece was specially made for Shaak Ti. She has two head-tails at the front and one at the back. Shaak is an adult so her head-tails are fully grown, unlike Ahsoka's.

Hollow horns on Shaak's head are called montrals and they can sense the space around her

Shaak Ti only fights with her lightsaber when all other options have been exhausted

White Togruta markings on a red head piece

Traditional Togruta akul-tooth headdress

Shaak Ti
JEDI GENERAL

Naturally red Togruta skin

DATA FILE

YEAR: 2011
FIRST SET: 7931
T-6 Jedi Shuttle
NO. OF SETS: 1
PIECES: 5
ACCESSORIES: Blue lightsaber
APPEARANCES: II, CW, III

LEGO bandanna piece is popular with rogues: Dengar, Kithaba, and Shahan Alama

Hondo Ohnaka is the fearsome leader of a gang of Weequay pirates. His minifigure wears mismatched clothes, a black bandanna, and green-eyed goggles—items he has scavenged on his many journeys. Hondo only appears in one LEGO set, but he and his pilfering gang are always plotting new ways to make a quick buck.

Pirate Tank (set 7753)

Hondo is the gunner on board the pirate tank in this 2009 set. The tank is equipped with flick missiles and a huge blaster cannon. Hondo and his gang of pirates are on a mission to kidnap Obi-Wan—the Jedi Master will fetch a good ransom!

Hondo's unique head is printed with wrinkly Weequay skin and goggles for swoop-piloting

Epaulet

The LEGO epaulet shoulder piece is worn by several minifigures across other LEGO themes, including pirates and soldiers. In LEGO *Star Wars*, however, only two minifigures wear this piece, Hondo and Embo.

Shoulder epaulets show all the other pirates who's in charge

Hondo's gray-and-tan, crinkly Weequay skin continues on his torso, under his open-necked shirt

Hondo Ohnaka
WEEQUAY PIRATE

Torso is printed with an elaborate jacket, which Hondo wears over a ragged white shirt. Hondo thinks the jacket gives him an air of grandeur

DATA FILE

YEAR: 2009
FIRST SET: 7753
Pirate Tank
NO. OF SETS: 1
PIECES: 5
ACCESSORIES: None
APPEARANCES: CW

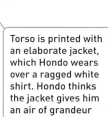

43

Turk Falso is a tough Weequay criminal. His minifigure is second-in-command in Hondo Ohnaka's pirate gang, and he wears clothes suitable for a pirate's life of planet-hopping and petty thieving. Turk searches for Jedi minifigures to hold for ransom, but he's also out to double-cross his fellow pirates. Luckily for everyone, this pirate appears in just one LEGO set.

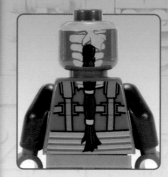

Pirate ponytail
Turk's black ponytail is printed on the back of his head—and continues down the back of his torso.

Turk's headband wraps all the way around the head piece and ties up at the back

DATA FILE

YEAR: 2009
FIRST SET: 7753
Pirate Tank
NO. OF SETS: 1
PIECES: 3
ACCESSORIES:
Twin gray pistols, cutlass
APPEARANCES: CW

Unique head piece is printed with Turk's leathery Weequay face

Turk Falso
DANGEROUS PIRATE

Turk carries a pair of ancient pistols

Weapon harness

Man of weapons
Turk wields many weapons in his crime-filled life. He uses this dark bluish-gray cutlass to threaten Jedi hostages.

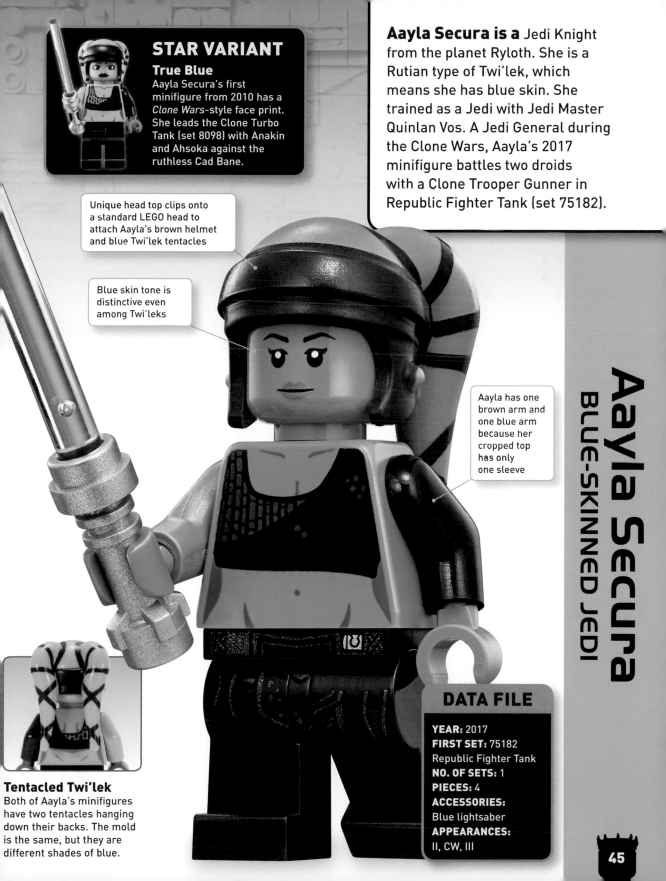

STAR VARIANT
True Blue
Aayla Secura's first minifigure from 2010 has a *Clone Wars*-style face print. She leads the Clone Turbo Tank (set 8098) with Anakin and Ahsoka against the ruthless Cad Bane.

Aayla Secura is a Jedi Knight from the planet Ryloth. She is a Rutian type of Twi'lek, which means she has blue skin. She trained as a Jedi with Jedi Master Quinlan Vos. A Jedi General during the Clone Wars, Aayla's 2017 minifigure battles two droids with a Clone Trooper Gunner in Republic Fighter Tank (set 75182).

Unique head top clips onto a standard LEGO head to attach Aayla's brown helmet and blue Twi'lek tentacles

Blue skin tone is distinctive even among Twi'leks

Aayla has one brown arm and one blue arm because her cropped top has only one sleeve

Aayla Secura
BLUE-SKINNED JEDI

Tentacled Twi'lek
Both of Aayla's minifigures have two tentacles hanging down their backs. The mold is the same, but they are different shades of blue.

DATA FILE
YEAR: 2017
FIRST SET: 75182 Republic Fighter Tank
NO. OF SETS: 1
PIECES: 4
ACCESSORIES: Blue lightsaber
APPEARANCES: II, CW, III

Cad Bane is a bounty hunter like no other, so it is fitting that his minifigure is unique, too. Blue-skinned and red-eyed, he comes in two variants, both with the same distinctive hat. The 2013 minifigure variant of this merciless mercenary zips around in a pirate speeder in HH-87 Starhopper (set 75024)—but Obi-Wan is hot on his tail.

STAR VARIANT
Ready for anything
The first Cad Bane minifigure wears detachable breathing apparatus, just in case! Found in two 2010 LEGO sets, he sports a tattered jacket and twin blasters.

Cad Bane
HUNTER FOR HIRE

With his wide-brimmed hat, Cad thinks of himself as a space cowboy

Typical Duros red eyes

Bulletproof panels worn over leather jacket

DATA FILE
YEAR: 2013
FIRST SET: 75024
HH-87 Starhopper
NO. OF SETS: 1
PIECES: 4
ACCESSORIES:
Blaster
APPEARANCES: CW

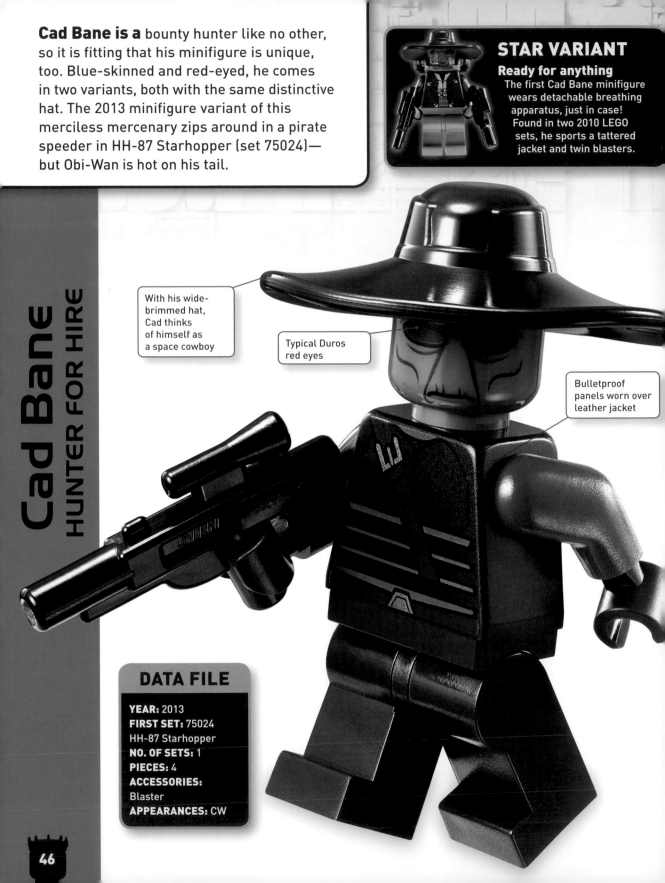

Hair is pulled into a neat top-knot so it does not get in Sugi's way during a mission

Bounty hunter Sugi is honest but deadly. Whether she is sent to capture a Jedi Knight or protect a family of poor farmers, she will not give up until her mission is complete. Sugi's minifigure wears functional clothes that help her get the job done. She doesn't need anything else—apart from her weapons! Sugi carries out many missions, but she appears in only one set.

Sugi is an Iridonian Zabrak. Her head piece has small printed horns and precise face tattoos

Sugi's unique torso is printed with her simple red vest and metal necklace—her most treasured possession

Vibroblade vibrates to make it more efficient than a regular blade

Sugi's weapon of choice is an EE-3 carbine rifle

Plain gray pants give Sugi ease of movement in combat

Sugi

HONORABLE BOUNTY HUNTER

47

Embo is a Kyuzo bounty hunter with sand-green, scaly skin and yellow eyes. He is part of Sugi's team of bounty hunters on board the Bounty Hunter Assault Gunship (set 7930). His minifigure carries a bowcaster and is made up of finely detailed pieces, including his hat, head, torso, and legs.

Embo's metal hat can also be thrown as a weapon or used as a shield

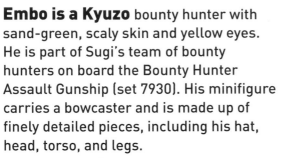

Embo
KYUZO BOUNTY HUNTER

Straps and armor
The back of Embo's torso contains more printed detail, which continues the pattern of his armor and ammo belt.

Black epaulet piece is also worn by Hondo Ohnaka

Embo wears a bronze breathing mask to filter moisture out of the air

Modified bowcaster

Ammunition strap

Utility belt printed on hip piece

Unique leg piece is printed with Embo's Kyuzo patterned wrap worn over a brown kama

DATA FILE

YEAR: 2011
FIRST SET: 7930
Bounty Hunter Assault Gunship
NO. OF SETS: 1
PIECES: 5
ACCESSORIES: Bowcaster
APPEARANCES: CW

Mandalorian Super Commando
This 2013 Clone Wars minifigure wears a version of Mandalorian armor, but it is colored to show his allegiance to Darth Maul. There are two variants, which are the same except for the head pieces under their helmets.

The Mandalorian is a deadly soldier from the planet Mandalore. He owns many weapons, but his distinctive blue-and-gray armor is his most treasured possession. Appearing in only two LEGO sets, this minifigure joins forces with the Separatists—even though his sturdy armor was the inspiration for clone trooper armor!

Ancient Mandalorian helmet design has similar markings to Jango Fett's helmet

DATA FILE

YEAR: 2011
FIRST SET: 7914 Mandalorian Battle Pack
NO. OF SETS: 2
PIECES: 5
ACCESSORIES: Blaster pistol/two blaster pistols/blaster rifle
APPEARANCES: CW

Jetpack fits around minifigure's neck

Under the helmet
Beneath the helmet is a new LEGO head piece printed with blue eyes and pale features. It is shared with one of the two Super Commando minifigures.

Mandalorian armor is famous in the LEGO *Star Wars* galaxy. It is made from an almost indestructible metal called beskar

Jetpack
The Mandalorian's armor is fitted with a jetpack. Jango Fett also wears a jetpack, which is sometimes attached to his helmet.

Mandalorian
ARMORED WARRIOR

Ruthless bounty hunter Aurra Sing will stop at nothing to get her prize. Her fearless minifigure is dressed in an orange jumpsuit laden with weapons, but wears no armor! Aurra appears in just one set and her minifigure is almost completely built out of unique pieces—only her arms and hands can be found on other minifigures.

Spoils of war
Aurra Sing knows exactly what will fetch the highest ransom. I Bounty Hunter Assault Gunshi (set 7930), she's managed to ge hold of a priceless Jedi holocron

Long brown hair is tied out of the way

Unique hairstyle
Aurra's long, brown LEGO hair piece was specially designed for her 2011 minifigure. It fits into the stud on top of Aurra's otherwise bald head piece and flows neatly down her back.

Weapons vest
The back of Aurra's unique torso is printed with her brown vest, in which she stores compact weapons and extra ammo.

Unique head piece is printed with Aurra's bright green eyes and confident smile

Shaak-hide utility belt

Functional orange jumpsuit allows Aurra to maneuver easily during combat

Holsters for Aurra's twin pistols

DATA FILE

YEAR: 2011
FIRST SET: 7930
Bounty Hunter Assault Gunship
NO. OF SETS: 1
PIECES: 4
ACCESSORIES:
Twin blaster pistols
APPEARANCES: I, CW

DATA FILE

YEAR: 2010
FIRST SET: 8128 Cad
Bane's Speeder
NO. OF SETS: 1
PIECES: 4
ACCESSORIES:
Blaster
APPEARANCES: CW

Shahan Alama was a pirate—until he was kicked out of the gang for being too nasty! Now he is a bounty hunter who works with Cad Bane. His mismatched clothing and bandanna point to his former life as a pirate, but Shahan's mean streak runs deep so he feels right at home among Bane's gang of hired brutes. Fortunately, Shahan wreaks havoc in just one LEGO set.

Dark red bandanna piece is also worn by the assassin Kithaba

Protective chestplate

Weequay skin pattern

Pearl-gold arm was taken from a combat droid to replace Shahan's destroyed right arm

Shahan's armor
Shahan's chestplate is printed on the back of his torso, too. Working together with Cad Bane has its risks!

Belt was stolen from a Twi'lek nobleman

Shahan Alama
PIRATE TURNED BOUNTY HUNTER

Weequay skin
There are four Weequay minifigures: Shahan, Hondo Ohnaka, the Weequay Skiff Guard, and Turk Falso. They all have faces printed with Weequay skin, but the patterns and colors vary from one villain to the next.

Quinlan Vos is an unconventional Jedi. He is an expert Force tracker, able to locate anybody by following their trail, but he has also teetered on the edge of the dark side. His unkempt minifigure has messy hair and stubble and wears a rusty chest plate over his Jedi tunic. He spends a lot of time undercover, which may be why this variant appears in only one LEGO set.

STAR VARIANT
First of his type
The first Quinlan has a printed hair braid on his torso in 2011. His hair is worn by male and female minifigures, including Hermione Granger and Molly Weasley in LEGO® Harry Potter™.

Longer flowing locks than Quinlan's first minifigure's shoulder-length hair piece

Yellow stripe across Quinlan's face is a reminder of his Kiffu heritage

Quinlan's blaster-proof chest plate is part of his Jedi uniform because he finds himself in danger more often than most Jedi

Quinlan Vos
JEDI TRACKER

Clone Turbo Tank (set 75151)
Quinlan Vos fights against a battle droid on Kashyyyk with this ten-wheeled tank. He is supported by Luminara Unduli, Clone Commander Gree, and an elite 41st Corps trooper.

Utility belt conceals Quinlan's Jedi items when he is undercover

Long Jedi robes continue on the leg piece

DATA FILE
YEAR: 2016
FIRST SET: 75151 Clone Turbo Tank
NO. OF SETS: 1
PIECES: 4
ACCESSORIES: Green lightsaber
APPEARANCES: CW

Sith Nightspeeder (set 7957)

Asajj Ventress, a Nightsister from Savage's home planet, pilots a striking Nightspeeder with Savage in this set.

The Dathomirian Nightbrother Savage Opress is on a secret mission. Hired by Asajj Ventress to destroy Count Dooku, this yellow-and-black minifigure poses as Dooku's new Sith apprentice. Savage appears in just one LEGO set, where his horned Dathomirian minifigure must decide who to attack: the Jedi Anakin Skywalker or Savage's two despised Sith Masters?

Savage's Zabrak horned head piece is the same mold as Darth Maul's, but it has yellow, not red, markings and a different pattern

LEGO spear piece with ax head attached

Nightbrother tattoos on yellow skin

Enchanted blade is a weapon from a clan of witches called the Nightsisters

Unique armor piece fits over the minifigure's neck. The Dathomirian armor protects Savage's torso and shoulders

Savage Opress
DARK APPRENTICE

DATA FILE

YEAR: 2011
FIRST SET: 7957 Sith Nightspeeder
NO. OF SETS: 1
PIECES: 5
ACCESSORIES: Double-bladed red lightsaber, enchanted blade
APPEARANCES: CW

53

Anakin Skywalker is now a celebrated Jedi Knight. His minifigure has a battle-scarred face and a cyborg hand after Anakin faced many trials during the Clone Wars, and proved himself to be a hero of the LEGO *Star Wars* galaxy. Anakin has 12 Jedi Knight variants, which appear in 20 different LEGO *Star Wars* sets.

STAR VARIANTS

Light look
Anakin's blue lightsaber is lit up by a battery in the minifigure's torso in 2005's Ultimate Lightsaber Duel (set 7257). A non-light-up variant appears in two sets, wearing a headset but no cape.

Dark look
This 2012 minifigure from Anakin's Jedi Interceptor (set 9494) has a double-sided head piece to show Anakin's transformation from Jedi to Sith.

Anakin Skywalker
JEDI KNIGHT

This shaggy hair piece appears on Anakin minifigures in dark brown and reddish-brown

Expression focused on flying a starfighter

Cyborg hand concealed by a black glove

Anakin wears darker robes than fellow Jedi, perhaps it is a sign of his future on the dark side of the Force

Hands-free
2005 saw the first Anakin minifigure to have a simple gold headset printed on his face. Three more Anakin minifigures with headsets followed, with more detailed prints.

DATA FILE

YEAR: 2018
FIRST SET: 75214 Anakin's Jedi Starfighter
NO. OF SETS: 1
PIECES: 4
ACCESSORIES: Blue lightsaber
APPEARANCES: CW, III

STAR VARIANTS

Light-up Jedi
A variant of Jedi Master Obi-Wan Kenobi appears in Ultimate Lightsaber Duel (set 7257). Pushing down the minifigure's head makes his blue lightsaber light up.

Pilot Jedi
This is the first Obi-Wan to have tan leg pieces. He wears a gold headset in Jedi Starfighter with Hyperdrive Booster Ring (set 7661) in 2007.

Obi-Wan Kenobi is now a Jedi Master, and he has achieved much military success as a general during the Clone Wars. His minifigure has appeared as slightly different variants in eight LEGO *Star Wars* sets. His minifigure in Anakin's Jedi Interceptor (set 9494), for example, is the only Jedi Master Obi-Wan Kenobi that has plain dark-tan leg pieces.

Six Obi-Wan minifigures have a pilot's headset, even though he dislikes flying

Utility belt with food capsules for long missions

Obi-Wan's Jedi Interceptor (set 75135)
Obi-Wan flies his Eta-2 *Actis*-class interceptor in the Battle of Coruscant alongside his trusty astromech droid, R4-P17, which can clip on to the wing.

Obi-Wan's robe printing extends to his legs

Cloaked Kenobi
Jedi Master Obi-Wan wears a Jedi cloak in four LEGO sets for passing unnoticed on Jedi business. The light-up lightsaber variant in Ultimate Lightsaber Duel (set 7257) also wears a Jedi hood for extra privacy.

DATA FILE

YEAR: 2016
FIRST SET: 75135 Obi-Wan's Jedi Interceptor
NO. OF SETS: 1
PIECES: 4
ACCESSORIES: Blue lightsaber
APPEARANCES: CW, III

More than 20 astromech droids help out with starship navigation and repair in the LEGO *Star Wars* galaxy. Most of these dependable droids work on the side of the Republic, but there are a few spies in the mix, too. All astromech droids have the same leg pieces (with a hidden pin), but their head pieces and torsos have printed details in various shapes and colors.

DATA FILE
NAME: R4-P17
YEAR: 2016
FIRST SET: 75135 Obi-Wan's Jedi Interceptor
NO. OF SETS: 2
PIECES: 4
ACCESSORIES: None
APPEARANCES: III

Radar eye records messages from Obi-Wan for the Jedi Council

More head detail than the 2013 variant

Heat exhaust

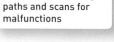

Radar eye tracks flight paths and scans for malfunctions

Movable legs attached with hidden pins

Astromechs
STARSHIP NAVIGATORS

DATA FILE
NAME: R2-R7
YEAR: 2007
FIRST SET: 7665 Republic Cruiser
NO. OF SETS: 1
PIECES: 4
ACCESSORIES: None
APPEARANCES: L

Gold metallic printing is not seen on any other astromech droid minifigure

Purple sensor for enhanced navigation

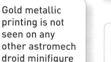

Ventilation grilles

Protruding lower body stores a third leg

Logic function display indicates what R7-A7 is thinking

DATA FILE
NAME: R7-A7
YEAR: 2009
FIRST SET: 7751 Ahsoka's Starfighter and Vulture Droid
NO. OF SETS: 1
PIECES: 4
ACCESSORIES: None
APPEARANCES: CW

Only this LEGO astromech has red legs

Recharge power coupling can be attached to the power source on Ahsoka's starship

DATA FILE
NAME: R8-B7
YEAR: 2011
FIRST SET: 7868 Mace Windu's Jedi Starfighter
NO. OF SETS: 1
PIECES: 4
ACCESSORIES: None
APPEARANCES: CW

DATA FILE

NAME: R5-D4
YEAR: 2012
FIRST SET: 9493
X-wing Starfighter
NO. OF SETS: 2
PIECES: 4
ACCESSORIES: None
APPEARANCES: IV

This head shape is new for this variant. The first two R5-D4 LEGO figures had domed heads

R5-series flower pot–shaped head piece

R5-J2 has the same torso piece as R2-Q5, his fellow Death Star astromech

LEGO robotic leg pieces are used only for astromech droids

Charging socket

DATA FILE

NAME: R2-Q5
YEAR: 2008
FIRST SET: 10188
Death Star
NO. OF SETS: 2
PIECES: 4
ACCESSORIES: None
APPEARANCES: VI

Radar eye can record surroundings

Rare bronze-printed panels

Functions include hidden spy devices

DATA FILE

NAME: R5-J2
YEAR: 2012
FIRST SET: 9492
TIE Fighter
NO. OF SETS: 1
PIECES: 4
ACCESSORIES: None
APPEARANCES: VI

Black leg pieces indicate that this is an Imperial droid

DATA FILE

NAME: R3-A2
YEAR: 2016
FIRST SET: 75098
Assault on Hoth
NO. OF SETS: 1
PIECES: 4
ACCESSORIES: None
APPEARANCES: V

Eye not surrounded by usual square plate

First ever transparent astromech head piece

Brick color is called transparent black

Kit Fisto is a green-skinned Jedi Master. The long tentacles that grow from his head can sense emotions in the people around him. As a respected Jedi General, Kit fights alongside other Jedi Knights and he leads troops into battle in four LEGO sets. The caped variant appears only in Palpatine's Arrest (set 9526).

STAR VARIANT
Lighter lightsaber
This Kit Fisto, with no cape, flies with Obi-Wan in the 2007 Jedi Starfighter with Hyperdrive Booster Ring (set 7661) and also stars in two other sets. His lightsaber is slightly lighter than the later variant's—fluorescent green instead of bright green.

Nautolan heads have green skin, black unblinking eyes, and head tentacles

Tentacles
The back of Kit Fisto's head piece displays more of his sensory tentacles.

Head of rubber
Kit Fisto was the first LEGO minifigure to have a head made from rubber. Other LEGO *Star Wars* minifigures, including Plo Koon and some variants of Yoda also have rubber heads.

Brown cape is worn by all five Jedi minifigures in the Palpatine's Arrest set

Tentacles sense emotions and give Kit Fisto an advantage in battle: he knows who is scared!

Only Kit Fisto has this torso with brown-and-gray Jedi robes and silver belt

Kit Fisto
JEDI GENERAL

DATA FILE

YEAR: 2012
FIRST SET: 9526
Palpatine's Arrest
NO. OF SETS: 1
PIECES: 4
ACCESSORIES:
Green lightsaber
APPEARANCES: CW, III

Luminara Unduli is a skilled and disciplined Jedi Master. In 2011, a *Clone Wars* minifigure was released in two sets. This third version is very similar, but it has a more classic style of face print and a brown headdress. It also has more detailed robes on the torso and legs and metallic printing.

Head piece is now brown instead of black and has a new mold with ruffled folds all around the back

Highly detailed torso with unique printing includes Jedi robes with colorful Mirialan symbol

DATA FILE

YEAR: 2016
FIRST SET: 75151
Clone Turbo Tank
NO. OF SETS: 1
PIECES: 5
ACCESSORIES:
Green lightsaber
APPEARANCES: CW, III

Mirialan facial tattoos on green-tinged skin

Luminara Unduli
JEDI MASTER

New cape
Unlike the previous Luminara minifigure from Battle for Geonosis (set 7869), this 2016 minifigure wears a cape. The new brown cape is exclusive to Luminara's minifigure in Clone Turbo Tank (set 75151).

Ornate Mirial sash made from heveng wool

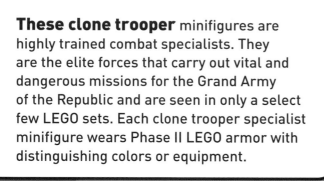

These clone trooper minifigures are highly trained combat specialists. They are the elite forces that carry out vital and dangerous missions for the Grand Army of the Republic and are seen in only a select few LEGO sets. Each clone trooper specialist minifigure wears Phase II LEGO armor with distinguishing colors or equipment.

Blaster rifle

DATA FILE

NAME: Clone trooper
SPECIALTY: Regular infantry
YEAR: 2010
FIRST SET: 8091 Republic Swamp Speeder
NO. OF SETS: 1
PIECES: 4
ACCESSORIES: Blaster rifle
APPEARANCES: III

Variants of this torso print are shared with other clone troopers, including one who wears a Santa hat in the 2014 LEGO *Star Wars* Advent Calendar

DATA FILE

NAME: V-Wing Pilot
SPECIALTY: Flying
YEAR: 2014
FIRST SET: 75039 V-wing Starfighter
NO. OF SETS: 1
PIECES: 4
ACCESSORIES: Blaster pistol
APPEARANCES: III

Helmet is marked with red-and-yellow Republic symbols

Life-support pack integrated into uniform. Back of the torso is also printed

DATA FILE

NAME: Airborne clone trooper
SPECIALTY: Aerial assaults
YEAR: 2014
FIRST SET: 75036 Utapau Troopers
NO. OF SETS: 1
PIECES: 5
ACCESSORIES: Stud-shooter
APPEARANCES: III

Scuff marks on helmet

Gray outfit is worn by this third variant. The first two clone pilot minifigures wear blue

Clone armor skirt

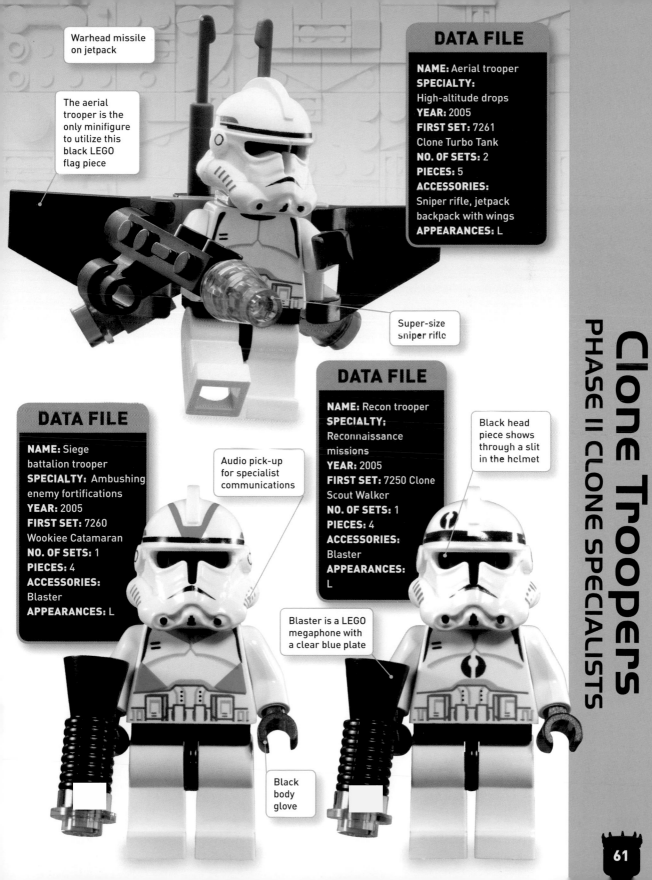

Warhead missile on jetpack

The aerial trooper is the only minifigure to utilize this black LEGO flag piece

DATA FILE

NAME: Aerial trooper
SPECIALTY:
High-altitude drops
YEAR: 2005
FIRST SET: 7261
Clone Turbo Tank
NO. OF SETS: 2
PIECES: 5
ACCESSORIES:
Sniper rifle, jetpack
backpack with wings
APPEARANCES: L

Super-size sniper rifle

DATA FILE

NAME: Recon trooper
SPECIALTY:
Reconnaissance
missions
YEAR: 2005
FIRST SET: 7250 Clone
Scout Walker
NO. OF SETS: 1
PIECES: 4
ACCESSORIES:
Blaster
APPEARANCES:
L

Black head piece shows through a slit in the helmet

DATA FILE

NAME: Siege
battalion trooper
SPECIALTY: Ambushing
enemy fortifications
YEAR: 2005
FIRST SET: 7260
Wookiee Catamaran
NO. OF SETS: 1
PIECES: 4
ACCESSORIES:
Blaster
APPEARANCES: L

Audio pick-up for specialist communications

Blaster is a LEGO megaphone with a clear blue plate

Black body glove

Clone Troopers
PHASE II CLONE SPECIALISTS

These minifigures carry out specialist missions for the Republic in several LEGO sets. Many of these troopers have unique markings, such as the orange flashes on the armor of the 212th Battalion and the special camouflage pattern of Kashyyyk troopers. They may also carry crucial equipment for their specific mission.

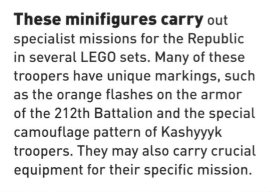

Orange markings of 212th Battalion

Scratches on armor

Leg prints are mostly seen on clone troopers from 2011 onward

DATA FILE

NAME: 212th Battalion trooper
SPECIALTY: Ground attacks
YEAR: 2014
FIRST SET: 75036 Utapau Troopers
NO. OF SETS: 1
PIECES: 4
ACCESSORIES: Stud-shooter
APPEARANCES: III

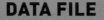

Clone Troopers
PHASE II CLONE SPECIALISTS

Helmet exclusive to Star Corps trooper

Pauldron in battalion colors

Undersuit is visible below helmet

DATA FILE

NAME: Star Corps trooper
SPECIALTY: Ground attacks
YEAR: 2005
FIRST SET: 7261 Clone Turbo Tank
NO. OF SETS: 2
PIECES: 5
ACCESSORIES: Twin gray blaster pistols
APPEARANCES: III

Double star
The Star Corps trooper minifigure is included in two sets between 2005 and 2007. In the 2007 Clone Troopers Battle Pack (set 7655), he appears without his pauldron.

Helmet shape was used for the original sand-green 41st Corps trooper in 2005

Torso print is similar to the 2014 variant

Pockets for ammo and supplies

DATA FILE
DATA FILE

NAME: 41st Elite Corps trooper
SPECIALTY: Kashyyyk deployment
YEAR: 2019
FIRST SET: 75234 AT-AP Walker
NO. OF SETS: 2
PIECES: 4
ACCESSORIES: Blaster
APPEARANCES: III

DATA FILE

NAME: Airborne Geonosis trooper
SPECIALTY: High-altitude drops
YEAR: 2015
FIRST SET: 75089 Geonosis Troopers
NO. OF SETS: 1
PIECES: 4
ACCESSORIES: Stud-shooter
APPEARANCES: L

DATA FILE

NAME: 41st Kashyyyk clone trooper
SPECIALTY: Camouflage
YEAR: 2014
FIRST SET: 75035 Kashyyyk Troopers
NO. OF SETS: 2
PIECES: 4
ACCESSORIES: Stud-shooter/blaster
APPEARANCES: L

Green visor assists vision in dense forest

Print is also used on a standard helmet mold for a non-airborne Geonosis trooper

Unique helmet mold

Camouflage pattern exclusive to 41st Elite Corps

Armored sleeves

Camouflage boots have high traction soles for unsteady ground

Reddish-sandy colors blend in on Geonosis

Clone Troopers
PHASE II CLONE SPECIALISTS

The Wookiee Chewbacca is a brave fighter and longtime companion of Han Solo. And just as Chewie towers over his friend in the *Star Wars* movies, his LEGO minifigure is notably taller than average, too. Chewbacca appears in 32 LEGO sets, ever ready to protect his home planet of Kashyyyk from invasion or to fight alongside his rebel friends.

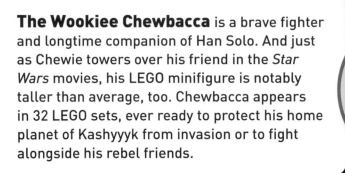

Comic-Con exclusive
In 2009, a handcuffed Chewbacca minifigure appeared in a collectible display made exclusively for San Diego's Comic-Con. The set also included Luke Skywalker and Han Solo disguised as stormtroopers.

DATA FILE
YEAR: 2014
FIRST SET: 75042 Droid Gunship
NO. OF SETS: 10
PIECES: 3
ACCESSORIES: Bowcaster/stud-shooter/handcuffs
APPEARANCES: CW, III, IV, V, VI

STAR VARIANTS

Original Wookiee
The first Chewbacca in 2000 was plain brown with only a little printing on the nose and bandolier. It was followed in 2004 with a second one from the same mold, but in reddish-brown.

Wintry Wookiee
A seasonal snow-furred Chewbacca starred in the 2016 LEGO *Star Wars* Advent Calendar. His usual mold was used to make all-white bricks, decorated with a holly-themed pattern on his bandolier.

Head sculpt designed for Chewbacca

The head and textured body are made from a single piece that fits over a standard dark-brown minifigure torso

Bandolier contains energy bolts for the Wookiee bowcaster

LEGO crossbow piece put to use as the distinctive Wookiee bowcaster

Chewbacca's two-tone fur first appeared on this 2014 minifigure

Chewbacca
WOOKIEE HERO

Sith lightning
During his "arrest" (set 9526), Palpatine uses deadly Sith lightning to defeat Mace Windu—the last of his Jedi attackers. During this battle, the Chancellor's face takes on its full Sith appearance.

When the Supreme Chancellor of the Republic is exposed as the Sith Lord Darth Sidious, a Jedi task force is sent to arrest him! Palpatine prepares for the coming conflict by retrieving his gold-hilted red Sith lightsaber from its hiding place in his office.

Hair piece is also worn by Count Dooku, but his is gray

Scary swap
The expression on the reverse of Palpatine's head piece is certainly not nice! The yellow Sith eyes and heavily wrinkled brow expose the Chancellor's true identity.

At first, Palpatine looks worried to have been exposed as a Sith

Trim pattern continues on the back of Palpatine's torso

Palpatine reveals his ornate Sith lightsaber for the first time

Gold lightsaber hilt is unique to Palpatine in the LEGO *Star Wars* theme

Torso is a similar design to Palpatine's 2009 minifigure, but with more detail

Palpatine wears his red chancellor's robes, but he does not need to hide his Sith identity any more

DATA FILE

YEAR: 2012
FIRST SET: 9526 Palpatine's Arrest
NO. OF SETS: 1
PIECES: 4
ACCESSORIES: Red lightsaber/Force lightning
APPEARANCES: III

Sith Lord Emperor Palpatine is the self-appointed ruler of the LEGO *Star Wars* galaxy. His minifigure dresses in simple black robes, and three of his six variants carry a cane to make him look weak, but don't be fooled! This is a man of terrible power who has made his presence felt in 11 LEGO sets.

Hologram
The Imperial Star Destroyer (set 6211) features Emperor Palpatine's minifigure as a hologram. His printed image appears on a sticker attached to a transparent-blue LEGO brick.

DATA FILE
YEAR: 2016
FIRST SET: 75159 Death Star
NO. OF SETS: 3
PIECES: 5
ACCESSORIES: Force lightning/red lightsaber
APPEARANCES: III, Reb, V, VI

Handheld LEGO Force Lightning pieces (first released in 2015)

Tan face (first used for the Palpatine minifigure that came with the DK book LEGO *Star Wars: The Dark Side* in 2014)

Emperor Palpatine
DARK DICTATOR

STAR VARIANTS
First emperor
The original Emperor Palpatine minifigure has different torso printing, yellow hands, and a yellow face with smaller eyes. He walks with a cane and appears in three 2000–2002 sets.

Imperial ruler
The 2008 revamp gave Palpatine a gray face with more wrinkles and big yellow eyes. He holds court in the Death Star (set 10188) and travels in Emperor Palpatine's Shuttle (set 8096).

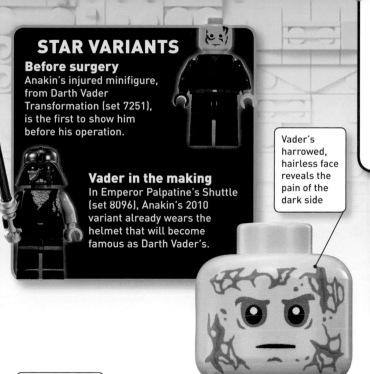

STAR VARIANTS

Before surgery
Anakin's injured minifigure, from Darth Vader Transformation (set 7251), is the first to show him before his operation.

Vader in the making
In Emperor Palpatine's Shuttle (set 8096), Anakin's 2010 variant already wears the helmet that will become famous as Darth Vader's.

Emotionally, Anakin Skywalker has succumbed to the dark side. Now his physical transformation is almost complete, too. Three charred and scarred Anakin minifigures receive life-saving and life-changing medical treatment in three LEGO sets.

Vader's harrowed, hairless face reveals the pain of the dark side

Transformation
A LEGO Technic mechanism flips the operating table between Anakin and Darth Vader. Another lets you place the iconic helmet on Vader's minifigure's head.

Burned remnants of Anakin's Jedi robes

Anakin's remaining flesh-colored arm is all that is left of his past humanity

Anakin Skywalker
FALLEN JEDI

DATA FILE

YEAR: 2017
FIRST SET: 75183 Darth Vader Transformation
NO. OF SETS: 1
PIECES: 3
ACCESSORIES: None
APPEARANCES: III

Before ... and after
All three of Anakin's injured minifigures come in sets which also include full Darth Vader minifigures so you can see his complete transition to the dark side.

It is very rare to see Darth Vader without his iconic black life-support suit. He cannot go anywhere without it. But, in the privacy and protection of his castle on Mustafar, he can relax in his own personal bacta tank. Floating in its rejuvenating fluid keeps him alive. Bacta heals his body—but his enemies believe his mind is corrupted beyond hope.

Darth Vader's Castle (set 75251)
Vader's healing bacta tank is deep within his fortress on Mustafar. He's attended by a Royal Guard and an Imperial Transport Pilot. The set also includes a fully dressed Darth Vader.

Darth Vader
BACTA TANK

White head piece was created in 2015 and features in four sets under Vader's helmet

Cybernetic arm has a metallic finish

Breathing mask clips between head and torso

DATA FILE

YEAR: 2019
FIRST SET: 75251 Darth Vader's Castle
NO. OF SETS: 1
PIECES: 4
ACCESSORIES: None
APPEARANCES: RO

Bacta tank
Vader floats in his curved transparent-blue tank in his meditation chamber. But beware: he may look vulnerable, but his Force powers never sleep!

Bacta bodies
Three other minifigures are dressed for bacta treatment. Two Luke Skywalkers in Hoth Echo Base (set 7879) and Hoth Medical Chamber (set 75203) and Finn in the third edition of DK's LEGO *Star Wars: Visual Dictionary* (in 2018).

Darth Vader's iconic look is instantly recognizable in his LEGO minifigure form, even though there are 17 variants. They differ in torso print, skin color, eye color, scar patterns, and in their capes. But they all wear one of two designs of his trademark helmet.

Welcome to Toy Fair
A 10th anniversary edition chrome-black Darth Vader minifigure was given out to lucky guests at the 2009 Toy Fair in New York in a special LEGO Collectors Event presentation box.

New head
Vader has gray, white, and tan head pieces under his helmets, but the 2017 variant's is peach colored.

This second helmet mold from 2015 is two pieces—the helmet and a mouth guard piece

This is the 2014 torso design. The original 1999 one was updated in 2008, 2010, and again in 2014

Santa Vader
Darth Vader wears a festive red cape to match his unique Santa-themed leg and torso printing in the 2014 LEGO *Star Wars* Advent Calendar.

Darth Vader
SITH LORD

DATA FILE

YEAR: 2017
FIRST SET: 75183 Darth Vader Transformation
NO. OF SETS: 2
PIECES: 5
ACCESSORIES: Red lightsaber
APPEARANCES: III, Reb, RO, IV, V, VI

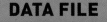

This fresh-faced minifigure is a young Han Solo. Dressed in scruffy clothes on his homeworld Corellia, he has not yet escaped the Imperial-controlled planet to start his life proper. Han is a scrumrat with the White Worms gang in the city of Coronet. He scratches a living stealing and running the black market for the White Worms.

Age-defying
This 2018 minifigure is much younger than previous Han Solos (particularly the gray-haired ones). It is one of five Han minifigures based on *Solo: A Star Wars Story*—a prequel movie about Han's youth.

Hair piece is also worn by seven older Han minifigures from 2016 onward

Corellian M-68 landspeeder
Han hot-wires a classic civilian repulsorlift street racer to escape the White Worms in Han Solo's Landspeeder (set 75209). Can he and Qi'ra make it off Corellia?

Tattered shirt from a tough life on the streets of Corellia

Clothes encrusted in salty water from the sewers that the White Worms call home

DATA FILE
YEAR: 2018
FIRST SET: 75209
Han Solo's Landspeeder
NO. OF SETS: 1
PIECES: 4
ACCESSORIES: Blaster pistol, wrench
APPEARANCES: S

Corellian hound
Anyone trying to scam or escape the White Worms gang should beware their Corellian hounds. This single-mold LEGO piece captures the ferocity of the vicious beast with its tiny red eyes and snarling yellow teeth.

An abandoned street urchin on Corellia, Qi'ra took refuge with the White Worms gang. She started out pickpocketing for them in exchange for meager food and shelter and soon progressed through the ranks to Head Girl thanks to her street smarts. Qi'ra's first minifigure, from 2018, shows the beginning of her journey and is literally marked with signs of her hard life in the dirty sewers.

Unique dress
Qi'ra's minifigure expresses her unique style. Her torso is printed with a wide faux-wool collar and a bright wrap-around shirt that makes a rare splash of color in the dingy sewers.

Qi'ra keeps spikes for picking locks in her belt loops

New LEGO hair piece falls as though it is tucked behind Qi'ra's ear

Metallic silver printing for jacket

Double header
All three of Qi'ra's minifigures have a face that looks serious and perhaps a little lost. The other side presents a crooked smile, full of bravado.

Legs are printed with a faux leather skirt, black pants, and black boots

Moloch is not a typical Grindalid—or minifigure! His fellow Grindalids prefer to stay in the sewers, away from harmful sunlight. They send humans out to do their hard work for them. But brutish Moloch likes to go above ground. He walks the streets of Corellia—and enforces the will of the White Worms gang himself.

Sidekick
When Han Solo and Qi'ra try to escape from the White Worms gang, Moloch's goon Rebolt helps go after them. Like Han and Qi'ra, Rebolt is a human working for the White Worms gang.

Moloch
WHITE WORMS ENFORCER

DATA FILE

YEAR: 2018
FIRST SET: 75210
Moloch's Landspeeder
NO. OF SETS: 1
PIECES: 3
ACCESSORIES:
Blaster pistol, scepter
APPEARANCES: S

Tightly fitting cowl protects Moloch's skin from lethal sunlight when he ventures outside

The specially molded head piece has ridges that fit over Moloch's back

Scepter with a clublike head

Moloch stands on his tail to "walk," so his long flowing robes are printed on a curved LEGO slope piece

Moloch's Landspeeder (set 75210)
Moloch's high-speed A-A4b truckspeeder zips through the narrow streets of Corellia, in hot pursuit of Han and Qi'ra.

Imperial forces come in many forms and so do their minifigures. Patrol troopers cruise the streets, enforcing Imperial rule on Corellia. And they pose an extra obstacle for Han and Qi'ra to evade after they escape from the clutches of the White Worms gang. Two of these minifigures come with the Imperial Patrol Battle Pack (set 75207).

Imperial Battle Pack (set 75207)
One of the patrol troopers chases after Han and Qi'ra on this fast bike. The Aratech C-PH patrol speeder has a cannon and two stud-shooters. He is determined to stop them!

DATA FILE

YEAR: 2018
FIRST SET: 75207 Imperial Patrol Battle Pack
NO. OF SETS: 1
PIECES: 4
ACCESSORIES: Stud-shooter
APPEARANCES: S

Wide black stripe goes all the way around the back of the helmet

Only the patrol trooper has a green light on his chest plate

Black pants rather than full plastoid armor give flexibility

Patrol trooper
IMPERIAL ENFORCER ON CORELLIA

Where do Imperial pilot cadets end up when they are expelled from flight school? Han Solo finds out: conscripted into the Imperial infantry and sent to the least desirable battlefields. Ex-cadet Han Solo finds himself bogged down in someone else's battle on the muddy planet of Mimban. He is now an Imperial Swamp Trooper.

STAR VARIANT

Mud, mud, mud
An extra-muddy variant of Han Solo's mudtrooper was released in 2018. Every piece is dripping with mud, and his hair piece has been changed to the same muddy color.

Han Solo Mudtrooper

Han Solo
MISERABLE MUDTROOPER

DATA FILE

YEAR: 2018
FIRST SET: 75211
Imperial TIE Fighter
NO. OF SETS: 1
PIECES: 5
ACCESSORIES:
Blaster rifle
APPEARANCES: S

Goggles are both molded and printed on the helmet

Han has a cocky expression and raised eyebrow, even in the depths of a muddy fight

Rare cape has a ragged edge and a printed hood on the back

Helmet with flair
The flared style of Han's LEGO helmet is seen on Imperial troopers, officers, and AT-DP and AT-ST pilots, but only he has goggles.

Token plates of green armor are worn over regular clothes

Army captain's cap is not armored because officers rarely go into battle

This minifigure looks like just another mudtrooper (albeit a captain), but it is actually Tobias Beckett. He has stolen the outfit to blend in among Imperial troops until his crew can escape off Mimban. His minifigure looks similar to Han Solo's mudtrooper, but all the pieces are unique. As an officer, Tobias wears a greatcoat over his standard uniform and an Imperial cap.

DATA FILE

YEAR: 2018
FIRST SET: 75211 Imperial TIE Fighter
NO. OF SETS: 1
PIECES: 4
ACCESSORIES: Twin silver blaster pistols
APPEARANCES: S

Mustache gives a hint that this is actually Tobias Beckett

Gray uniform soon becomes camouflaged on Mimban—thanks to all the mud

Mud stains give the Imperial swamp troopers their nickname of "mudtrooper"

Tobias Beckett
DISGUISED MUDTROOPER

Mimban stormtroopers are the elite Imperial troops on the muddy, swampy planet Mimban. The minifigure is well-protected from the boggy conditions, unlike the regular Mimban infantry soldiers. His strong armor is camouflaged with mud splatters and his helmet has a built-in mask for filtering the hazardous Mimban air.

Imperial TIE Fighter (set 75211)
A Mimban stormtrooper comes with the 2018 LEGO TIE Fighter. He is accompanied by a TIE pilot and two familiar mudtroopers—but are they friends or foes?

Mimban Stormtrooper
WET-WEATHER SOLDIER

Caped crusader
The Mimban stormtrooper's dark-gray feathery-edged cloak has a black printed hood on the back. It's also worn by Han Solo's mudtrooper.

Helmet hides the regular peach-toned head piece used for clones and stormtroopers

Respirator cleans polluted Mimban air

Waterproof cape is nicknamed a "slick" by troopers

LEGO stormtrooper pieces in light gray are unique to this minifigure

DATA FILE
YEAR: 2018
FIRST SET: 75211 Imperial TIE Fighter
NO. OF SETS: 1
PIECES: 5
ACCESSORIES: Blaster
APPEARANCES: S

STAR VARIANT

Goggle-eyed
The second young Chewbacca minifigure has goggles printed directly onto his head. He's ready to help Tobias Beckett's crew raid the Imperial Conveyex Transport (set 75217).

There are six different Chewbacca minifigures. This one shows a younger Chewbacca back when he first met his future friend and copilot Han Solo. Chewbacca is visibly younger in this mold—and he is looking good for only 190 years old! Like his previous minifigures, he has a sandwich-board piece over a plain torso, but this one is a new mold for 2018.

Furrier, fluffier head mold makes Chewie look younger than his previous minifigures

No-caster
Chewbacca's two *Solo* minifigures are the only ones to not carry his trademark bowcaster. When you escape prison, you have to improvise with what you can get—and this blaster rifle serves Chewie well.

Greatest space saga of them all
Chewie joined Han Solo in the *Millennium Falcon* cockpit in a 203-piece 2018 San Diego Comic-Con exclusive set.

For the first time, Chewie's minifigure has a pouch and a double bandolier

A second shade of brown was added to the Wookiee leg piece in 2014

Chewbacca
WOOKIEE ESCAPEE

DATA FILE

YEAR: 2018
FIRST SET: 75212 Kessel Run *Millennium Falcon*
NO. OF SETS: 2
PIECES: 3
ACCESSORIES: Blaster rifle
APPEARANCES: S

Han Solo is still young, but he has already had an eventful life. Now he has fallen in with Tobias Beckett—a professional thief who helped him flee the Imperial army. Han has waited a long time for a shot to make his fortune. Now free to be his own man, he adopts the pants, open-shirt, and jacket combo that becomes his trademark look.

STAR VARIANT
Buckle up
Han helps Beckett's crew raid the Imperial Conveyex Transport (set 75217). He has flying goggles and a fur coat, but he keeps his ammo belt and gun holster on hand, on top of his new overcoat.

Kessel Run *Millennium Falcon* (set 75212)
Han Solo makes history in Kessel Run *Millennium Falcon* (set 75212) when his crew travels the dangerous smuggling route in just 12 parsecs.

Hair piece was first used for Han Solo in 2016 and is exclusive to his minifigures

Leather jacket is made of nerf hide

Han's jacket has no lapels, and his black shirt has a folded-over flap, like Lando Calrissian's

27 Han Solo minifigures have a print of his gunslinger belt and holster on his pants

Han Solo
BECKETT'S CREW MEMBER

DATA FILE
YEAR: 2018
FIRST SET: 75212 Kessel Run *Millennium Falcon*
NO. OF SETS: 2
PIECES: 4
ACCESSORIES: Blaster
APPEARANCES: S

Tobias Beckett lives in a dangerous underworld of shady characters. He is always looking for schemes to make money—like stealing from a heavily armed and armored Imperial train traveling at high speed. He leads his own crew, but he is not the real boss. There is always someone higher up he has to answer to, which could explain his minifigure's troubled look.

Cloud-Rider Swoop Bikes (set 75215)
Tobias's heist seems to be going according to plan, but then a rival gang, the Cloud-Riders, swoop in to swipe his hard-earned prize for themselves.

Same head piece as Beckett's mudtrooper minifigure

Coaxium canister
The target of Beckett's plan is coaxium—a rare, very valuable, powerful fuel used for traveling in hyperspace.

Leather-gloved hand carries a heavy blaster pistol

Double holsters for his twin pistols under his greatcoat

Tobias Beckett
CREW LEADER

DATA FILE

YEAR: 2018
FIRST SET: 75215 Cloud-Rider Swoop Bikes
NO. OF SETS: 1
PIECES: 4
ACCESSORIES: Twin silver blaster pistols
APPEARANCES: S

Val's minifigure relishes dangerous missions with Tobias Beckett's crew. She is an expert climber and has an encyclopedic knowledge of weapons and explosives. For the raid on Vandor, she prepares her own homemade baradium bombs. Only she can set them off because the detonator responds to her biological signature and no one else's.

Weapons cache

As a weapons expert, Val knows how to make good use of the weapon rack that comes with her set. It holds four long rifles and is hidden in the cargo container.

Blastproof glasses

On the reverse side of Val's head, she wears protective flying goggles and has a look of focused concentration. The task ahead has high stakes.

Grapple gun was adapted by Val to reel rope 600 meters (2,000 feet)

Jacket with fur from a mastmot (a big four-legged creature with shaggy fur)

Climbing gloves are powered with an electromagnetic grip

Red ropes and a brown harness for climbing and rappelling

DATA FILE

YEAR: 2018
FIRST SET: 75219
Imperial AT-Hauler
NO. OF SETS: 1
PIECES: 4
ACCESSORIES: Silver grapple gun
APPEARANCES: S

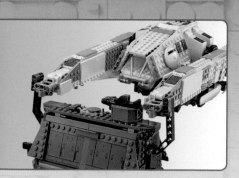

Great train robbery
Rio Durant puts his piloting skills to the test in the Imperial AT-Hauler (set 75219). Beckett's crew use the cargo carrier to swipe a carriage from the high-speed conveyex train.

Rio Durant is an Ardennian—a six-limbed creature from the planet Ardennia—and an excellent pilot. Rio and Tobias Beckett go way back, and so do their schemes. Rio is a key member of Tobias's crew and he loves outlandish capers—the more outrageous the better! He chances his four arms flying dangerous missions and is a fun companion on them, too. He always has a story to tell.

DATA FILE

YEAR: 2018
FIRST SET: 75219
Imperial AT-Hauler
NO. OF SETS: 1
PIECES: 4
ACCESSORIES: Blaster
APPEARANCES: S

Four-armed first
Rio is the first minifigure to have four arms on a standard torso. Four-armed Lord Garmadon from LEGO® Ninjago® has two torsos on top of each other.

Goggles piece from 2016 can pivot up to sit on Rio's head

Print of a Torplex LVD-41 pilot life-support system

Short leg piece: the Ardennian is only 1.49m (4 ft 11 in) tall

Rio Durant
FOUR-ARMED PILOT

Range troopers are the Empire's first line of defense on remote worlds. On Vandor, they must keep the conveyex train running on time. It carries valuable cargo like coaxium, which attracts the attention of many brave criminals. Two range trooper minifigures come with the train, but is that enough to protect it from Tobias Beckett's gang?

Collared
Some LEGO *Star Wars* troopers wear fabric kamas or pauldrons, but this set is the first to introduce a fabric collar. Range troopers wear it in white and the Imperial conveyex gunner wears the same piece in black.

Metallic copper visor printed on a unique helmet mold

Cloth collar

Range Trooper
CONVEYEX PATROLLERS

Walking on the walls
Range troopers can patrol any side of the train thanks to their magnetomic gription boots. They cling to the train walls—even at 90 kilometers (56 miles) an hour.

Rugged blaster is enhanced with a lightsaber hilt and clip piece

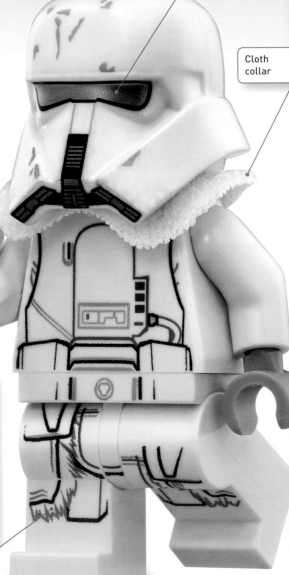

DATA FILE

YEAR: 2018
FIRST SET: 75217 Imperial Conveyex Transport
NO. OF SETS: 1
PIECES: 5
ACCESSORIES: Modified white blaster
APPEARANCES: S

Clothes are lined with an artificial insulating fabric called synthfur

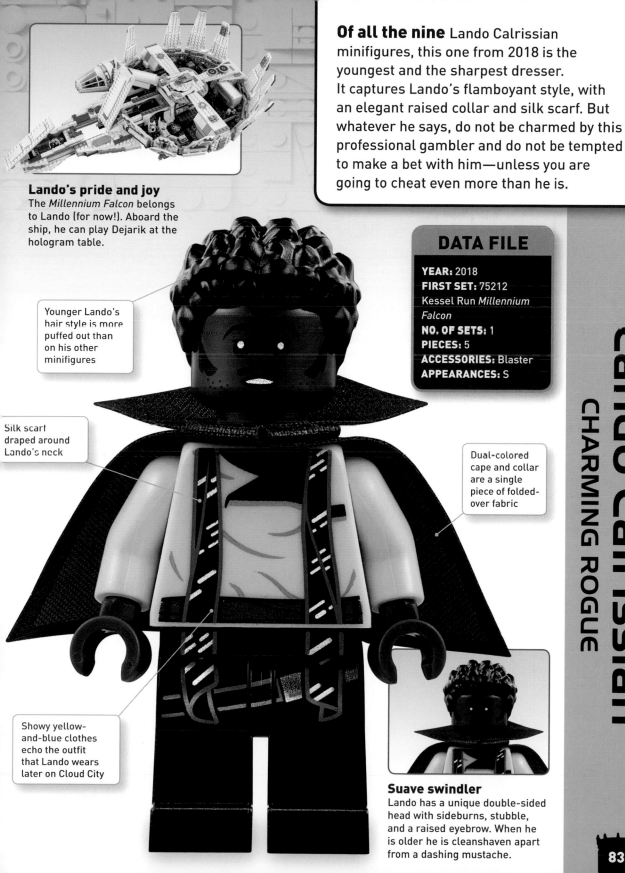

Of all the nine Lando Calrissian minifigures, this one from 2018 is the youngest and the sharpest dresser. It captures Lando's flamboyant style, with an elegant raised collar and silk scarf. But whatever he says, do not be charmed by this professional gambler and do not be tempted to make a bet with him—unless you are going to cheat even more than he is.

Lando's pride and joy
The *Millennium Falcon* belongs to Lando (for now!). Aboard the ship, he can play Dejarik at the hologram table.

Younger Lando's hair style is more puffed out than on his other minifigures

Silk scarf draped around Lando's neck

DATA FILE

YEAR: 2018
FIRST SET: 75212
Kessel Run *Millennium Falcon*
NO. OF SETS: 1
PIECES: 5
ACCESSORIES: Blaster
APPEARANCES: 5

Dual-colored cape and collar are a single piece of folded-over fabric

Showy yellow-and-blue clothes echo the outfit that Lando wears later on Cloud City

Lando Calrissian
CHARMING ROGUE

Suave swindler
Lando has a unique double-sided head with sideburns, stubble, and a raised eyebrow. When he is older he is cleanshaven apart from a dashing mustache.

Qi'ra has come a long way from her salt-encrusted clothes on Corellia. No longer a scrumrat urchin, she has risen through the ranks of the criminal organization Crimson Dawn. She is now a trusted lieutenant with serious power. Her stylish new clothes fit her new sophisticated position, but they're still practical for on-the-ground missions.

Ponytail chic
Both variants of Qi'ra's Crimson Dawn minifigures have the same ponytail. It is made from a more flexible type of plastic than most LEGO hair and was originally created for the LEGO® Friends theme.

Qi'ra
CRIMSON DAWN LIEUTENANT

DATA FILE
YEAR: 2018
FIRST SET: 75219
Imperial AT-Hauler
NO. OF SETS: 1
PIECES: 4
ACCESSORIES:
Blaster
APPEARANCES: S

Unique torso has a fur coat for frozen Vandor over a tailored pale moof-leather jacket

Qi'ra's head piece is shared by all three of her minifigures

Belt has a silver printed buckle and loops for ammunition

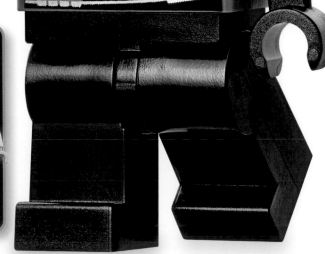

STAR VARIANT

Kessel runner
Aboard the Kessel Run *Millennium Falcon* (set 75212) is another Qi'ra. She has all the same pieces except for the torso. She has taken off her gloves and fur coat, and her tailored moof-leather jacket is now open, revealing her Crimson Dawn necklace.

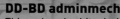

This red-and-white droid works in the control center in the Kessel mines. His head piece also features on R5-series droids and Chopper (C1-10P). His legs are skeleton leg pieces on a T-piece under an upside-down jumper plate.

S1D6-SA-5 works in the miserable Kessel spice mines. Protocol droids are designed for brainy work, not hard labor, but the mine owners do not care. The Pyke Syndicate use whomever they can enslave to mine their spice in appalling conditions. When the Kessel Run *Millennium Falcon* (set 75212) arrives at the mines, the droids are liberated and S1D6-SA-5 is free.

Restraining bolt keeps the droid subdued and subservient in terrible conditions

Photoreceptor

Wiring print is inspired by LEGO protocol droid minifigures

S1D6-SA-5's once shiny red coating is now tarnished and dirty from life down the mines

S1D6-SA-5
KESSEL OPERATIONS DROID

DATA FILE

YEAR: 2018
FIRST SET: 75212 Kessel Run *Millennium Falcon*
NO. OF SETS: 1
PIECES: 3
ACCESSORIES: None
APPEARANCES: S

Quay Tolsite is a Pyke who works for the Pyke Syndicate—a criminal network that controls the illegal spice trade. As Director of Operations, he is in charge in the Kessel spice mines, but that means little. The people who are really in control stay far away from the nasty place. The arrival of the *Millennium Falcon* at the mines spells Tolsite's end.

Hexagonal hood
Many minifigures wear hoods, but none is like Quay Tolsite's head protector. It is based on three hexagons with two breathing tube connectors at the bottom.

Pearl-gold head under the hood has printed eyes and breathing tube connectors

Large angular helmets are worn by all Pykes, but this is the only LEGO one

DATA FILE

YEAR: 2018
FIRST SET: 75212 Kessel Run *Millennium Falcon*
NO. OF SETS: 1
PIECES: 4
ACCESSORIES: Blaster pistol
APPEARANCES: S

Breathing tubes enable Pykes to breathe on Kessel. They are allergic to its atmosphere

Long robes are on a curved LEGO slope piece and are printed with dirt from the underground mines

Agent in the mines
Quay Tolsite has to put up with agents sent by the Mining Guild. One of them comes in Kessel Mine Worker (set 40299) with his own stand.

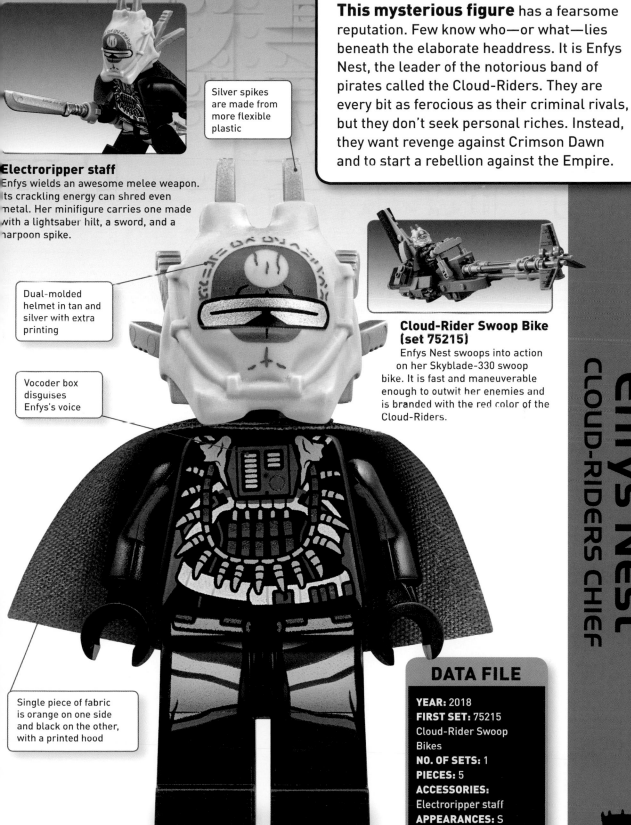

This mysterious figure has a fearsome reputation. Few know who—or what—lies beneath the elaborate headdress. It is Enfys Nest, the leader of the notorious band of pirates called the Cloud-Riders. They are every bit as ferocious as their criminal rivals, but they don't seek personal riches. Instead, they want revenge against Crimson Dawn and to start a rebellion against the Empire.

Silver spikes are made from more flexible plastic

Electroripper staff
Enfys wields an awesome melee weapon. Its crackling energy can shred even metal. Her minifigure carries one made with a lightsaber hilt, a sword, and a harpoon spike.

Cloud-Rider Swoop Bike (set 75215)
Enfys Nest swoops into action on her Skyblade-330 swoop bike. It is fast and maneuverable enough to outwit her enemies and is branded with the red color of the Cloud-Riders.

Dual-molded helmet in tan and silver with extra printing

Vocoder box disguises Enfys's voice

Single piece of fabric is orange on one side and black on the other, with a printed hood

Enfys Nest
CLOUD-RIDERS CHIEF

DATA FILE
YEAR: 2018
FIRST SET: 75215 Cloud-Rider Swoop Bikes
NO. OF SETS: 1
PIECES: 5
ACCESSORIES: Electroripper staff
APPEARANCES: S

Weazel is second-in-command to Enfys Nest in the Cloud-Riders band of marauders. His elaborate head gear hides his identity and makes him look ferocious. Weazel has been pursuing Tobias Beckett with a tracking device and he tracks him down in Cloud-Rider Swoop Bikes (set 75215). He wants Beckett's coaxium fuel!

Master of disguise
Weazel's helmet is dual-molded in tan and red with silver printing on the front and black printing on the back. The sides of the black head underneath have dark-brown printing for the flaps.

Rangefinder and a comms device in the Kalevalan helmet keep Weazel in touch with Enfys

Double swoop
Unlike Enfys, who flies alone, Weazel has a swoop bike with a sidecar. The marauders often fly in pairs so one pirate can jump from the sidecar to raid other ships in flight—even at high speeds!

Slit in the dual-molded helmet reveals the black head underneath

DATA FILE
YEAR: 2018
FIRST SET: 75215 Cloud-Rider Swoop Bikes
NO. OF SETS: 1
PIECES: 4
ACCESSORIES: Ordnance launcher
APPEARANCES: I, S

K21c portable ordnance launcher

Darth Maul appears as a shadowy figure in *Solo: A Star Wars Story*, but his matching minifigure is very solid. This is Maul's second one since losing his legs in a fierce duel with Obi-Wan Kenobi. The first had specially molded LEGO robotic legs. However, now that Maul has more sophisticated mechanical legs, this minifigure has a regular leg piece with a new print.

Zabrak horn piece is shared with five Maul minifigures

Criminal master
Darth Maul ruthlessly controls the criminal network called Crimson Dawn. A former Sith, he uses his trademark double-bladed red lightsaber for this dangerous work.

Tattooed head print of Maul's older, more weathered face

Crimson Dawn pendant

Exclusive
This Darth Maul minifigure comes with LEGO *Star Wars Character Encyclopedia: New Edition*. It shares characteristics with other Darth Maul minifigures, but has exclusive printing on the chest.

This is the only Darth Maul torso to show red skin under black robes

New robotic legs printed onto a regular leg piece

Mechanical toes

Darth Maul
CRIMSON DAWN CRIME LORD

DATA FILE

YEAR: 2019
BOOK: LEGO *Star Wars Character Encyclopedia: New Edition*
NO. OF SETS: N/A
PIECES: 4
ACCESSORIES: Double-bladed red lightsaber
APPEARANCES: S

This gutsy green Twi'lek is ready to make history! Hera Syndulla is one of the first minifigures in the subtheme, LEGO *Star Wars Rebels*. Owner of the rebel starship the *Ghost*, she joins her rebel pals as they take on the evil Empire and travel the galaxy in pursuit of justice. Hera appears in the *Ghost* (set 75053) and later the microfighter *Ghost* (set 75127).

All smiles?
Hera has a double-sided head piece, with a neutral face on one side and a lopsided grin on the other.

Pilot helmet with flying goggles

Hera Syndulla
REBEL PILOT

Hera's lekku (head-tails) sprouting out of her helmet

Twi'leks
Not all Twi'leks are green-skinned. Jedi Aayla Secura has also been made in LEGO minifigure form, but she is a distinctive bright blue color. Bib Fortuna's minifigure is tan.

Orange pilot jumpsuit with brown plates of protective armor

Lekku
Twi'leks are sometimes nicknamed "tail heads" because of their lekku (head-tails). Hera's lekku feature a white tattoo design.

Hera conceals a secret blaster in her boot—just in case

DATA FILE

YEAR: 2014
FIRST SET: 75053
The *Ghost*
NO. OF SETS: 2
PIECES: 4
ACCESSORIES:
Blaster pistol
APPEARANCES: Reb

C1-10P, normally known as Chopper, is a stubborn little astromech droid who keeps all systems running aboard rebel starship the *Ghost*. Built mostly from secondhand parts, Chopper's figure has a uniquely small stature—smaller even than other LEGO *Star Wars* astromechs—thanks to his new short leg and torso pieces. He beeps at crew members and saves the day in four sets.

The *Phantom* and the *Ghost*

Chopper fits into the back of the *Phantom* attack shuttle, ready to guide rebel hero Ezra through battle. Chopper is always happy when the *Phantom* docks back safely to the larger starship, the *Ghost*.

C1-series

Chopper is unique in LEGO *Star Wars*—as the only C1-series astromech figure. C1 droids are very old models, which perhaps explains why Chopper is so fond of "old-fashioned" starship maintenance.

Head piece is the same mold as R5 figures, but with unique coloring and details

Mechanical arms can zap enemies with an electroshock

Articulated arms extend from side compartments in Chopper's head

DATA FILE

YEAR: 2014
FIRST SET: 75048
The *Phantom*
NO. OF SETS: 4
PIECES: 5
ACCESSORIES: None
APPEARANCES: Reb, RO

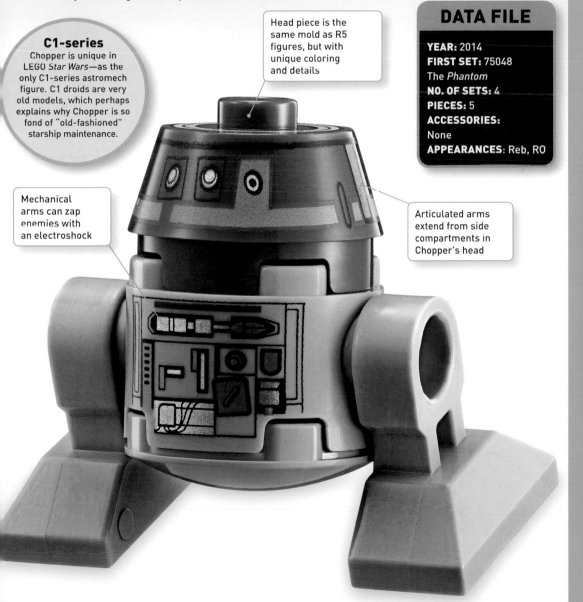

C1-10P
ECCENTRIC ASTROMECH

A former Jedi Padawan, Kanan Jarrus was forced into hiding following Order 66. Now he is a rebel leader and freedom fighter. When Kanan's minifigure was first released in 2014, he had black hair and black facial hair. His minifigure was later updated with brown hair to reflect his appearance on the TV show *Star Wars Rebels*.

STAR VARIANT

Blind Kanan
In the *Phantom* (set 75170) Kanan has a green mask molded to his hair piece after being blinded by Darth Maul.

Ponytailed hair piece was designed for Kanan and is later used in black for Bodhi Rook

Wookiee Gunship (set 75084)
Kanan joins Wullffwarro and the Wookiees aboard their gunship. Equipped with front cannons, rapid-fire shooters, and a mobile gun post, Kanan and his crew are ready for battle!

Right arm is a darker green because Kanan wears a shoulder and arm protector

Kanan Jarrus
JEDI IN TRAINING

Armored pads strapped around knees

DATA FILE

YEAR: 2015
FIRST SET: 75084
Wookiee Gunship
NO. OF SETS: 3
PIECES: 4
ACCESSORIES: Blue lightsaber/blaster
APPEARANCES: Reb

DLT-20A laser rifle
The perfect weapon for long-range accurate fire, many stormtroopers are equipped with this heavy but powerful blaster rifle.

This stormtrooper enforces the Empire's rule across the galaxy in the TV series *Star Wars Rebels*. His armor details are similar to the 2014 classic stormtrooper minifigure, but he has his own "cartoon" style in keeping with the TV show. Beneath the helmet, however, his grimacing head piece is the same as other clone troopers since 2012.

STAR VARIANT

Stormtrooper Sergeant

In 2015, a stormtrooper Sergeant (set 5002938) wears a white pauldron and has the right to order around regular stormtroopers.

Air vents are only bright blue on stormtroopers from the Rebels subtheme

DATA FILE

YEAR: 2014
FIRST SET: 75053
The *Ghost*
NO. OF SETS: 6
PIECES: 4
ACCESSORIES:
Blaster rifle/blaster/stud-shooter
APPEARANCES: Reb

Environmental controls are useful for different planetary atmospheres

Knee protector plate for when assuming a sniper position

Black body glove is visible at knee joint

Stormtrooper
IMPERIAL WARRIOR

93

Sabine Wren is one of the youngest rebels, but she has an explosive reputation! This Mandalorian minifigure is skilled in blowing up key Imperial targets. Sabine is also a graffiti artist who loves to customize her armor and tag downed TIE (Twin Ion Engine) fighters. Sometimes she combines her talents by planting paint bombs.

STAR VARIANT

Blue hair day

Sabine's original minifigure from 2015 has blue hair with orange streaks. Her outfit has a similar decoration and color palette as her later minifigure, but in a different combination.

Hair piece is the same mold as 2015, but it's now dark blue, light blue, and green

DATA FILE

YEAR: 2016
FIRST SET: 75150
Vader's TIE Advanced
vs A-Wing Starfighter
NO. OF SETS: 2
PIECES: 4
ACCESSORIES:
Single or double blasters
APPEARANCES: Reb

About face

Both of Sabine's minifigures share the same double-sided head. One side has her battle face, with gritted teeth. Turn it around to see a concentrated expression for when she is planting explosives.

Sabine Wren
EXPLOSIVES EXPERT

Torso shows Mandalorian armor that is decorated with Sabine's own colorful designs

Tan legs have unique printing with chaps, gun belt, and graffiti on the knee pads

Military man
Zeb is the only one of his rebel crew with military training, having been a member of the Lasan Honor Guard. He controls the *Ghost*'s rotating gun turret and can't wait to launch an attack on the Empire!

A fierce alien rebel from the planet Lasan, Zeb wants to end Imperial rule once and for all, with good reason—the Empire wiped out most of his species. Zeb joins the crew of the *Ghost* (set 75053) as their straight-talking gunner. He cuts a striking figure among his rebel friends with his purple skin, yellow battle suit, and unique head piece with bright green eyes.

DATA FILE

YEAR: 2014
FIRST SET: 75053
The *Ghost*
NO. OF SETS: 1
PIECES: 3
ACCESSORIES:
Bo-rifle
APPEARANCES: Reb

AB-75 bo-rifle
Part-blaster, part electrostaff, Zeb's bo-rifle weapon is unique to the Lasan Honor Guard. It is built with two LEGO blasters connected with a lightsaber hilt piece.

Green eyes are a distinctive feature of the Lasat species

Goatee is a status symbol among the Lasat

Belt and neck plate design continue on back of torso

Zeb has more powerful legs than humans

Zeb Orrelios
ALIEN ALLY

A Force-sensitive young thief from the planet Lothal, Ezra is surprised to find friendship among a group of rebels. He begins his Jedi training under the guidance of fellow rebel Kanan Jarrus. But instead of carrying a standard lightsaber, gadget-loving Ezra has one with a blaster built in to its hilt!

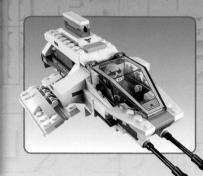

**The *Phantom*
(set 75048)**
Ezra pilots the *Phantom*, a speedy attack shuttle that launches from the larger rebel ship, the *Ghost*. Ezra unfolds the wings and takes control of the two-way shooters. Stormtroopers, beware!

Ezra Bridger
YOUNG REBEL

Helmet collector
Ezra has an unusual hobby: collecting Imperial helmets! His minifigure comes with a salvaged helmet in The *Phantom* (set 75048).

Lothal logo
The back of Ezra's torso is printed with a vintage logo—a remnant of Ezra's former life on the streets of Lothal.

Unique torso printed with pockets to hold Ezra's stolen goods

Utility belt holds all sorts of gadgets

Knee pad and shin guard printed on leg piece

DATA FILE

YEAR: 2014
FIRST SET: 75048
The *Phantom*
NO. OF SETS: 3
PIECES: 4
ACCESSORIES:
Customized blue lightsaber
APPEARANCES: Reb

A high-ranking officer in the Imperial Security Bureau, Agent Kallus is ready to crush any rebellion on the planet Lothal. He commands an AT-DP (set 75083), transports TIE fighters in Imperial Assault Carrier (set 75106) in 2015, and battles the Rebel Combat Frigate (set 75158) in 2016.

All his own hair
Imperial Assault Carrier (set 75106) includes Agent Kallus. Instead of a helmet, Kallus has a unique hair piece. With his helmet off, he can show off his very impressive sideburns.

Textured helmet, issued by the Imperial Security Bureau, is designed to scare people into obedience

Insignia denotes senior rank

DATA FILE

YEAR: 2015
FIRST SET: 75083 AT-DP
NO. OF SETS: 3
PIECES: 4
ACCESSORIES: Bo-rifle
APPEARANCES: Reb

Rifle made from two blasters connected by a black lightsaber hilt element

Lightweight combat armor

Agent Kallus
IMPERIAL ENFORCER

Rebel look
Like all the *Rebels* minifigures, Agent Kallus has a subtly different look from other LEGO *Star Wars* characters. This is because the designs are based on the stylized look of the *Star Wars Rebels* TV show.

Tasked to track down any remaining Jedi, the Inquisitor has carefully cultivated a fearsome reputation. The dreaded Jedi-hunter certainly looks the part, dressed in menacing black-and-gray armor, with an intimidating chest plate and helmet. Beneath the helmet, this minifigure's head piece is pale, lined, and marked with tattoos. This is not a minifigure to be messed with!

TIE Advanced Prototype (set 75082)
Aboard his starfighter, the Inquisitor has many advantages over his rebel enemies. Unlike standard TIE fighters, this prototype has a hyperdrive and protective shields.

Chest plate and shoulder protectors are a single piece. It connects to the head piece

Faced with fear
The Inquisitor, with his white face, is the only Pau'an minifigure.

Double-bladed lightsaber with a new hilt piece

Black armor

DATA FILE
YEAR: 2015
FIRST SET: 75082 TIE Advanced Prototype
NO. OF SETS: 1
PIECES: 5
ACCESSORIES: Double-bladed red lightsaber
APPEARANCES: Reb

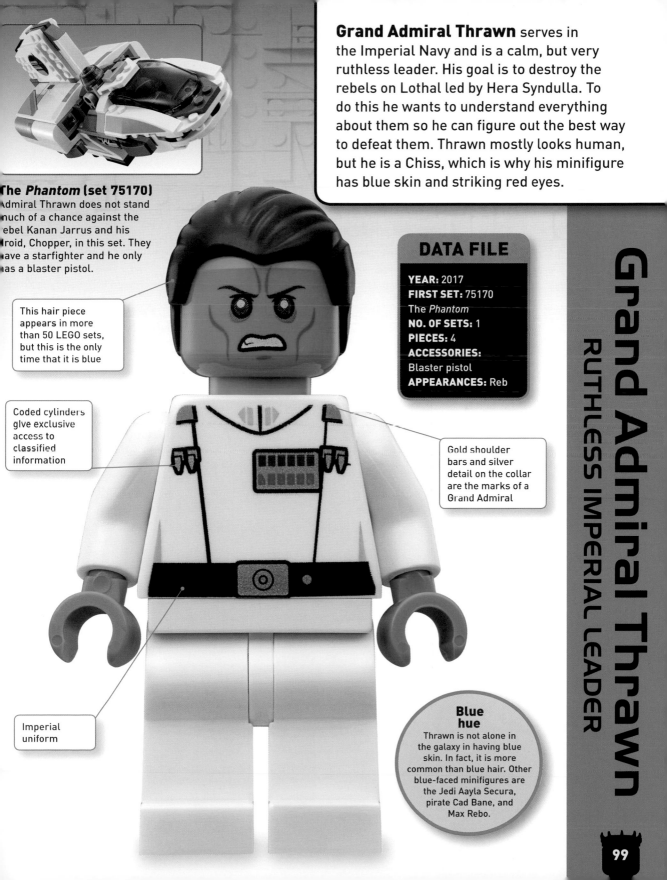

Grand Admiral Thrawn serves in the Imperial Navy and is a calm, but very ruthless leader. His goal is to destroy the rebels on Lothal led by Hera Syndulla. To do this he wants to understand everything about them so he can figure out the best way to defeat them. Thrawn mostly looks human, but he is a Chiss, which is why his minifigure has blue skin and striking red eyes.

The *Phantom* (set 75170)

Admiral Thrawn does not stand much of a chance against the rebel Kanan Jarrus and his droid, Chopper, in this set. They have a starfighter and he only has a blaster pistol.

This hair piece appears in more than 50 LEGO sets, but this is the only time that it is blue

Coded cylinders give exclusive access to classified information

Imperial uniform

DATA FILE

YEAR: 2017
FIRST SET: 75170
The *Phantom*
NO. OF SETS: 1
PIECES: 4
ACCESSORIES:
Blaster pistol
APPEARANCES: Reb

Gold shoulder bars and silver detail on the collar are the marks of a Grand Admiral

Blue hue

Thrawn is not alone in the galaxy in having blue skin. In fact, it is more common than blue hair. Other blue-faced minifigures are the Jedi Aayla Secura, pirate Cad Bane, and Max Rebo.

Grand Admiral Thrawn
RUTHLESS IMPERIAL LEADER

Jyn Erso had a tough start in life because she lost her parents to the Empire, and she is angry with the whole LEGO *Star Wars* galaxy. Hostile to everyone, she eventually finds a cause she can make a positive difference to. Her life's work is to steal the plans of the Death Star and pass them to the rebels. This is a huge leap forward for the Rebellion.

Complex feelings
One half of Jyn's double-sided face is calm and collected, even in the face of great danger. The other side expresses her rage against everyone who has ever let her down.

DATA FILE
YEAR: 2016
FIRST SET: 75155
Rebel U-Wing Fighter
NO. OF SETS: 1
PIECES: 6
ACCESSORIES:
Silver blaster pistol, shoulder bag, HH-12 rocket launcher
APPEARANCES: RO

Comms headset and Jyn's hair are molded into the flight helmet

Stolen A180 blaster pistol

HH-12 rocket launcher is built around a LEGO lightsaber hilt

Jyn Erso
A BORN REBEL

Poncho is the same shape as Princess Leia's on Endor, but it is worn the reverse way

STAR VARIANT

U-wing passenger
In a long insulated blue coat and dark-orange pants, an earlier version of Cassian Andor flies aboard the Rebel U-Wing Fighter (set 75155) in 2016.

Compared to many minifigures in the LEGO *Star Wars* galaxy, Captain Cassian Andor looks very ordinary—and that is just what he hopes to achieve. As an intelligence officer with the Rebel Alliance, he wants to blend in. Spies collect more information about their enemies if they can pass unnoticed. But appearances can be deceiving and Captain Andor is anything but ordinary!

Rebel Prince Charming?
Cassian shares his hair piece with his other variant as well as with Prince Charming from the LEGO® Disney Princess theme. His beard printing is unique to him, though.

DATA FILE

YEAR: 2017
FIRST SET: 75171
Battle on Scarif
NO. OF SETS: 1
PIECES: 4
ACCESSORIES:
Blaster
APPEARANCES: RO

Two green circles indicate rank of captain

Heavy brown canvas jacket with a mandarin collar is worn over a tan top

Cassian Andor
REBEL INTELLIGENCE OFFICER

Scarif mission
Watch out for that soldier, Cassian! No, it's OK, it's just Jyn Erso in disguise. They work together to locate the Death Star plans.

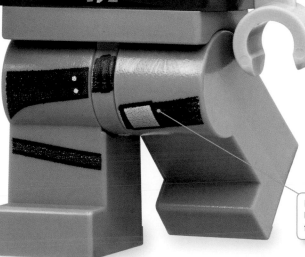

Dark brown leather holster for a blaster

101

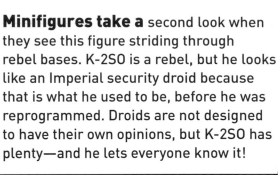

Minifigures take a second look when they see this figure striding through rebel bases. K-2SO is a rebel, but he looks like an Imperial security droid because that is what he used to be, before he was reprogrammed. Droids are not designed to have their own opinions, but K-2SO has plenty—and he lets everyone know it!

Walking tall
K-2SO stands taller than LEGO minifigures. He has the legs of a super battle droid and an extra-tall single torso-and-head piece, which was specially molded for him.

Exclusive torso also has a connector on the back for a backpack or other accessories

Black arm pieces are also used for LEGO skeletons, and battle droids have them in tan

Imperial symbol on each shoulder can be useful for getting into enemy territory

This leg piece was molded for super battle droids, but only K-2SO has it in black

Imperials reunited
K-2SO encounters his former employer, the Empire, in Krennic's Imperial Shuttle (set 75156). He joins Orson Krennic and two death troopers along with Bodhi Rook and Pao.

DATA FILE

YEAR: 2016
FIRST SET: 75156 Krennic's Imperial Shuttle
NO. OF SETS: 1
PIECES: 4
ACCESSORIES: None
APPEARANCES: RO

Action packed
A LEGO piece around Bodhi's neck supports his backpack. The new Rebel recruit carries a long cable to connect his ship with the communications network on Scarif.

This minifigure has an important message, but it could cost him his life. Bodhi Rook was a pilot who delivered cargo for the Empire until someone gave him information that caused him to defect, join the rebels, and ultimately take part in a mission to steal the plans to the Death Star. He goes from having an ordinary life to battling the Empire in Krennic's Imperial Shuttle (set 75156).

Swept-back hair, tied in a short ponytail, was first used for Kanan Jarrus

DATA FILE

YEAR: 2016
FIRST SET: 75156 Krennic's Imperial Shuttle
NO. OF SETS: 1
PIECES: 5
ACCESSORIES: Blaster pistol, backpack
APPEARANCES: RO

Double stubble
Experienced pilot Bodhi has goggles for flying, but his double-sided head has another print, too. He looks happier to have his feet on the ground.

Aircrew survival vest has lots of pockets and its detailed print continues on the back of the torso

Imperial comlink clips to vest

Imperial-issue gray flightsuit

Bodhi Rook
IMPERIAL DEFECTOR

This minifigure cannot see with his eyes, but his deep affinity with the Force connects him with the world around him. Chirrut Îmwe is a Guardian of the Whills, which is an ancient order of warrior monks on the planet Jedha. He is also a fearsome warrior and he takes up weapons to fight against the Empire.

Dangerous hovertank
On the crowded streets of Jedha, Chirrut Îmwe battles an Imperial Assault Hovertank (set 75152). It is protected by two Imperial hovertank trooper minifigures.

Chirrut Îmwe
BLIND WARRIOR MONK

DATA FILE

YEAR: 2016
FIRST SET: 75152 Imperial Assault Hovertank
NO. OF SETS: 1
PIECES: 6
ACCESSORIES: Lightbow, staff
APPEARANCES: RO

Blank eyes cannot see

Traditional Jedha lightbow fires energy blasts

Walking staff is a dangerous weapon in Chirrut's hands

Echo-box transmitter helps Chirrut know what is around him

One hand is white because Chirrut wears a gauntlet for firing his lightbow

DATA FILE

YEAR: 2016
FIRST SET: 75153
AT-ST Walker
NO. OF SETS: 1
PIECES: 5
ACCESSORIES: Repeating blaster cannon with backpack generator
APPEARANCES: RO

Baze likes to blow things up and he has some powerful weapons such as his devastating repeating blaster. Baze used to be a Guardian of the Whills, like his friend Chirrut Îmwe, but now he follows his own mission. He wants revenge against the Empire for destroying his home city on Jedha. He joins the Rogue One team and provides a lot of firepower on the mission to Scarif.

**AT-ST Walker
(set 75153)**
Baze and a rebel trooper battle an AT-ST driver in this Imperial walker. In the narrow streets of holy Jedha City, it spells devastation.

Generator's exhaust pipe

Repeating blaster cannon

Transparent neck brace

Baze Malbus
FREELANCE ASSASSIN

Firepower
Baze's repeating blaster is so devastating it needs its own generator, which he carries on his back. Both parts are brick-built, and the weapon connects to its power source with a LEGO chain.

Kneepad for kneeling on the ground to fire large weapon

Bistan is the only Iakaru to join the Rogue One mission against the Empire and the only one of his species to come in minifigure form. He is a friendly and well-liked member of the rebels, but the warriorlike Iakaru is a dangerous enemy to have. He enjoys the thrill of battle and puts all his energy into the Battle of Scarif.

Agile Iakaru
Stocky Bistan has a sturdy minifigure, but he is more agile than he looks. Iakaru evolved to live in trees, so Bistan is comfortable perching on the side of a fast-moving U-wing.

DATA FILE
YEAR: 2016
FIRST SET: 75155
Rebel U-Wing Fighter
NO. OF SETS: 1
PIECES: 3
ACCESSORIES:
Blaster
APPEARANCES: RO

Bistan
U-WING DOOR GUNNER

Hair piece is printed with hair—and streaks of bald patches

Bushy eyebrows help Bistan sense the space around him, like whiskers

Red Iakaru eyes have excellent eyesight and depth perception

Metal sealing ring for attaching a flight helmet is molded to Bistan's unique head

Safety harness on the torso and leg continues around the back of the torso

Air power
Bistan perches in the open doorway of a U-wing to fire his M-45 repeating ion blaster at ground targets in U-Wing Fighter (set 75155).

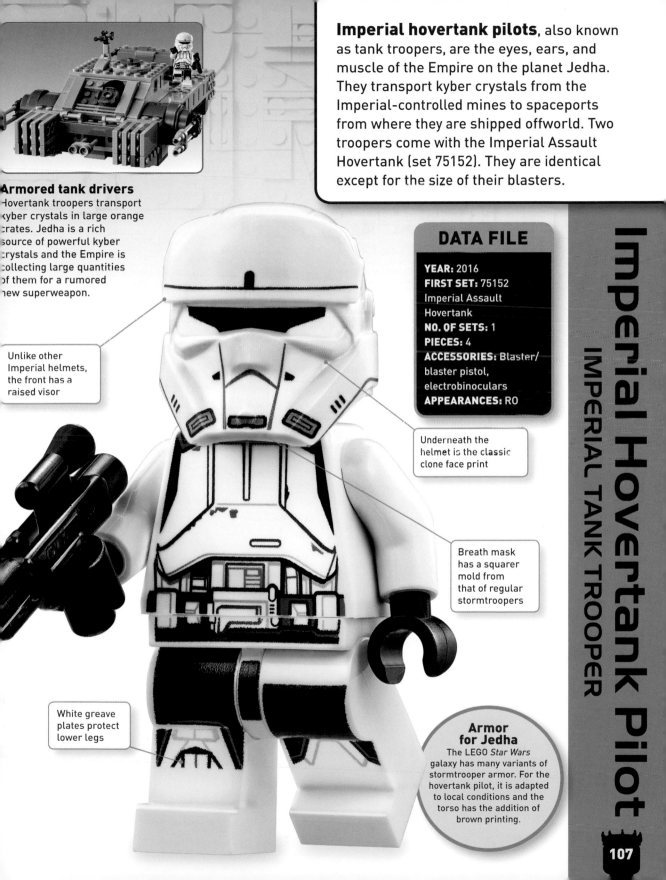

Imperial hovertank pilots, also known as tank troopers, are the eyes, ears, and muscle of the Empire on the planet Jedha. They transport kyber crystals from the Imperial-controlled mines to spaceports from where they are shipped offworld. Two troopers come with the Imperial Assault Hovertank (set 75152). They are identical except for the size of their blasters.

Armored tank drivers
Hovertank troopers transport kyber crystals in large orange crates. Jedha is a rich source of powerful kyber crystals and the Empire is collecting large quantities of them for a rumored new superweapon.

DATA FILE
YEAR: 2016
FIRST SET: 75152 Imperial Assault Hovertank
NO. OF SETS: 1
PIECES: 4
ACCESSORIES: Blaster/blaster pistol, electrobinoculars
APPEARANCES: RO

Unlike other Imperial helmets, the front has a raised visor

Underneath the helmet is the classic clone face print

Breath mask has a squarer mold from that of regular stormtroopers

White greave plates protect lower legs

Armor for Jedha
The LEGO Star Wars galaxy has many variants of stormtrooper armor. For the hovertank pilot, it is adapted to local conditions and the torso has the addition of brown printing.

107

Orson Krennic, the Director of Imperial Advanced Weapons Research, is a very clever but very cruel man. He goes everywhere with his death trooper bodyguards, who will fire immediately on his command. Krennic dreams of creating a moon-sized superweapon and he will do anything to make his scientists build it.

Krennic's Imperial Shuttle (set 75156)
Krennic has his own personal starship. He travels on it to inspect the building progress of the Death Star, known as the Tarkin Initiative.

Director Orson Krennic
DIRECTOR OF WEAPONS RESEARCH

DATA FILE

YEAR: 2016
FIRST SET: 75156
Krennic's Imperial Shuttle
NO. OF SETS: 1
PIECES: 5
ACCESSORIES: Silver blaster
APPEARANCES: RO

Wrinkled brow tells of the pressure of the Death Star project

Rank plaque shows Krennic is the equivalent of Admiral

Code cylinders give Krennic access to top-secret places and information

Rebel cape
White is a rare color for a cape in the LEGO *Star Wars* galaxy and Krennic is the only Imperial minifigure to wear one. Two rebel minifigures, Mon Mothma (2009) and Princess Leia (2012), also have one.

Crisp white uniform is still clean because other people do Krennic's dirty work for him

STAR VARIANT
Commander
Two senior Imperial death troopers accompany Krennic in Krennic's Imperial Shuttle (set 75156) in 2016. They have a simple torso print and wear fabric pauldrons on their shoulder.

These sinister stormtroopers look as mean as their name suggests. Imperial death troopers are part of Imperial intelligence and they work as elite bodyguards for senior Imperial personnel like Director Orson Krennic. Their black armor has a special coating that makes it hard for enemy sensors to detect—which also makes them well suited to stealth missions.

Battle Pack (set 75165)
Two death trooper minifigures join forces with two regular stormtroopers in this set. One trooper can sit atop an Imperial walker, which has posable legs.

DATA FILE
YEAR: 2017
FIRST SET: 75165 Imperial Trooper Battle Pack
NO. OF SETS: 2
PIECES: 5
ACCESSORIES: Stud-shooter/blaster
APPEARANCES: Reb, RO

Imperial Death Trooper
ELITE STORMTROOPER

Only death troopers have green spots on their helmets. The lights are part of their improved sensor system

Fragmentation grenades are carried on torso

Black troopers
At first glance, death trooper minifigures look like TIE pilots because they wear black. However, their prints have more in common with white stormtrooper minifigures.

109

Rebel Jyn Erso is determined to bring down the Empire. She will do anything, even dress up as an Imperial ground trooper. It is the best way to sneak inside the Imperial base on Scarif. She wants to steal the plans to the superweapon that the Empire is building. If the rebels know more about the Death Star, they might be able to destroy it.

Under the helmet
When not in danger of being spotted, Jyn's minifigure can swap her Imperial helmet for a ponytailed hair piece. This hair piece is also used by Kordi from *Star Wars: The Freemaker Adventures.*

Jyn Erso
IMPERIAL GROUND CREW DISGUISE

Front of helmet juts forward and upward in front of the recessed visor

Helmet protects ground crew from engine blast

Torso identical to the Imperial Ground Trooper minifigures from 2016 and 2017

DATA FILE

YEAR: 2017
FIRST SET: 75171
Battle on Scarif
NO. OF SETS: 1
PIECES: 4
ACCESSORIES:
Blaster, helmet
APPEARANCES: RO

Geographically, the planet Scarif is a tropical paradise. It has sun, sea, surf, and . . . stormtroopers. They are Imperial coastal defender stormtroopers, also known as shoretroopers, who are trained to fight on the beach. Scarif is protected by a shield gate so a posting here is quiet and pleasant—until the rebels arrive. No one gets to enjoy the beach in Battle on Scarif (set 75171).

DATA FILE

YEAR: 2017
FIRST SET: 75171
Battle on Scarif
NO. OF SETS: 1
PIECES: 4
ACCESSORIES:
Modified gray blaster
APPEARANCES: RO

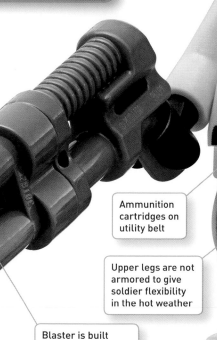

Helmet filters sand from the air and contains cooling fans

Armor has a special coating to strengthen it against sea salt

Ammunition cartridges on utility belt

Upper legs are not armored to give soldier flexibility in the hot weather

Blaster is built with space gun and binoculars pieces

Shoretrooper
SCARIF STORMTROOPER

The Drabatan minifigure called "Paodok'Draba'Takat Sap'De'Rekti Nik'Linke'Ti 'Ki'Vef'Nik'NeSevef'Li'Kek" is generally known just as Pao. An amphibian from the marshy, freshwater planet Pipada, Pao believes in the Resistance cause. He works as a mechanic on the D'Qar base and takes up arms to fight in the Battle of Scarif.

Small but fierce
One side of Pao's head looks calm. The other shows his large mouth roaring in a war cry. Pao's loud voice encourages his allies and terrifies his enemies.

Backpack antenna

Helmet with flared neck guard

Neck brace connects to a stickered backpack

Illegal blaster rifle has a chamber on top for tibanna gas, which gives it extra power

Pao
REBEL FIGHTER

DATA FILE

YEAR: 2016
FIRST SET: 75156
Krennic's Imperial Shuttle
NO. OF SETS: 1
PIECES: 5
ACCESSORIES: Modified blaster rifle, backpack
APPEARANCES: RO

Waterproof fatigues

U-wings and Y-wings
This unnamed pilot has a lot in common with General Merrick—most of their bodies are the same. He flies two types of ships in Rebel U-Wing Fighter (set 75155) in 2016 and Y-Wing Starfighter (set 75172) in 2017.

General Antoc Merrick is a loyal Rebel pilot who commands Blue Squadron. He was an excellent pilot in the Rarified Air Cavalry on Virujansi until the Empire took over the planet and he left to join the Rebel Alliance. As well as flying for the rebels, he also has a place on the rebel council. During the Battle of Scarif, his pilots get through the shield gate and into Scarif's atmosphere to fight.

All smiles
Christmas is the time to be jolly, and Merrick is enjoying the season in his LEGO *Star Wars* advent calendar. One side of his head smiles and the other has a bigger open-mouthed grin.

Ruffled, windswept hair piece suits the dashing pilot

Torso piece is shared with the U-wing pilot minifigure. The print is the same as the Y-wing pilot's, but he has black hands

DATA FILE

YEAR: 2018
FIRST SET: 75213
LEGO *Star Wars*
Advent Calendar
NO. OF SETS: 1
PIECES: 4
ACCESSORIES:
Blaster pistol, helmet
APPEARANCES: RO

Leg piece shared with two other LEGO *Star Wars* pilot minifigures

Borrowed helmet
A snowman is keeping Merrick's helmet cool for him in the same set, the 2018 LEGO *Star Wars* Advent Calendar (set 75213).

Brave **Admiral Raddus is** a Mon
Calamari. He commands the *Profundity* MC75
Star Cruiser and the whole Rebel Alliance
fleet. Admiral Raddus never shies away from
a fight and he plays a big role in the Battle of
Scarif when his ship takes on the Imperial
Navy. Many years later, the Resistance names
a flagship in his honor.

Fishy colors
Mon Calamari
subspecies have different
skin tones from each other.
Admiral Ackbar and the Mon
Calamari officer minifigures
have orangey-brown
mottled skin.

Eye printing
has much
more detail
than the first
two 2009
Mon Calamari
minifigures

DATA FILE
YEAR: 2017
FIRST SET: 75172
Y-Wing Starfighter
NO. OF SETS: 1
PIECES: 3
ACCESSORIES:
Blaster pistol
APPEARANCES: RO

Gray jerkin worn
over blue Fleet
service uniform

City crest awarded
for Raddus's service
to his city, Nystullum

Admiral Raddus
PROFUNDITY COMMANDER

Watertight
pockets

Y-Wing Starfighter (set 75172)
Raddus can fly the Y-wing in this
set or take over from the Y-wing
pilot minifigure in the crane and
use it to load the starfighter.

Loaded up
Moroff's tall backpack includes a battery, a survival pack, and clip on the side for his brick-built gun. His gun is a rotary cannon blaster made with a LEGO agent's gun and a LEGO Technic axle piece.

This tall ball of fur is not cuddly. Moroff is a heartless, ruthless minifigure who will happily go after anyone in the LEGO *Star Wars* galaxy for the right price. The very strong Gigoran is not interested in who is right and who is wrong, he just wants to get paid. Moroff joins a group of mercenaries on the planet Jedha and is part of the team that brings Bodhi Rook in for questioning.

Vocoder box translates Gigoran into Galactic Basic

DATA FILE

YEAR: 2017
FIRST SET: 75172
Y-Wing Starfighter
NO. OF SETS: 1
PIECES: 3
ACCESSORIES: Rotary blaster cannon, backpack
APPEARANCES: RO

Moroff
GIGORAN MERCENARY

Gray flecked print on white fur continues on both the front and back of the torso

Dual-molding
The gray vocoder and chest panel on Moroff's sandwich-board piece are not printed. The whole element is molded in two colors of plastic, so the gray goes all the way through to the inside.

Utility pouches are on leg straps rather than on a belt around the waist like most minifigures have

Loyal to the Empire and highly disciplined, an Imperial stormtrooper is built to succeed in combat. Shielded in white armor, many have blank heads under their helmets to hide their identity. Stormtroopers reach into every corner of the galaxy and 13 types make their presence felt in 38 sets.

Stormtrooper
IMPERIAL SOLDIER

Heads up
Early variants of the stormtrooper minifigure have blank heads: the first ones were plain yellow, then peach, and then, in 2008, black. Stormtroopers with faces beneath their helmets were released in 2012.

Helmet had a revised LEGO mold in 2019. It is now dual-molded so the eyes are no longer printed

Striped mouth grilles have been seen on stormtroopers since 2007

Printed legs are not identical

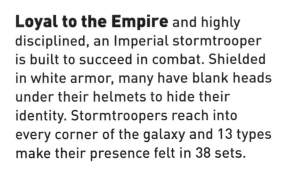

STAR VARIANTS

Original stormtrooper
This is the first stormtrooper minifigure. He hides a blank yellow head under his helmet and appears in four sets from 2001 to 2003.

Armor detail
First released in a 2012 battle pack, this variant has torso armor detail and plain legs. It also comes with DK's LEGO *Minifigure Year by Year: A Visual History* (2013).

Super trooper
This shiny silver chrome stormtrooper was released in a promotional polybag in 2010. It was sold exclusively at Toys "R" Us stores throughout March of that year.

Utility belt with blaster power cell reserves

DATA FILE

YEAR: 2019
FIRST SET: 75229 Death Star Escape
NO. OF SETS: 3
PIECES: 4
ACCESSORIES: Blaster/stud-shooter
APPEARANCES: Reb, IV, V, VI, M

STAR VARIANTS

True original

The first C-3PO appears in five sets between 2001 and 2005 with a light pearl-gold finish. Another one, in a richer pearl-gold, appears in five more sets from 2008 to 2010.

Red arm

In *The Force Awakens*, C-3PO has replaced his left arm with a red metallic one, in order to remember another droid's brave sacrifice.

Chrome gold

This limited-edition chrome gold C-3PO was randomly placed in 10,000 sets to celebrate the 30th anniversary of *Star Wars* in 2007. The LEGO Group also made five of this minifigure in real 14-carat gold.

C-3PO-ho-ho

In the 2015 Advent Calendar (set 75097), a festive C-3PO carries a red sack of presents.

Fretful C-3PO has found himself in 26 sets since he was first released in 2001. The original protocol droid, C-3PO now has eight variants. Up to 2012, all C-3PO minifigures have the same printing, but come in different tones of gold. Since 2012, C-3PO has had new head and torso printings that show his eyes, his colorful wires, an oil stain, and even the restraining bolt put on him by the Jawas on Tatooine.

Audiosensor— C-3PO has one on each side of his head

Warm gold finish

Behind you!

C-3PO's shiny gold armor continues on the back of his torso, along with his backplate and mid-body section.

C-3PO's connection wires are exposed in his mid-body section. They have been brightly colored since 2012

C-3PO
PROTOCOL DROID

DATA FILE

YEAR: 2016
FIRST SET: 75136 Droid Escape Pod
NO. OF SETS: 9
PIECES: 3
ACCESSORIES: None except for air traffic paddles in 75247 *Star Wars* Rebel A-Wing Starfighter
APPEARANCES: II, CW, III, Reb, IV, V, VI, VII, VIII, IX

This rebel trooper is ready to fight for the Alliance! His minifigure comes well equipped for battle with his custom-made blast helmet and plenty of firepower. Four rebel scout troopers have starred in six sets alongside a scout speeder, an advent calendar, and three versions of the *Tantive IV*, including one that comes with Alderaan.

STAR VARIANT
First trooper
The original rebel scout trooper is almost the same as the second one, but he is not smiling. He appears with several comrades in Rebel Scout Speeder (set 7668) and onboard *Tantive IV* (set 10198).

Rebel Scout Trooper
SOLDIER OF THE REBEL ARMY

Removable blast visor clips into holes at the sides of the helmet

Only the rebel scout trooper and Captain Antilles wear this blast helmet

Face and chin-strap print is new for 2019

Secret info
The rebel command center in TIE Fighter Attack (set 75237) has a transparent brick with the plans of the Death Star to help the rebels.

New detail on the previously plain vest

DATA FILE
YEAR: 2019
FIRST SET: 75237
TIE Fighter Attack
NO. OF SETS: 2
PIECES: 5
ACCESSORIES:
Silver blaster
APPEARANCES: RO, IV

Plain gray pants are common to all three rebel scout troopers (and they appear in more than 100 other LEGO sets!)

STAR VARIANTS

Original Leia
A yellow-faced Leia flew into the LEGO *Star Wars* galaxy on the original *Millennium Falcon* (set 7190). A similar Leia with peach-colored head and hands stars in four sets from 2007 to 2010.

Celebration cape
In Gold Leader's Y-Wing Starfighter (set 9495) in 2012, Leia is dressed up for an awards ceremony. She presents the heroic pilot Dutch Vander with a medal.

As a member of the Galactic Senate and a secret sympathizer with the Rebel Alliance, Princess Leia Organa is a symbol of hope across the LEGO *Star Wars* galaxy. She dresses in the traditional white robes of the Alderaan royal family. Her eight variants bring her calm voice of reason into 11 sets, including very significant models like three *Millennium Falcon*s, two Death Stars, and two *Tantive IV* ships.

Leia's famous double braided-bun hair style got an updated LEGO piece in 2011

Leia probably stole this blaster from Imperial forces!

Torso was also worn in 2014 and in 2019 with a sloped brick skirt in *Tantive IV* (set 75244)

Symbolic silver belt of Alderaan royalty

Serious side
Princess Leia's double-sided head was updated for her 2019 minifigures. She does not look happy!

Princess Leia
SENATOR OF ALDERAAN

DATA FILE
YEAR: 2019
FIRST SET: 75229 Death Star Escape
NO. OF SETS: 1
PIECES: 4
ACCESSORIES: Blaster
APPEARANCES: IV

Luke Skywalker is a poor farmboy who dreams of becoming a space pilot. He longs to escape the daily drudgery of life on his uncle's moisture farm. When he meets exiled Jedi Obi-Wan Kenobi, Luke's life changes forever and he finally has something to smile about. Nine Luke minifigures in his white Tatooine robes appear in 17 sets.

STAR VARIANTS

First Luke
The young Luke variant with short tan hair and a yellow face and hands appears in three LEGO sets from 1999 to 2004. He also appears in LEGO *Star Wars: The Visual Dictionary* (2014) with updated printing.

Long locks
Ultimate Collector's *Millennium Falcon* (set 10179) comes with a Luke with long hair. There is a similar variant—but with white eye details—on Luke's Landspeeder (set 8092).

Mop head
The other side of Luke's 2011 head has a printed blindfold for when he practices with his lightsaber. The same mop of hair appears on the smiling Luke given away at New York Comic-Con 2012.

Luke Skywalker
FARMBOY OF TATOOINE

DATA FILE

YEAR: 2016
FIRST SET: 75159
Death Star
NO. OF SETS: 3
PIECES: 4
ACCESSORIES: Electrobinoculars
APPEARANCES: IV

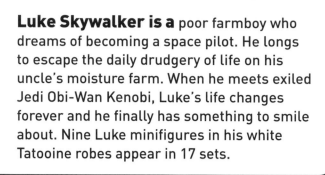

The same simple farm tunic is also worn by Luke Skywalker in three 2014 LEGO *Star Wars* sets

Utility belt holds Luke's farm tools

Leg bindings keep out the desert sand

Visual treat
The revised edition of DK's LEGO *Star Wars: Visual Dictionary* (2014) came with a Luke minifigure. He was an updated version of the first Luke minifigure with extra creases printed on his shirt.

Sandcrawler (set 75220)
In this set, unwary droids need to watch out for the two Jawas on the prowl for scrap metal to sell. Droids are loaded onto the sandcrawler with a LEGO Technic crane and put into a custom-built droid prison.

Indigenous to the desert planet Tatooine, Jawas are small, industrious creatures, always on the lookout for items to scavenge and sell. Their humanoid shape is reflected in a standard minifigure form, though they have short, unposable legs and a mysterious face. Fortunately, the LEGO plastic doesn't recreate the Jawa's distinctive body odor.

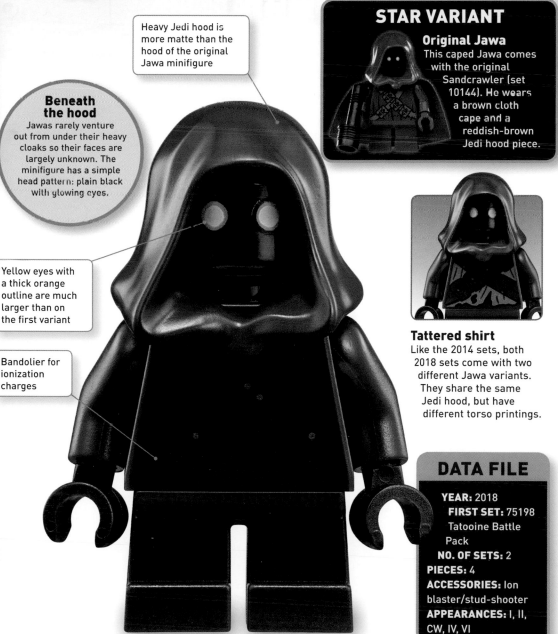

Heavy Jedi hood is more matte than the hood of the original Jawa minifigure

Beneath the hood
Jawas rarely venture out from under their heavy cloaks so their faces are largely unknown. The minifigure has a simple head pattern: plain black with glowing eyes.

Yellow eyes with a thick orange outline are much larger than on the first variant

Bandolier for ionization charges

STAR VARIANT

Original Jawa
This caped Jawa comes with the original Sandcrawler (set 10144). He wears a brown cloth cape and a reddish-brown Jedi hood piece.

Tattered shirt
Like the 2014 sets, both 2018 sets come with two different Jawa variants. They share the same Jedi hood, but have different torso printings.

Jawa
DESERT SCAVENGER

DATA FILE
YEAR: 2018
FIRST SET: 75198 Tatooine Battle Pack
NO. OF SETS: 2
PIECES: 4
ACCESSORIES: Ion blaster/stud-shooter
APPEARANCES: I, II, CW, IV, VI

Now an old man, Obi-Wan Kenobi is a Jedi in exile. He lives a hermit's existence on Tatooine and goes by the name of Ben Kenobi. However, his minifigure shows signs of the dramatic, exciting life he once led. He wears Jedi robes and a brown cloak and keeps his blue lightsaber close at hand. "Ben" Kenobi appears in ten LEGO *Star Wars* sets.

Obi-Wan "Ben" Kenobi
EXILED JEDI

Original Obi-Wan
In 1999, the aged Obi-Wan has a yellow head and hands and a simple torso printing. In 2004 he was given new gray hair and printing, and in 2007 a peach-skinned version was released.

Hood and cape
In the *Millennium Falcon* (set 7965), Obi-Wan hides his identity with a hood and cape—the only other aged Obi-Wan with these clothes is in the 2011 Death Star (set 10188).

White details in the eyes first appeared on a variant in Luke's Landspeeder (set 8092) in 2010

Only Obi-Wan has this head with a printed gray beard and wrinkles

Jedi-type robes are similar to Tatooine fashion, so Ben does not look suspicious

DATA FILE

YEAR: 2014
FIRST SET: 75052
Mos Eisley Cantina
NO. OF SETS: 4
PIECES: 4
ACCESSORIES:
Blue lightsaber
APPEARANCES: Reb, IV

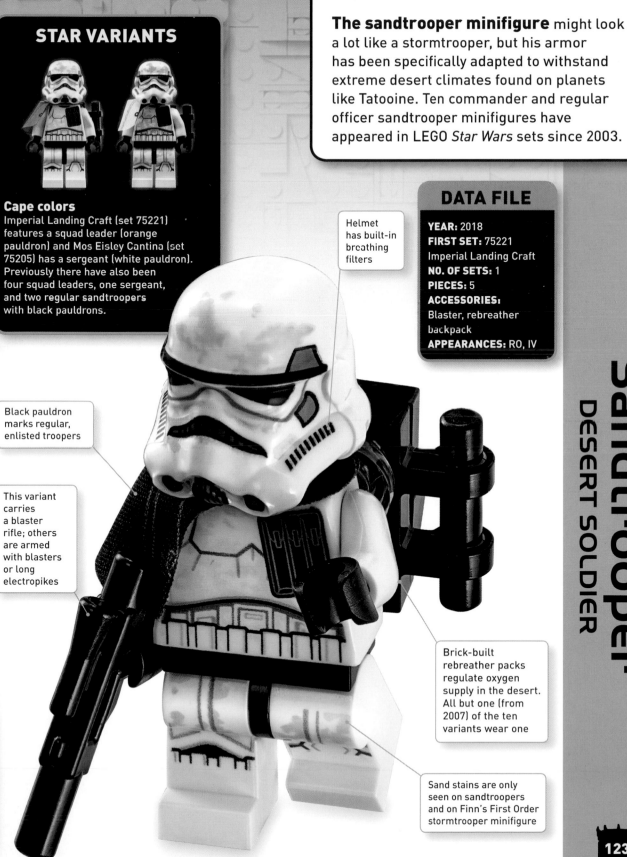

STAR VARIANTS

Cape colors
Imperial Landing Craft (set 75221) features a squad leader (orange pauldron) and Mos Eisley Cantina (set 75205) has a sergeant (white pauldron). Previously there have also been four squad leaders, one sergeant, and two regular sandtroopers with black pauldrons.

The sandtrooper minifigure might look a lot like a stormtrooper, but his armor has been specifically adapted to withstand extreme desert climates found on planets like Tatooine. Ten commander and regular officer sandtrooper minifigures have appeared in LEGO *Star Wars* sets since 2003.

Helmet has built-in breathing filters

DATA FILE

YEAR: 2018
FIRST SET: 75221 Imperial Landing Craft
NO. OF SETS: 1
PIECES: 5
ACCESSORIES: Blaster, rebreather backpack
APPEARANCES: RO, IV

Black pauldron marks regular, enlisted troopers

This variant carries a blaster rifle; others are armed with blasters or long electropikes

Brick-built rebreather packs regulate oxygen supply in the desert. All but one (from 2007) of the ten variants wear one

Sand stains are only seen on sandtroopers and on Finn's First Order stormtrooper minifigure

Sandtrooper
DESERT SOLDIER

There are three LEGO sets of the cantina in Mos Eisley (from 2004, 2014, and 2018), but only this one includes its server, Wuher. The hairy, unfriendly-looking man serves drinks to criminals and unsavory characters—but not to droids. Droids are not allowed in the cantina so no droids are included in the set.

Mos Eisley Cantina (set 75205)
Wuher stands behind his curved bar and watches his shifty customers like Han Solo and Greedo, who are eyeing each other in a booth.

Wuher serves up special Cantina drinks in this transparent mug, which appears in 21 LEGO sets

Bala-Tik, DJ, and Cassian Andor also have this hair piece

First LEGO *Star Wars* minifigure with two colors of sideburns printed on the head

Tan clothes are cool in the desert and are very popular on Tatooine

Wuher
CANTINA SERVER

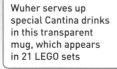

DATA FILE

YEAR: 2018
FIRST SET: 75205
Mos Eisley Cantina
NO. OF SETS: 1
PIECES: 4
ACCESSORIES:
Blaster pistol, tankard
APPEARANCES: IV

The Bith musician Figrin D'an and his band, the Modal Nodes, are a regular fixture at the Mos Eisley Cantina. Large heads and finely tuned senses are characteristics of the Bith species. Many Bith are artists or musicians. The Bith musician minifigure wears dark clothing to reflect the cool, mellow tone of his band's wailing jazz music.

Mos Eisley Cantina (set 75052)
The seedy Mos Eisley Cantina is a favorite performance spot for Figrin D'an and the Modal Nodes. There is a darkly lit stage, a well-stocked bar, and plenty of customers who appreciate some of the best music in the galaxy.

DATA FILE

YEAR: 2014
FIRST SET: 75052
Mos Eisley Cantina
NO. OF SETS: 1
PIECES: 3
ACCESSORIES: Kloo horn/fizzz/ommni box
APPEARANCES: IV

Kloo horn instrument made from a LEGO lightsaber hilt and a faucet piece

New large head mold for the highly evolved Bith species

Huge eyes are incredibly receptive to colors and shapes

Black jacket is printed with silver buttons and detailing, which continues on back of the torso

Tuneful trio
Three Bith musicians are included in the Mos Eisley Cantina set. Their minifigures are identical, but each has a different instrument. In addition to the kloo horn, there is a fizzz and an ommni box.

Bith Musician
CANTINA BAND MEMBER

This bold minifigure is a lovable LEGO *Star Wars* rogue! The unlikely hero who found himself mixed up in the Rebellion against the Empire has now starred in 17 LEGO *Star Wars* sets. Like his beat-up ship, the *Millennium Falcon*, Han's minifigure has been modified over the years—but he has retained his confident smile.

STAR VARIANTS

Three Solos
Han Solo has 15 minifigures relating to Han's everyday clothes. Seven with blue pants match his appearance in Episode IV, while his four brown-legged variants represent Episode VI. All are printed with a belt for a blaster. In 2017, Han swapped his black vest for a blue long-sleeved jacket in *Millennium Falcon* (set 75192) and three more figures with blue arms followed.

20th anniversary Han
The original Han Solo is very rare and it came in the first-ever LEGO *Millennium Falcon* (set 7190), released in 2000. His minifigure was re-released in Imperial Dropship—20th Anniversary Edition (set 75262).

Han Solo
BRAVE BRAGGART

Since 2011, Han has had a peach-colored head with white eye detailing

Harrison Ford
Han Solo is the first LEGO minifigure to be based on the likeness of actor Harrison Ford, who plays Han Solo in the *Star Wars* movies—but he is not the only one to be based on Ford! There is also a LEGO® *Indiana Jones*™.

Blue arms replaced white and beige ones in 2017

This is the only Han Solo to have dual-molded legs

DATA FILE

YEAR: 2018
FIRST SET: 75222 Betrayal at Cloud City
NO OF SETS: 1
PIECES: 4
ACCESSORIES: Blaster pistol
APPEARANCES: IV, V, VI

Mos Eisley Cantina (set 75052)
This second LEGO model of the seedy saloon on Tatooine from 2014 is the setting for the confrontation between the second Greedo minifigure and Han Solo. The pair discuss Han's unpaid debts at a table in a shady alcove.

Rodian bounty hunter Greedo is looking for Han Solo to recover money that Han owes to his boss, Jabba the Hutt. He finally catches up with Han in three LEGO sets of the noisy Mos Eisley Cantina on Tatooine. There is going to be a showdown—but will greedy Greedo be able to persuade Han Solo to settle his debt?

STAR VARIANT

First Greedo
The original Greedo minifigure appears only in the 2004 Mos Eisley Cantina (set 4501). With his exclusive dark-turquoise head, he is highly sought after by LEGO *Star Wars* collectors.

DATA FILE

YEAR: 2018
FIRST SET: 75205
Mos Eisley Cantina
NO OF SETS: 1
PIECES: 3
ACCESSORIES: Blaster pistol
APPEARANCES: IV

Large disk-shaped eyes with light reflectors

Head is sand-green, like the second variant

Tan vest over sky-blue jumpsuit

Bright-blue legs have a low-slung brown blaster belt with a silver buckle

First Rodian
Greedo was the first Rodian minifigure. His pimpled head mold was designed just for him, but later used in other colors for fellow Rodians Wald and Onaconda Farr. LEGO designers updated Greedo's own head printing for the 2014 and the 2018 variants.

Greedo
BOUNTY HUNTER

127

Governor of the Imperial Outland Regions, Grand Moff Tarkin has appeared in four LEGO *Star Wars* sets since 2006, including two large models of the Death Star and the Imperial Star Destroyer—the jewels in the Empire's fleet. Tarkin's intimidating countenance and obvious rank make him one of the Empire's most feared men.

STAR VARIANTS

First Moff
Tarkin's original variant came with the first large Death Star (set 10188) and the Imperial Star Destroyer (set 6211).

Tanned Tarkin
For the *Star Wars Rebels* TV series, Tarkin's minifigure swaps his gray Imperial uniform for a tan one.

Death Star (set 75159)
Grand Moff Tarkin is one of 27 minifigures included in the Death Star set. Tarkin just needs to say the word and the Death Star's powerful superweapon can fire a laser beam powerful enough to destroy Alderaan—the planet seen through the window.

Light peach head with drawn cheekbones and a scowl is only used for Grand Moff Tarkin

Unique rank badge indicates military status. As Grand Moff, Tarkin has two rows of colored squares

Black belt with silver Imperial officer's disc

DATA FILE

YEAR: 2016
FIRST SET: 75159 Death Star
NO. OF SETS: 1
PIECES: 4
ACCESSORIES: Blaster
APPEARANCES: Reb, RO, IV

Admiral Wullf Yularen has had a long and varied military career. First, he fought with the Grand Army of the Republic, leading clone troopers. During the Clone Wars he was assigned to the Jedi General Anakin Skywalker. Then when Order 66 was issued, he, along with his clone troopers, turned against the Jedi. He has been part of the Imperial Army ever since.

May the fourth be with you
Admiral Yularen's exclusive minifigure was released in a polybag as the May 4th promotion in 2015.

Stern expression with wrinkles, bushy eyebrows, and mustache

Swept-back hair piece in white is exclusive to this minifigure

Pristine
Imperial uniforms come in black, dark and light gray, dark and light tan, and blue, but only three minifigures wear a white one. Krennic and Thrawn do, but Yularen's has the cleanest and neatest print.

Imperial rank insignia

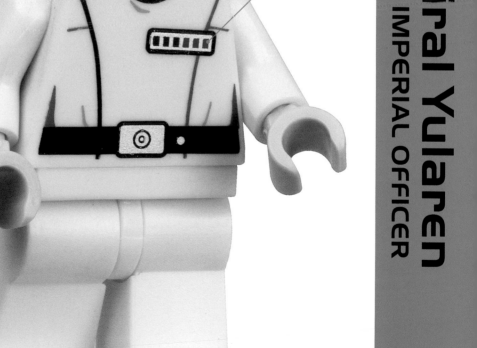

Admiral Yularen
SENIOR IMPERIAL OFFICER

DATA FILE

YEAR: 2015
FIRST SET: 5002947
Admiral Yularen
NO. OF SETS: 1
PIECES: 4
ACCESSORIES: None
APPEARANCES: CW, Reb, IV

Wearing a starched gray uniform with a gray or black hat, the eight Imperial officer minifigure variants are an essential part of the Emperor's vast army. The high-ranking soldiers work far from the battlefield, aboard starships such as the 2012 TIE Fighter (set 9492) and the Imperial Star Destroyers (sets 6211 and 75055) from 2006 and 2014.

STAR VARIANTS

First officer
This original variant is found only in the 2002 set Final Duel II (set 7201). He has a sunnier disposition than his later counterpart! Before the 2010 redesign, all Imperial officer minifigures had smiling faces.

Stern face
This 2010 variant from the Imperial Shuttle (set 10212) has the same torso as two earlier officers released in 2005 and 2006, but each one has different face printing.

LEGO crested command cap introduced in 2014

Printed facial hair was first seen on the 2014 variant

Imperial code cylinder—only important military officers carry these sophisticated keycards

Imperial kepi
Many members of the LEGO Star Wars security forces have a flat, peaked cap called a kepi. The Imperial pilot also wears one. However, in 2010 the kepi was replaced with a uniquely shaped hat and then a command cap in 2014.

Red-and-blue rank insignia is on all variants, except for 2016, which has red and yellow

Black belt was first used in 2012

Imperial Officer
EMPEROR'S HENCHMAN

DATA FILE

YEAR: 2017
FIRST SET: 75184
LEGO Star Wars Advent Calendar 2017
NO. OF SETS: 1
PIECES: 4
ACCESSORIES: Blaster pistol
APPEARANCES: Reb, IV, V, VI

The RA-7 droid is informally known as a Death Star droid because it is often found on the Imperial battle station, and two black RA-7 minifigures come with Death Star sets. They are protocol droids like C-3PO, but they have low intelligence and are programmed to be stern, not helpful. A blue-gray one is in a set based on *Star Wars: The Yoda Chronicles*, and a dark-gray one is sold by Jawas in Sandcrawler (set 75220).

Photoreceptors are a droid's visual organs. The RA-7 uses his to spy on officials

Death Star (set 10188)
The first Death Star droid from 2008 is exclusive to this set. If in need of repairs, he can take the turbolift to the droid maintenance room (top right in picture). The facility has a work bench and tool rack.

Vocabulator allows the RA-7 to speak—and pass on secrets

Chestplate was redesigned in 2014 and has been made in three color combinations

Internal wires show through

STAR VARIANT
Black protocol droid
The first RA-7 droid was the same shape as C-3PO and other protocol droids. Even his chestplate print was used on their minifigures.

Death Star Droid
RA-7 PROTOCOL DROID

Head start
The first RA-7 head shared the protocol droid mold, then RA-7 got a more accurate, bug-eyed mold in 2014. Three droids have it in black, dark gray, and bluish gray, and also bounty hunter 4-LOM.

DATA FILE

YEAR: 2016
FIRST SET: 75159
Death Star
NO. OF SETS: 1
PIECES: 3
ACCESSORIES: None
APPEARANCES: IV

This Luke Skywalker minifigure is exclusive to the Death Star (set 75159). Luke is there to rescue Leia, but first he must get past the Death Star's tough security forces. So, if you can't beat 'em, join 'em! Luke is disguised in stormtrooper armor. He can wear either a helmet or his (more recognizable) tan hair.

Death Star (set 75159)
In the depths of the Death Star, Luke, Leia, Chewbacca, and Han find themselves in the stinking trash compactor! Because of a LEGO mechanism, the walls are closing in—can they escape in time?

STAR VARIANT

First disguise
Luke also poses as a stormtrooper in 2008 to sneak aboard the Death Star (set 10188). He has flatter, longer hair, which is worn by four other early Luke minifigures.

Shaggy hair piece is seen on six other Luke minifigures released since 2011

The other side of Luke's head has downturned eyebrows and mouth

White armor is not only a good disguise— it also protects Luke from blaster bolts

Stormtrooper armor is more detailed than on Luke's first variant in 2008

Luke Skywalker
STORMTROOPER DISGUISE

DATA FILE

YEAR: 2016
FIRST SET: 75159 Death Star
NO. OF SETS: 2
PIECES: 4
ACCESSORIES: Blaster, stormtrooper helmet
APPEARANCES: IV

Detention block rescue

Both Han and Luke repeat their gallant breaking and entering in this stand-alone scene. It is a promotional set, that was exclusive to Celebration 2017.

The quickwitted scoundrel

Han Solo wears stolen armor to disguise himself on the Death Star. Like Luke, Han comes with both his standard reddish-brown hair and a stormtrooper helmet. He certainly needs it to hide that trademark smirk! An earlier minifigure of Han disguised as a stormtrooper infiltrated the Death Star (set 10188) in 2008.

This hair piece is exclusive to Han Solo minifigures

Black, temperature-controlled body glove is worn under armor

This stormtrooper torso has appeared in 12 LEGO *Star Wars* sets from 2014

DATA FILE

YEAR: 2016
FIRST SET: 75159
Death Star
NO. OF SETS: 2
PIECES: 4
ACCESSORIES: Blaster, stormtrooper helmet
APPEARANCES: IV

Han Solo
STORMTROOPER DISGUISE

Collectibles

The first variants of Han Solo and Luke Skywalker in stormtrooper disguises were also part of the LEGO Collectible Display Set 3, along with Chewbacca. The set was available for one day only at San Diego Comic-Con 2009.

White stormtrooper legs and black hips have printing—unlike the piece on Han's first variant

Now part of the Rebel Alliance, Luke Skywalker is ready for action against the Imperial forces as an X-wing pilot! This version of Luke wears an orange pressurized g-suit and unique helmet. The minifigure has appeared in 16 LEGO *Star Wars* sets, in nine different variations.

STAR VARIANTS
Rare rebel
The first X-wing pilot Luke (*right*) appears in only one 2003/4 set: Rebel Snowspeeder (set 4500). He has bluish-gray hips and a less detailed helmet and face design than the 2006 variant (*left*). Luke gets a more detailed torso in 2010.

Insulated helmet has red rebel markings and is also worn by Luke in Snowspeeder— 20th Anniversary Edition (set 75259)

Orange visor and chin strap are printed on the face

Deadly pilot
This 2018 Luke has the same flight suit as in 2019, but his visor is built into the helmet, not printed. He can leap out of his X-Wing Starfighter (set 75218) and strike with his lightsaber.

Minifigure torso is shared with five other pilots including Dak Ralter, Dutch Vander, and Biggs Darklighter

Luke's blue lightsaber once belonged to his father, Anakin Skywalker

Luke Skywalker
X-WING PILOT

DATA FILE
YEAR: 2019
FIRST SET: 75235 X-Wing Starfighter Trench Run
NO. OF SETS: 2
PIECES: 4
ACCESSORIES: Blue lightsaber
APPEARANCES: IV, V

X-wing pilots boldly fly into battle, often heavily outnumbered by Imperial foes. This may explain this minifigure's somber expression. Many rebel pilots wear a standard orange jumpsuit with plain legs, but this one has a brand-new flight suit with detail on the front and back of his torso that continues onto his legs. Some pilot minifigures are not named, but this is Theron Nett from Red Squadron.

Helmet decoration is individual to each pilot

Head piece is shared with the rebel pilot in the 2014 LEGO *Star Wars* Advent Calendar (set 75056)

Facing fear
In his microfighter X-wing with the dome of a green-and-white astromech droid, Theron reveals the terrified expression on the other side of his head.

Life-support unit strapped over flak vest

Deep pockets carry vital supplies

X-wing Pilot
FEARLESS FLYER

DATA FILE
YEAR: 2014
FIRST SET: 75032
X-Wing Fighter
NO. OF SETS: 1
PIECES: 4
ACCESSORIES: Blaster pistol
APPEARANCES: Reb, RO, IV, V, VI

135

These elite pilots of the Imperial Navy are referred to as "bucketheads" by rebel pilots because of their bulky helmets. Their unique headgear and flight suits are a self-contained life-support system that helps them survive in the vacuum of space. TIE pilot minifigure variants have fought in 23 LEGO sets since 2001.

Changing headgear

The original 2001 TIE pilot's helmet (left) was from a stormtrooper helmet mold. Its shape was updated in 2010 (second). The 2013 helmet (third) first appears in the TIE Bomber and Asteroid Field (set 75008). The fourth helmet is from the *Solo* movie in 2018.

TIE Pilot
ELITE IMPERIAL PILOT

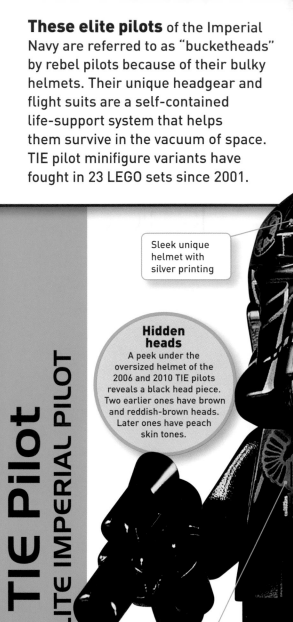

Sleek unique helmet with silver printing

Hidden heads
A peek under the oversized helmet of the 2006 and 2010 TIE pilots reveals a black head piece. Two earlier ones have brown and reddish-brown heads. Later ones have peach skin tones.

Beneath the helmet
Variants of the TIE pilot released in 2012 and 2013 have printed faces on a black head piece, making them look as if they are wearing hoods. The 2014 and 2016 variants have nothing to keep out the cold—no wonder he is frowning!

Torso printing includes a life-support system that helps the pilot adapt to changing altitudes

Breather tubes transfer oxygen

DATA FILE

YEAR: 2016
FIRST SET: 75154 TIE Striker
NO. OF SETS: 3
PIECES: 4
ACCESSORIES: Blaster, electrobinoculars/ blaster pistol
APPEARANCES: Reb, S, RO, IV, V, VI

Bookish Luke
Luke with his medal of honor has not been seen in LEGO sets. It only comes in DK books, including LEGO *Star Wars: The Visual Dictionary* (2009).

This Luke Skywalker

minifigure was specially created to celebrate ten years of LEGO *Star Wars*. The minifigure himself has cause for celebration—Luke has been honored with a medal for his bravery. Destroying the first Death Star was quite a feat!

This long, tan hair piece is also seen on Tatooine Luke and Luke in his stormtrooper disguise

Pants pair
Luke is not the only minifigure to sport pants with a gun-belt pattern. They are also worn by his friend Han Solo's minifigure. Han has worn the pants on Tatooine, Hoth, and the moon of Endor.

Sparkling eyes
There is a second variant of the ceremonial Luke minifigure, which has white in his eyes.

Princess Leia Organa awards Luke with this medal of bravery for destroying the first Death Star at the Battle of Yavin

Luke might be celebrating, but he stays armed with this gun belt

DATA FILE

YEAR: 2009
FIRST SET: LEGO *Star Wars: The Visual Dictionary*
NO. OF SETS: None
PIECES: 4
ACCESSORIES: None
APPEARANCES: IV

This proud Han Solo minifigure is exclusive to the first release of this book! Han has received the highest medal of honor for his role in the destruction of the first Death Star. Cocky Han doesn't feel the need to dress up for the medal ceremony—what could look better than his cool blue jeans and black vest?

Standard reddish-brown LEGO hair

DK exclusive
This Han Solo minifigure, with his celebratory medal, featured in the first edition of the LEGO *Star Wars Character Encyclopedia* in 2011.

Classic hair
There are 21 Han Solo minifigures with this hairstyle, including his first three in 2000. Some wear it in brown and others in reddish brown. He later acquired a more tousled look, but this special edition harks back to the early days.

Princess Leia Organa awards Han with this medal of honor for his heroics in the Battle of Yavin

Han Solo
DECORATED HERO

Han's unique torso features his favorite black vest and light-colored shirt

Gun belt wraps around leg

DATA FILE

YEAR: 2011
FIRST SET: LEGO *Star Wars: Character Encyclopedia*
NO. OF SETS: None
PIECES: 4
ACCESSORIES: None
APPEARANCES: IV

White LEGO snow goggles were first used in 2009 for Hoth rebel minifigures

Commander Luke Skywalker is stationed with his Rebel Alliance squadron on the ice planet Hoth. The minifigure finds himself in a chilling situation when he is captured by a wampa ice creature in Assault on Hoth (set 75098). Luckily, LEGO Luke is braced to withstand subarctic temperatures in his insulated uniform and snow goggles.

Luke's face is happy and well, but on the other side of his head are wampa scratches, new for 2016

Rebel rank insignia shows that Luke is a commander

Communications chip helps Luke give signals to his squadron

Luke Skywalker
HOTH REBEL COMMANDER

Deadly wampa cave
Poor Luke dangles from the roof of a cave awaiting his fate at the hands of the hungry wampa in this 2016 set. Can he escape and get back to Echo Base in Assault on Hoth (set 75098)?

DATA FILE

YEAR: 2016
FIRST SET: 75098
Assault on Hoth
NO. OF SETS: 1
PIECES: 5
ACCESSORIES:
Blue lightsaber
APPEARANCES: V

Rebel Captain Han Solo is stationed on the ice planet Hoth. Han hates the cold, so his minifigure wraps up warm in a removable fur-lined parka hood and gray snow boots. Between 2004 and 2011, four Han minifigures wore blue parkas and tan pants. In 2013, Han switched to a long brown coat for three variants. These seven Han minifigures in cold-weather gear appear in eight Hoth sets.

Hoodless Han
Han has a removable parka in Hoth Echo Base (set 7879). His body and legs are the same as the 2004 variant, but he has a new head and hair. The 2006 variant also has holster printing, but on reddish-brown legs.

Yellow Han
This rare yellow variant of Han Solo in Hoth gear appears in a promotional *Millennium Falcon* (set 4504). A 2009 variant is much the same, but it has peach-colored head and hands.

Han Solo
HOTH HERO

Han has interchangeable parka hood and hair

Knotted neckerchief to keep out the chill

Coat printing continues onto legs

DATA FILE

YEAR: 2016
FIRST SET: 75138 Hoth Attack
NO. OF SETS: 1
PIECES: 4
ACCESSORIES: Blaster pistol
APPEARANCES: V

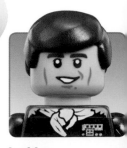

Insider
In Assault on Hoth (set 75098), Han is dressed for staying inside Echo Base—he has hair instead of a hood.

STAR VARIANTS

First Leia

This variant of Leia in her Hoth gear appears in two sets: *Millennium Falcon* (set 4504) and X-Wing Fighter (set 6212). She wears Leia's trademark two-bun hair piece. She also has a new head and torso, and peach-colored hands.

Leia in 2011

In Hoth Echo Base (set 7879), Leia has a new head piece and hair style and she wears the first insulated vest rather than a jacket.

On duty on Hoth, Leia wears her braided hair tied up. This LEGO hair piece is also seen on her 2011 Hoth variant

Princess Leia has pulled back her hair, donned insulated gear, and is now ready for action on Hoth! Leia is an inspirational leader of the Rebel Alliance. She is a key command figure, organizing troops and tactics from her command post. This version of Leia in her Hoth gear has four variants, which have starred in six LEGO sets.

Leia's torso has a white insulated vest, rather than tan, and a zipped-up jumpsuit

Leia still wears the symbolic white clothing of Alderaan royalty

Head first

Before 2011, all LEGO Leia minifigures had the same head, which they shared with three other minifigures: Mon Mothma in LEGO *Star Wars* and two female soccer players in LEGO® Soccer.

Rebel rank insignia shows Leia is a rebel leader

White-gloved hand

Patterned leg and torso pieces are shared with Leia's 2017 variant—it is the same except for her facial expressions

Princess Leia
HOTH COMMANDER

DATA FILE

YEAR: 2018
FIRST SET: 75203 Hoth Medical Chamber
NO. OF SETS: 2
PIECES: 4
ACCESSORIES: Blaster
APPEARANCES: V

After a near-death experience in the frozen wilderness of Hoth, Luke Skywalker is injured and unconscious in the Hoth Medical Chamber (set 75203). It is lucky that the rebels are equipped with a healing LEGO bacta tank to aid his recovery! His minifigure looks familiar from 2011, but the details on the face, torso and legs make all these pieces unique.

Bacta tank
Injured Luke fits in the large bacta tank in the Hoth Medical Chamber (set 75203). A 2-1B medical droid is on hand to oversee his recovery and nurse him back to health. A very similar Luke undergoes the same treatment in Hoth Echo Base (set 7879) in 2011.

Luke Skywalker
AT THE INFIRMARY

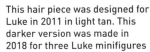

Feeling better
Swiveling Luke's head reveals a different face. He's now awake and without the mask, but his bruise still lingers.

This hair piece was designed for Luke in 2011 in light tan. This darker version was made in 2018 for three Luke minifigures

A breathing mask provides Luke with oxygen while he is submerged in a rejuvenating bacta tank

These arm straps are also on the back of Luke's torso piece. They are used to hang him from a harness during his bacta treatment

Luke wears white briefs at the Hoth infirmary

DATA FILE
YEAR: 2018
FIRST SET: 75203
Hoth Medical Chamber
NO. OF SETS: 1
PIECES: 4
ACCESSORIES: None
APPEARANCES: V

The AT-AT driver is a top Imperial soldier. His minifigure commands a deadly AT-AT (All Terrain Armored Transport) walker. Four variations of the AT-AT driver have appeared in six LEGO sets since 2003. His minifigure wears a gray or sand-blue jumpsuit under blaster-proof armor. He also has a specialized helmet.

Helmet is marked with Imperial symbols

Specialized AT-AT helmet has a breathing apparatus that enables the driver to breathe on any terrain he explores

Energy monitor

Life-support system connects the air supply to the helmet through two tubes

Identity chip

DATA FILE

YEAR: 2014
FIRST SET: 75054 AT-AT
NO. OF SETS: 2
PIECES: 4
ACCESSORIES: Blaster pistol
APPEARANCES: Reb, V

Imperial pilots
The AT-AT driver is sometimes considered to be a pilot, even though AT-ATs are not flying machines. He shares his helmet mold with the Imperial TIE pilot, who has a black version of it and a similar torso.

This highly specialized Imperial snowtrooper has ten minifigures, all built to survive in 22 subzero LEGO sets. His airtight white body glove provides insulation from the cold as well as camouflage on icy planets, while his masked helmet and backpack have been created specifically for his use.

Standard snowtrooper
Most snowtroopers are exclusive to one LEGO *Star Wars* set—but not this one! He appears in eight sets (2007–2011). He has a plain black head. The first snowtrooper with a printed head comes with the 2012 LEGO *Star Wars* Advent Calendar.

This second helmet mold was new in 2014. It has printed eyes instead of holes

STAR VARIANT
Snow clone
This 2013 snowtrooper has black hands, gray hips, and clone-trooper armor printed on his torso. It wears the first generation helmet with eye holes and appears in the *Millennium Falcon* (set 4504, blue box edition only).

Controls for heating the suit and communication

This is the first snowtrooper to have printing on its legs

Tan gloves are unique to this snowtrooper

Snowtrooper
SUBARCTIC STORMTROOPER

DATA FILE
YEAR: 2019
FIRST SET: 75239 Hoth Generator Attack
NO. OF SETS: 2
PIECES: 4
ACCESSORIES: Blaster
APPEARANCES: V

STAR VARIANT

Early settler

The first Yoda to flee to Dagobah has a molded, print-free head. He trains Luke in X-wing Fighter (set 4502), which also includes a model of his modest hut.

Yoda is more than 900 years old. He was once the great, respected Grand Master of the Jedi Order, but now the Jedi are banished and almost destroyed. Yoda is in hiding on the remote world of Dagobah. Here he leads a simple life in Yoda's Hut (set 75208), foraging for yarum seeds and mushroom spores and cooking rootleaf stew. He has a very peaceful existence, until Luke Skywalker arrives in an X-wing to be trained as a Jedi.

Yoda I heart

A special-edition sand-green Yoda minifigure with a "NY I heart" torso (printed with black letters and a red heart shape) was given away at the 2013 New York Toy Fair and at an event in Times Square.

Head mold in olive green is in four sets and is based on prequel trilogy movies and *Star Wars: The Clone Wars*

Wooden gimer stick is Yoda's staff

DATA FILE

YEAR: 2018
FIRST SET: 75208
Yoda's Hut
NO. OF SETS: 1
PIECES: 3
ACCESSORIES: Gimer stick
APPEARANCES: V

Musical instrument called a blissl is worn around Yoda's neck

Olive-green skin replaced sand green in 2013

Yoda
JEDI IN EXILE

On a quest to become a Jedi, Luke Skywalker is dressed for extreme training. His tank top and pants are easy to maneuver in, and the color combinations on his two minifigure variants provide camouflage on the swamp planet Dagobah. Luke's face is set in a determined expression— his mentor, Master Yoda, is a hard taskmaster and Luke must use all his strength to succeed!

In the LEGO *Star Wars* theme, this hair piece in tan is used only for Luke minifigures

Yoda's Hut (set 75208)
Luke can practice his Jedi skills away from prying eyes on distant Dagobah. Yoda's cozy hut has a Force jump feature, fold-out training sections, and a secret compartment under the floor.

Jedi training
Luke's first trainee minifigure in 2003 works hard to improve his strength and willpower, with Yoda carried on his back. Yoda's minifigure is small enough to stand on Luke's backpack.

Luke Skywalker
JEDI IN TRAINING

Feel the Force
The reverse side of Luke's face shows him deeply in tune with the Force. This is a core part of learning to be a Jedi.

Neck can hold a transparent brace for attaching a backpack

Torso print is similar to the 2003 variant, but the tank top is now light tan instead of green

DATA FILE
YEAR: 2018
FIRST SET: 75208
Yoda's Hut
NO. OF SETS: 1
PIECES: 5
ACCESSORIES:
Blue lightsaber, backpack
APPEARANCES: V

Deep pockets for foraging for Dagobah seeds and berries

Single Trandoshan

Bossk's head, with smooth horns and sharp teeth, was specially cast for his minifigure. Like Yoda and the Gamorrean guard, Bossk started out with sand-green skin, which was later revamped in olive green.

Flying in style

Both of Bossk's flight suit torsos have details on the back as well as the front.

This dangerous Trandoshan minifigure is the bounty hunter Bossk. He is best known for working with Boba Fett and his cronies, but his latest minifigure appears in a speeder bike set based on the LEGO *Star Wars: The Freemaker Adventures* subtheme with fellow terrible bounty hunter villains, 4-LOM, IG-88, and Dengar.

Eyes see in the infrared spectrum

Printed white teeth

STAR VARIANT

Original hunter

The first Bossk has the same head mold but with sand-green reptilian skin and a brighter yellow flight suit. He appears alongside Boba Fett and Han Solo in 2010's *Slave I* (set 8097).

Vicious Trandoshan claws

BOSSK
ALIEN BOUNTY HUNTER

DATA FILE

YEAR: 2017
FIRST SET: 75167 Bounty Hunter Speeder Bike Battle Pack
NO. OF SETS: 1
PIECES: 3
ACCESSORIES: Stud-shooter
APPEARANCES: CW, V, VI

This minifigure might wear makeshift armor, but don't underestimate him! Dengar is a dangerous bounty hunter. He is hired by Darth Vader to capture the *Millennium Falcon* and its passengers. Three variants of Dengar appear in four LEGO *Star Wars* sets, all with his Valken-38 blaster rifle close at hand.

STAR VARIANTS

Ninja bandage
The 2006 Dengar variant comes with the LEGO set *Slave I* (set 6209). His torso and legs are different and the minifigure's standard LEGO head piece is covered with a white ninja hood.

Printed bandages
In 2011, Dengar boards Vader's Super Star Destroyer (set 10221). His torso shows more details of his armor which is built from discarded bits of sandtroopers, snowtroopers, and stormtroopers.

Dengar always wears a head bandage because of a severe head injury from long ago

Scarred face from a swoop-bike crash

White gloves to protect hands

Dengar
BANDAGED BOUNTY HUNTER

DATA FILE
YEAR: 2016
FIRST SET: 75145 Eclipse Fighter
NO. OF SETS: 2
PIECES: 5
ACCESSORIES: Backpack, stud-shooter/backpack, blaster rifle
APPEARANCES: CW, V, VI

STAR VARIANTS

Bronze Boba
There are only two of these solid bronze Boba Fetts in existence. One was given away to a lucky competition winner as part of the LEGO "May the Fourth" promotion in 2010.

Cloud City
This is the first Boba variant to have leg and arm printing and is unique to Cloud City (set 10123), released in 2003. A similar variant with plain gray legs and arms was released in 2000.

New blue pants
This 2010 Boba Fett is the first to feature blue legs. The pale-blue part features in five later variants, all of which have additional printing on top of the blue base.

Mandalorian bounty hunter Boba Fett appears in 16 LEGO *Star Wars* sets as an adult, with 13 variations. Boba's latest incarnation is battle-worn, but equipped with all he needs to catch his quarry: a probing rangefinder, a powerful jetpack, and unbeatable firepower.

Detachable rangefinder

DATA FILE

YEAR: 2018
FIRST SET: 75222 Betrayal at Cloud City
NO. OF SETS: 1
PIECES: 7
ACCESSORIES: Modified blaster
APPEARANCES: IV, V, VI

Only two Boba Fett variants have printing on the arms

Captured Wookiee hair is worn as a prize

Tattered fabric pauldron with an orange stripe is unique to Boba Fett

Boba Fett
INFAMOUS BOUNTY HUNTER

EXCLUSIVE

Cover star
Available only with the second edition of this book, white Boba Fett is based on concept designs for the character. A 2010 variant with the first Boba helmet has a simpler white look.

This cool customer is the baron administrator of Cloud City. Lando Calrissian is known for his flamboyant personality and sense of style—and this is reflected in his LEGO minifigure. It has an extravagant yellow-lined cape and an elegant baronial outfit. Three Lando variants in all their finery star in three sets, alongside Lando's old gambling partner and longtime fellow scoundrel Han Solo.

STAR VARIANT

The first baron
2003 Lando oversees Cloud City (set 10123). He carries a blaster made from a LEGO loudhailer. A matching 20th anniversary minifigure was also released in 2019.

Lando Calrissian
BARON OF CLOUD CITY

DATA FILE

YEAR: 2018
FIRST SET: 75222
Betrayal at Cloud City
NO. OF SETS: 1
PIECES: 5
ACCESSORIES:
None
APPEARANCES: V

Previously smooth hair piece is now textured

Lando's unique face print has his suave mustache, raised eyebrow, and winning smile

Blue torso has updated creases for 2018

Baron administrator state belt has been revised since the 2003 print

New yellow-lined cape has the addition of a pattern inside

Betrayal on Cloud City (set 75222)
As Lando's assistant, Lobot is involved in Lando's deal to help Darth Vader capture the rebels. But when Lando has a change of heart, Lobot switches sides, too, and helps the rebels escape.

Half-man, half-robot, Lobot is Lando Calrissian's cyborg assistant. Lobot's double-sided head is the only clue that he is not fully human: One side has a human face, while the other is printed with a computer implant. As Cloud City's computer liaison officer, Lobot is one of a kind—though his LEGO variants are three of a kind.

STAR VARIANT

In communication
This Lobot comes with the 2002 Twin-Pod Cloud Car (set 7119). Like his 2012 variant, he has a unique head that shows his implant. Instead of a blaster, however, he carries a radio.

Cybernetic head implant

DATA FILE

YEAR: 2018
FIRST SET: 75222
Betrayal at Cloud City
NO. OF SETS: 1
PIECES: 3
ACCESSORIES: None
APPEARANCES: V

Belt projects clear-signal field

Torso is a unique variation of the 2012 design printed with Lobot's plain, functional gray tunic and black belt

Super computer
The backs of both Lobot's 2012 and 2018 head variants show the computer device that has been implanted into his brain. It allows him to control Cloud City's computer system with his mind.

Unusual behavior
Lobot's first two minifigures both come with twin-pod cloud cars, but it is only in the LEGO *Star Wars* galaxy that Lobot would pilot one. Usually, he leaves that to cloud car pilots, and he focuses on the day-to-day running of Cloud City.

Ugnaughts have a reputation for working hard. This one is certainly dedicated to his task of turning Han Solo's minifigure into carbonite. Ugnaughts are piglike humanoids and many of them live on the floating city near Bespin. They keep Cloud City running and do many different jobs, including working in the giant tibanna gas mine.

STAR VARIANT
Carbonite technician
A second Ugnaught appears in a later set with carbon-freezing: Betrayal at Cloud City (set 75222). This 2018 variant wears a pale-gray tunic and black pants when he turns Han to carbonite.

Ugnaught
CLOUD CITY WORKER

Carbon-Freezing Chamber (set 75137)
The Ugnaught has his trotters on the controls of the freezing chamber. Darth Vader gives the order, the Ugnaught pushes the buttons, and Han becomes frozen.

DATA FILE

YEAR: 2016
FIRST SET: 75137 Carbon-Freezing Chamber
NO. OF SETS: 1
PIECES: 3
ACCESSORIES: None
APPEARANCES: V

Bald head with mottled piglike skin

Detailed mold has nostrils in the upturned nose

Printed facial hair wraps around the jowls and joins with white molded hair at the back

Short leg piece because Ugnaughts are lower than humans in height—as well as status

Believing she is safe on Cloud City, Princess Leia dresses in a regal outfit and is not armed with a blaster. But it is not long before Darth Vader and his stormtroopers show up and Princess Leia must try to hide. This Leia minifigure is hard to find in the LEGO *Star Wars* galaxy: she only appears in *Betrayal at Cloud City* (set 75222), released in 2018.

Hair braided and wrapped on top of Leia's head

Brick skirt

All but three of Leia's 23 minifigures wear practical pants. One has a cloth skirt over bare legs, and this Cloud City one and a Death Star variant from 2019 are the only Leia minifigures to have a sloped, skirt-shaped brick.

Head piece is first used in 2015 and appears with Leia in four sets

Radial pattern is new, but is based on the torso of Leia's earlier variant

Long flowing dress is pulled in with a wide belt

Sloped brick piece for Leia's long skirt

Princess Leia
CLOUD CITY CAPTIVE

DATA FILE

YEAR: 2018
FIRST SET: 75222
Betrayal at Cloud City
NO. OF SETS: 1
PIECES: 4
ACCESSORIES: None
APPEARANCES: V

Luke arrives on Cloud City to rescue his friends, but it is a trap! Darth Vader is waiting for him. Luke's two Cloud City variants are dressed in a tan jumpsuit, which is not restrictive, allowing him to put up a good fight against Vader. But there is nothing Luke can do to protect his minifigure's right hand, which he loses in battle.

Betrayal at Cloud City (set 75222)

Luke's minifigure wields his blue lightsaber against Darth Vader. But Vader uses the Force to make a LEGO wall collapse! They do battle on a platform, which is supported by transparent panel pieces and can swing out from the main model. Watch out, Luke!

Luke Skywalker
CLOUD CITY

Two other 2018 Luke minifigures have this hair piece—one in the bacta tank and one on Dagobah

STAR VARIANT

2003 dueler

The first Luke to battle Vader on Cloud City (set 10123) has a torso that has been used for farmers and workers in other LEGO themes, but his right hand can be removed after his duel with Darth Vader.

Luke's face is injured and alarmed after his duel. On the other side it has a neutral expression for when he arrives

Silver belt buckle was previously on Luke's hip piece, but now it is higher up

DATA FILE

YEAR: 2018
FIRST SET: 75222
Betrayal at Cloud City
NO. OF SETS: 1
PIECES: 4
ACCESSORIES: Blaster pistol, blue lightsaber
APPEARANCES: V

Luke's tan jumpsuit has plenty of utility pockets

STAR VARIANTS

Uncreased
The original variant of this minifigure has yellow skin, light eyebrows, and no creases on his shirt—even though it appears in Desert Skiff (set 7104), when Han has just escaped after a few days in a cramped carbonite prison.

Creased
Han's torso with a creased white shirt features in six sets from 2010 to 2018 and on the 2011 exclusive young Han minifigure.

Han Solo has been caught by Darth Vader! His outfit of casual brown pants and a plain white shirt is seen on eight minifigure variants, but the pants on this one are the darkest brown. These minifigures appear in sets relating to moments from both *The Empire Strikes Back* and *Return of the Jedi* films.

Trapped!
Han has been frozen in a block of carbonite! In 2000 he was a printed brick. In 2010, a molded element followed that cleverly traps Han inside.

Blaster pistol appears in more than 120 LEGO *Star Wars* sets

Exposed chest features on most of Han's minifigures— apart from his Hoth variants

Plain brown pants are worn by minifigures in many LEGO sets, including LEGO Pirates of the Caribbean and LEGO® City

Han Solo
FROZEN IN CARBONITE

DATA FILE

YEAR: 2017
FIRST SET: 75174 Desert Skiff Escape
NO. OF SETS: 2
PIECES: 4
ACCESSORIES: Blaster pistol/handcuffs
APPEARANCES: V, VI

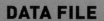

Three Gamorrean guard minifigures protect Jabba the Hutt in four LEGO sets. Brutish, strong, and dull-witted, this porky henchman does whatever his ruthless boss Jabba tells him. The green-skinned guard is also armed with a deadly vibro-ax.

DATA FILE

YEAR: 2012
FIRST SET: 9516
Jabba's Palace
NO. OF SETS: 2
PIECES: 3
ACCESSORIES:
Vibro-ax/chicken drumstick
APPEARANCES: CW, VI

Gamorreans are boarlike creatures, so the guard's unique head mold has horns, tusks, and a snout

Gamorrean Guard
JABBA'S PIG GUARD

Head and torso armor are a single sandwich-board piece. It fits over a plain reddish-brown LEGO torso with olive arms

Vibro-ax can inflict a lethal wound with minimal effort

Fur is not the guard's own—it is animal fur made into clothing

STAR VARIANTS

Gray-armed guard
The original variant of this minifigure comes in the 2003 set Jabba's Prize (set 4476), guarding the Han Solo frozen in carbonite. He has gray arms, green hands, and a brown hip piece.

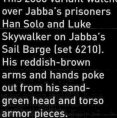

Red-handed
This 2006 variant watches over Jabba's prisoners Han Solo and Luke Skywalker on Jabba's Sail Barge (set 6210). His reddish-brown arms and hands poke out from his sand-green head and torso armor pieces.

Bygone Bib
The first Bib Fortuna variant dates back to 2003. This malevolent minifigure from Jabba's Message (set 4475) does not have the bared teeth of the 2012 variant, but he does have menacing red eyes and lips.

Bib Fortuna is Jabba the Hutt's eerie assistant. The Twi'lek minifigure decides who gets to speak to Jabba—and who doesn't. His minifigure comes in two LEGO sets and in two variants, both dressed in dark blue robes with a metal chestplate and black cape. His chestplate protects him from armed intruders, but it's no good against Jedi mind tricks!

Unique headtop piece depicts Bib's bulging forehead and fully grown Twi'lek tentacles. It attaches on top of a regular head piece and curls around it

Bib is very old, and has lived in Jabba's palace for many years. His skin is pale and wrinkled from decades without sunlight

Metal chestplate sits on top of Bib's robes, but under the blue belt that fastens them

BIB FORTUNA
TWI'LEK ASSISTANT

Twi'leks
Four LEGO Star Wars Twi'lek minifigures have been released: Bib Fortuna, Aayla Secura, Hera Syndulla, and Oola. The Twi'leks have tentacles that clip onto a standard LEGO head piece, although Bib's are longer, because he is older.

DATA FILE

YEAR: 2012
FIRST SET: 9516
Jabba's Palace
NO. OF SETS: 1
PIECES: 5
ACCESSORIES: None
APPEARANCES: I, VI

Luke Skywalker is now a brave Jedi Knight. He appears as 12 minifigures in 14 sets. They all look slightly different, often with changes to his head and hands. He has a new green lightsaber, but sometimes he has to fight with what he can find—like a bone!

This head with Luke's distinctive eyebrows and chin dimple was new for 2013. It also appears on the Luke in Ewok Village (set 10236). Han and Leia from that set also have white in their eyes

Bone of a former victim of Jabba's rancor beast

STAR VARIANTS

Two-handed
Jedi Knight Luke has peach-colored hands in the 2006 Jabba's Sail Barge (set 6210). His head piece also appears on the 2006 pilot Luke and on a 2007 young Obi-Wan.

Hooded figure
Four Jedi Knight Luke variants have yellow faces. This one has a black hood and cape to keep a low profile in the *Star Wars #2* LEGO minifigure pack (set 3341). He doesn't come with hair.

Handy
Six of Luke's Jedi Knight minifigures have identical hands. However, one day when he is a Jedi Knight, he loses his right hand in a duel with Darth Vader. To reflect this, his other six variants have one black gloved cybernetic hand.

This gray-and-black torso piece appears on only one other variant of Luke as a Jedi Knight—the one in Desert Skiff (set 9496)

Luke Skywalker
JEDI KNIGHT

All 12 variants of Jedi Knight Luke have the same black legs

DATA FILE

YEAR: 2013
FIRST SET: 75005 Rancor Pit
NO. OF SETS: 1
PIECES: 4
ACCESSORIES: Bone
APPEARANCES: VI

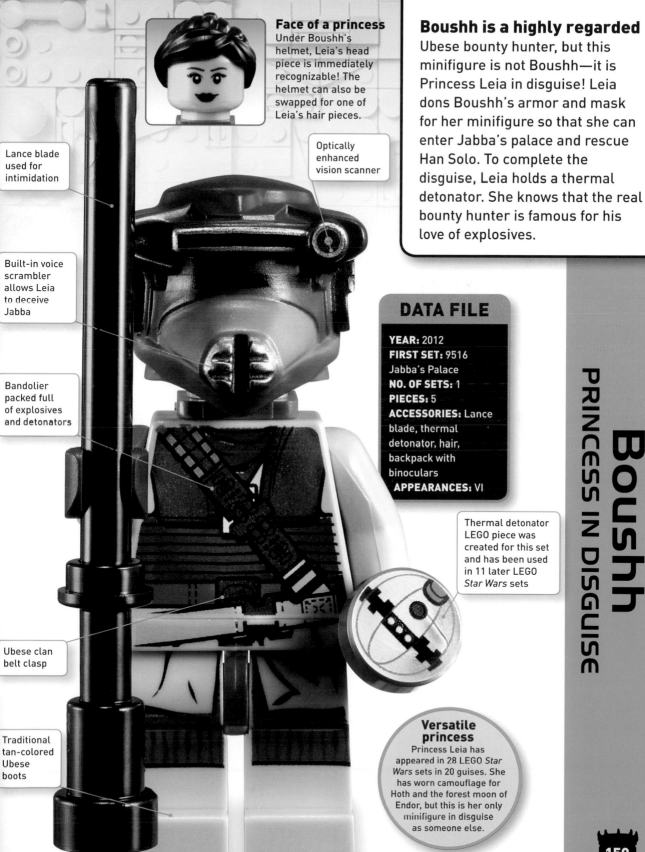

Face of a princess
Under Boushh's helmet, Leia's head piece is immediately recognizable! The helmet can also be swapped for one of Leia's hair pieces.

Lance blade used for intimidation

Optically enhanced vision scanner

Boushh is a highly regarded Ubese bounty hunter, but this minifigure is not Boushh—it is Princess Leia in disguise! Leia dons Boushh's armor and mask for her minifigure so that she can enter Jabba's palace and rescue Han Solo. To complete the disguise, Leia holds a thermal detonator. She knows that the real bounty hunter is famous for his love of explosives.

Built-in voice scrambler allows Leia to deceive Jabba

Bandolier packed full of explosives and detonators

DATA FILE

YEAR: 2012
FIRST SET: 9516
Jabba's Palace
NO. OF SETS: 1
PIECES: 5
ACCESSORIES: Lance blade, thermal detonator, hair, backpack with binoculars
APPEARANCES: VI

Thermal detonator LEGO piece was created for this set and has been used in 11 later LEGO Star Wars sets

Ubese clan belt clasp

Boushh
PRINCESS IN DISGUISE

Traditional tan-colored Ubese boots

Versatile princess
Princess Leia has appeared in 28 LEGO Star Wars sets in 20 guises. She has worn camouflage for Hoth and the forest moon of Endor, but this is her only minifigure in disguise as someone else.

Lando Calrissian is disguised as Tamtel Skreej, a skiff guard on the Desert Skiff (set 9496). Don't blow his cover, or he won't manage to rescue his friend Luke from the clutches of bounty hunter Boba Fett. Boba Fett wants Luke to walk the plank and fall into the jaws of the ferocious Sarlacc.

STAR VARIANT

Mustachioed hero
Lando first adopts his guard disguise in Jabba's Sail Barge (set 6210), released in 2006. This variant's helmet is silver and his chest armor is gold.

Lando Calrissian
SKIFF GUARD

Integrated face guard

Lando's dark brown skiff guard helmet is unique to this minifigure

Double trouble— Lando's ax-head is mounted on a spear

Ornate silver chest armor

Desert Skiff (set 9496)
Lando delivers Luke and Han to the Sarlacc Pit on Jabba's sand skiff. There, the minifigures will be fed to the ferocious LEGO Sarlacc beast!

DATA FILE

YEAR: 2012
FIRST SET: 9496
Desert Skiff
NO. OF SETS: 1
PIECES: 4
ACCESSORIES:
Vibro-ax
APPEARANCES: VI

STAR VARIANT

First Weequay guard

Aboard Jabba's Sail Barge (set 75020), the 2013 Weequay has blue arms and plain tan legs. His outfit is different, but he has the same sour expression.

This 2017 minifigure makes a short appearance traveling aboard Jabba's Desert Skiff. The Weequay guard jumps into the fray against Jabba's prisoners over the Great Pit of Carkoon. His surly expression may be some hint of his impending doom—despite his efforts and heavy weapon, this minifigure becomes just another meal for the hungry Sarlacc.

Just a few

Only three other Weequay minifigures exist—and they are all pirates: Hondo Ohnaka, Turk Falso, and Shahan Alama.

Leathery Weequay skin does not use same pattern as printed on previous Weequay minifigures

Heavy leather vest for desert combat

Ax head appears in other LEGO themes, including LEGO® *The Lord of the Rings*™

Long hair

Both minifigure variants have hair printed on the back of the head. This earlier one has tails of hair flowing down the back. On the newer version, one of the ponytails is on the front of the torso.

Weequay Skiff Guard
JABBA'S HENCHMAN

DATA FILE

YEAR: 2017
FIRST SET: 75174
Desert Skiff Escape
NO. OF SETS: 1
PIECES: 3
ACCESSORIES:
Vibro-ax
APPEARANCES: VI

This half-mad musician is a reckless character who will do anything for a free meal. In fact, his wages as Jabba the Hutt's personal keyboard player are paid entirely in food form! The Ortolan band leader played at Jabba's palace and was onboard Jabba's sail barge when Luke Skywalker arrived to rescue Han Solo. This minifigure appears in just one set.

Jabba's Sail Barge (set 75020)
This is the only set to contain the blue Ortolan. Perhaps Max's sweet music will distract Jabba while prisoners Princess Leia, in a slave costume, and R2-D2 make their escape.

Mad maestro
Max—real name Siiruulian Phantele—plays the nalargon keyboard, also known as a red ball jet organ. The wild performer has his own music room at the back of Jabba's barge.

DATA FILE

YEAR: 2013
FIRST SET: 75020
Jabba's Sail Barge
NO. OF SETS: 1
PIECES: 3
ACCESSORIES: None
APPEARANCES: VI

Max Rebo
BAND LEADER

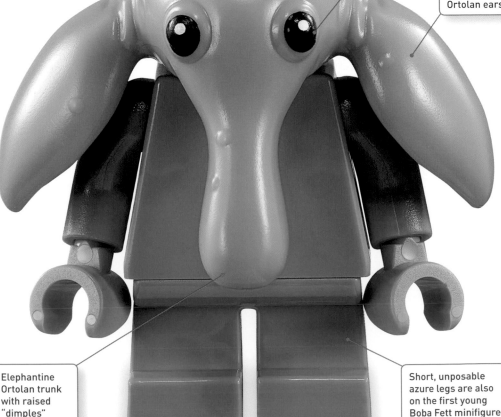

Rubbery blue head piece is unique to this minifigure

Molded and printed eyes

Long, floppy Ortolan ears

Elephantine Ortolan trunk with raised "dimples"

Short, unposable azure legs are also on the first young Boba Fett minifigure

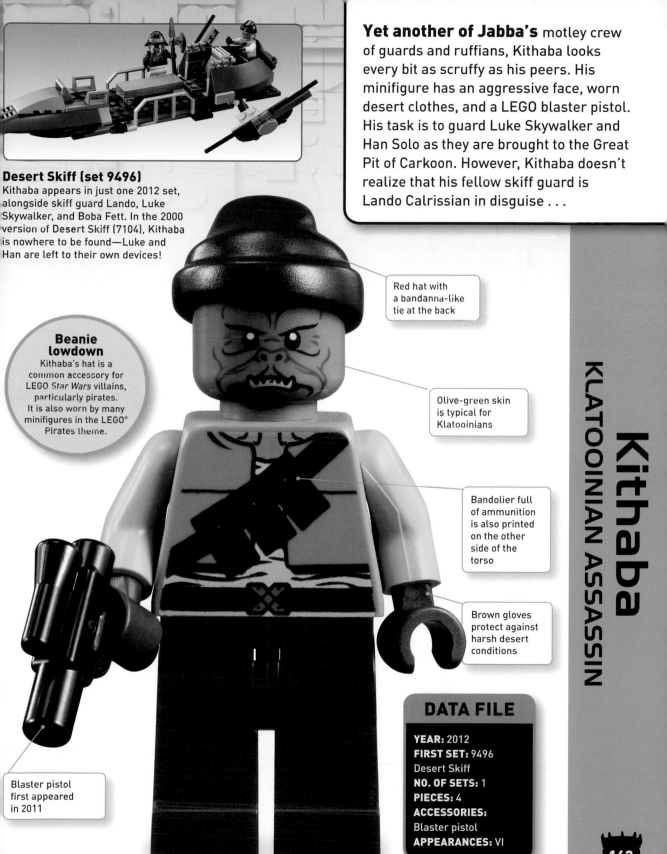

Desert Skiff (set 9496)
Kithaba appears in just one 2012 set, alongside skiff guard Lando, Luke Skywalker, and Boba Fett. In the 2000 version of Desert Skiff (7104), Kithaba is nowhere to be found—Luke and Han are left to their own devices!

Yet another of Jabba's motley crew of guards and ruffians, Kithaba looks every bit as scruffy as his peers. His minifigure has an aggressive face, worn desert clothes, and a LEGO blaster pistol. His task is to guard Luke Skywalker and Han Solo as they are brought to the Great Pit of Carkoon. However, Kithaba doesn't realize that his fellow skiff guard is Lando Calrissian in disguise . . .

Beanie lowdown
Kithaba's hat is a common accessory for LEGO *Star Wars* villains, particularly pirates. It is also worn by many minifigures in the LEGO® Pirates theme.

Red hat with a bandanna-like tie at the back

Olive-green skin is typical for Klatooinians

Bandolier full of ammunition is also printed on the other side of the torso

Brown gloves protect against harsh desert conditions

Blaster pistol first appeared in 2011

Kithaba
KLATOOINIAN ASSASSIN

DATA FILE

YEAR: 2012
FIRST SET: 9496 Desert Skiff
NO. OF SETS: 1
PIECES: 4
ACCESSORIES: Blaster pistol
APPEARANCES: VI

The mysterious Royal Guard is the Emperor's deadly personal bodyguard. Four minifigure variants have protected Palpatine and they vary only slightly. They all wear a full crimson uniform and cape. In this bright outfit, the Royal Guard stands out among other minifigures—he'll make anyone think twice about attacking the Emperor!

STAR VARIANT
Spear holder
This Royal Guard variant with black hands from 2008 wields a LEGO spear as his force pike. The original 2001 minifigure is the same, but wears red gloves.

Death Star Troopers (set 75034)
Two 2014 Royal Guards come in this battle pack, along with two Death Star gunners. Together, they will try to repel rebel attackers with their powerful laser cannon.

Royal Guard
CRIMSON PROTECTOR

Vibroactive Force pike stuns opponents with vibrating energy

Hood mold was designed especially for the Royal Guard

A standard black head piece and a slit in the helmet make it look like the minifigure is wearing a black visor

The material of the cape is the only difference between the 2014 and 2016 variants

Dark red arms and hands appear on two variants; the other two have bright red arms and either black or red hands

DATA FILE
YEAR: 2016
FIRST SET: 75159 Death Star
NO. OF SETS: 2
PIECES: 5
ACCESSORIES: Force pike
APPEARANCES: II, CW, III, Reb, RO, VI

***Home One* Mon Calamari Star Cruiser (set 7754)**
On board rebel ship *Home One*, Mon Mothma briefs the other rebel leaders about plans for attacking the second Death Star. They gather in the command center around an orange hologram of the Death Star.

Former senator Mon Mothma is the Supreme Commander of the Rebel Alliance. In her all-white outfit and rare white LEGO cape, her minifigure commands respect from all the rebel leaders. Mon Mothma is exclusive to the LEGO *Star Wars* set *Home One* Mon Calamari Star Cruiser (set 7754), where she discusses the latest rebel plans to defeat the Empire.

DATA FILE

YEAR: 2009
FIRST SET: 7754 *Home One* Mon Calamari Star Cruiser
NO. OF SETS: 1
PIECES: 5
ACCESSORIES: None
APPEARANCES: CW, III, Reb, VI

Same head piece as Princess Leia, another former senator

Unique torso printed with silver Chandrilian Freedom Medal

Princess Leia wears the same white cape in Gold Leader's Y-wing Starfighter (set 9495)

Mon Mothma
REBEL COMMANDER

Tousled hair
Mon Mothma's tousled reddish-brown hair is the same piece used for seven versions of Anakin Skywalker's minifigure.

Admirable Admiral Ackbar commands the rebel assault on the second Death Star from his flagship *Home One* (set 7754). This young Ackbar minifigure appears in four LEGO sets and plays a pivotal part in LEGO *Star Wars* history. He is one of four orange-brown skinned Mon Calamari minifigures, but his senior commander's uniform makes him stand out from the others.

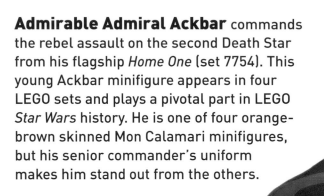

Mon Calamari officer
This officer maintains and repairs *Home One* (set 7754). His head mold is the same as the admiral's, but he has his own torso. The dark bib protects his tan uniform from oil and dirt, while the utility belt has a pair of storage pockets.

Admiral Ackbar
REBEL SUPREME COMMANDER

Solid Mon Calamari head with large, bulbous eyes

A cream Mon Calamari naval jerkin over a white space suit

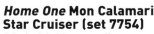

Home One Mon Calamari Star Cruiser (set 7754)
Admiral Ackbar coordinates the rebel assault on the second Death Star in this set. He has a swiveling and sliding command chair and a tactical computer that can mount his lap.

Metallic command insignia denotes Ackbar's high rank

Reddish-brown webbed hands

DATA FILE

YEAR: 2009
FIRST SET: 7754
Home One Mon Calamari Star Cruiser
NO. OF SETS: 3
PIECES: 3
ACCESSORIES: None
APPEARANCES: VI

Special set
Admiral Ackbar also appears in the exclusive LEGO *Star Wars* Collectible Display Set 2, which was available for one day only at the 2009 San Diego Comic-Con. Crix Madine and Jedi Knight Luke Skywalker are also included in the set.

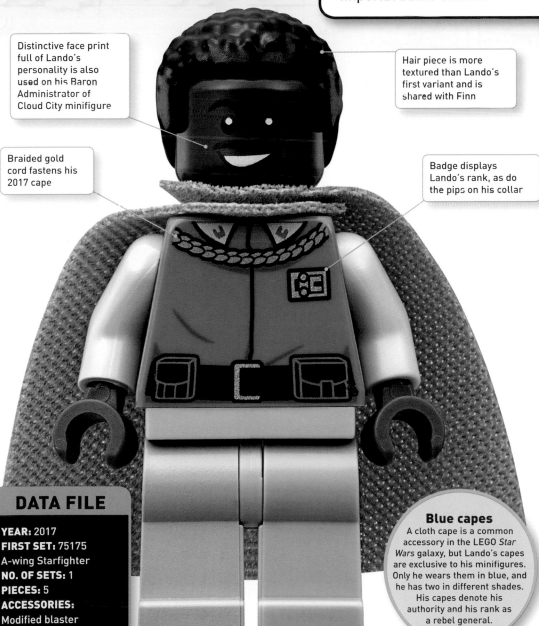

STAR VARIANT
Classic general
The first Lando minifigure from 2009 has a flatter hair piece and a simpler face print. He is recognizable from his sand-blue cape and well-groomed mustache.

General Lando Calrissian is one of the rebel generals onboard the *Home One* Mon Calamari Star Cruiser (set 7754), which is in battle against the second Death Star. His minifigure has a rare blue LEGO cape which makes him even more boldly confident than usual. He wears it to help him direct a particularly assertive attack on the colossal Imperial battle station.

Distinctive face print full of Lando's personality is also used on his Baron Administrator of Cloud City minifigure

Hair piece is more textured than Lando's first variant and is shared with Finn

Braided gold cord fastens his 2017 cape

Badge displays Lando's rank, as do the pips on his collar

Lando Calrissian
REBEL GENERAL

DATA FILE
YEAR: 2017
FIRST SET: 75175
A-wing Starfighter
NO. OF SETS: 1
PIECES: 5
ACCESSORIES:
Modified blaster
APPEARANCES: VI

Blue capes
A cloth cape is a common accessory in the LEGO *Star Wars* galaxy, but Lando's capes are exclusive to his minifigures. Only he wears them in blue, and he has two in different shades. His capes denote his authority and his rank as a rebel general.

The B-wing pilot is ready to fly the largest single-seat starship in the rebel fleet! He has had three minifigure variants, in three sets since 2000, always with his B-wing starfighter. Like his fellow rebel pilots, he wears a jumpsuit and a life-support pack, but he is distinguished by his uniform's bright red coloring.

Reddish-brown flying helmet with a fluorescent green visor piece

Pilot torsos
The first two B-wing pilot minifigures share a red torso, but with similar printing to that seen on many other rebel pilot minifigures, such as Y-wing pilot Dutch Vander and X-wing ace Wedge Antilles.

B-Wing Pilot
SPACE ACE

STAR VARIANTS

Yellow face

This yellow-faced variant appears in the 2000 LEGO set B-Wing at Rebel Control Center (set 7180). Apart from skin color, variations include a face with eyebrows and a translucent yellow visor instead of a black one.

Cheerful chap
This cheery pilot with a non-yellow head flies the 2006 B-Wing Fighter (set 6208). He wears the same silver helmet with yellow and black as the 2000 variant does, but his visor is translucent black, not yellow.

Standard head printing shows the pilot concentrating hard

Life-support pack

Breathing tube

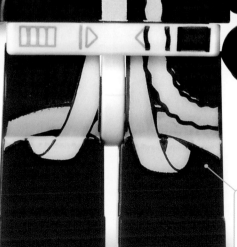

Torso and leg pieces very similar to those used for fellow B-wing pilot Ten Numb

DATA FILE

YEAR: 2013
FIRST SET: 75010 B-Wing Starfighter & Planet Endor
NO. OF SETS: 1
PIECES: 5
ACCESSORIES: Blaster pistol
APPEARANCES: VI

Rotating cockpit
The Gray Squadron pilot prepares for battle in B-Wing (set 75050). Its rotating cockpit gives a clear view of whatever is ahead, so the craft's spring-loaded shooters are sure to hit their Imperial targets.

In the pink
In contrast to the pilot's gray suit, the visor on one side of his reversible head piece is a vivid pink color. He also has a determined expression, rather than a faint smile.

Formed shortly after the Battle of Hoth, Gray Squadron is one of several rebel starfighter units who take their name from a color. While other rebel pilots wear brightly colored flight suits, the Gray Squadron pilot has a light gray suit with a unique helmet mold and new printed detail on his torso and legs.

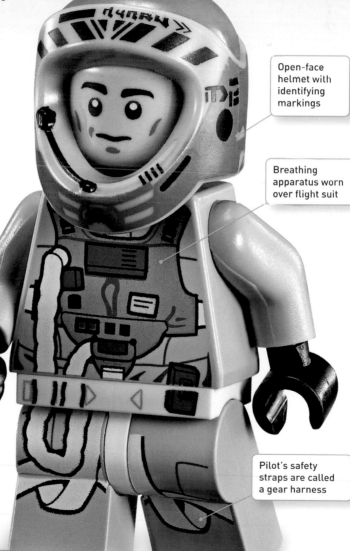

Open-face helmet with identifying markings

Breathing apparatus worn over flight suit

Pilot's safety straps are called a gear harness

Gray Squadron Pilot
REBEL FLYER

DATA FILE

YEAR: 2014
FIRST SET: 75050
B-Wing
NO. OF SETS: 1
PIECES: 4
ACCESSORIES:
Blaster pistol
APPEARANCES: VI

The A-wing pilot is part of a flying force known as Green Squadron because of the color of their jumpsuits. The A-wing pilot minifigure plays a crucial role in the Battle of Endor, flying A-wing fighters in six LEGO *Star Wars* sets. There are five variants of the green-suited minifigure, plus a red one and a pale-blue one from the *Star Wars Rebels* subtheme.

STAR VARIANTS

Yellow pilot
The original A-wing pilot has a yellow face with a printed headset and appears only in the A-Wing Fighter (set 7134), released in 2000. He also has a different helmet design than later variants.

Revealing visors
Two A-wing pilots appear in sets in 2006 and 2009. Near-identical, the 2006 pilot from A-Wing Fighter (set 6207) has a dark visor, while the 2009 pilot has a yellow one.

A-Wing Pilot
REBEL AIRMAN

DATA FILE
YEAR: 2017
FIRST SET: 75175
A-Wing Starfighter
NO. OF SETS: 2
PIECES: 4
ACCESSORIES:
Blaster pistol
APPEARANCES: Reb, VI

Comms unit is built into the helmet

A Rebels rebel
This A-wing pilot in a red flightsuit and fuller helmet is from a special edition polybag based on the *Star Wars Rebels* TV series.

Flight vest with life-support unit

Printing on the legs only appears on the 2013 and 2017 variants

Flying colors
Only the A-wing pilot wears a bright-green flight suit in the LEGO *Star Wars* galaxy. Most X-wing and Y-wing pilots wear orange, while most B-wing pilots wear red.

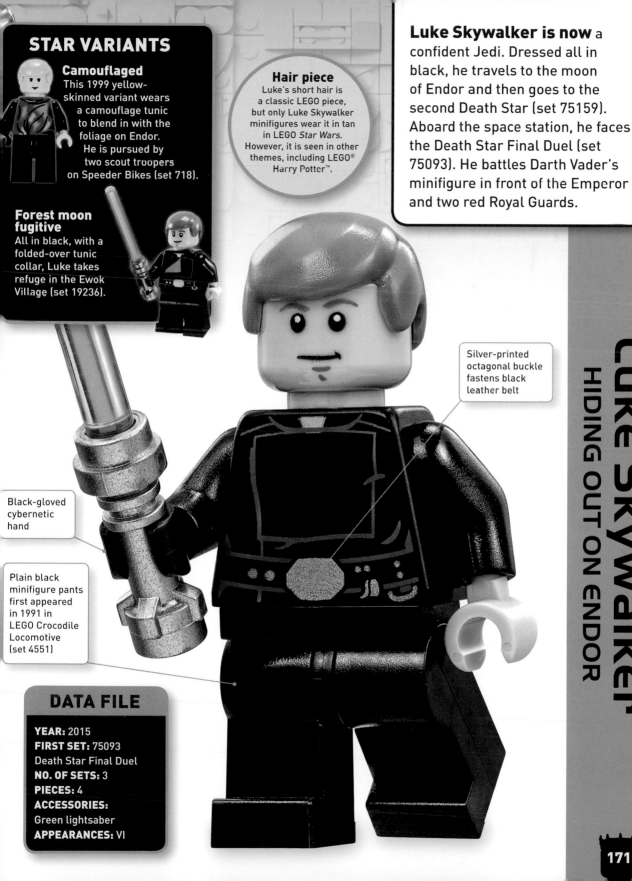

Camouflaged
This 1999 yellow-skinned variant wears a camouflage tunic to blend in with the foliage on Endor. He is pursued by two scout troopers on Speeder Bikes (set 718).

Forest moon fugitive
All in black, with a folded-over tunic collar, Luke takes refuge in the Ewok Village (set 19236).

Hair piece
Luke's short hair is a classic LEGO piece, but only Luke Skywalker minifigures wear it in tan in LEGO *Star Wars*. However, it is seen in other themes, including LEGO® Harry Potter™.

Luke Skywalker is now a confident Jedi. Dressed all in black, he travels to the moon of Endor and then goes to the second Death Star (set 75159). Aboard the space station, he faces the Death Star Final Duel (set 75093). He battles Darth Vader's minifigure in front of the Emperor and two red Royal Guards.

Silver-printed octagonal buckle fastens black leather belt

Black-gloved cybernetic hand

Plain black minifigure pants first appeared in 1991 in LEGO Crocodile Locomotive (set 4551)

Luke Skywalker
HIDING OUT ON ENDOR

DATA FILE

YEAR: 2015
FIRST SET: 75093 Death Star Final Duel
NO. OF SETS: 3
PIECES: 4
ACCESSORIES: Green lightsaber
APPEARANCES: VI

Han Solo's minifigures come in many costumes, but he did not get an Endor outfit until 2015. It marks the newly promoted General's triumph on the forest moon, where he leads a strike team. His minifigure, Leia, Chewbacca, and two nonidentical Endor troopers destroy the shield generator that is protecting the second Death Star.

Mission to Endor
Han and his team steal the Imperial Shuttle *Tydirium* (set 75094). They fly the *lambda*-class T-4a shuttle to the forest moon of Endor, where they play a crucial role in the Battle of Endor.

DATA FILE

YEAR: 2015
FIRST SET: 75094
Imperial Shuttle *Tydirium*
NO. OF SETS: 1
PIECES: 4
ACCESSORIES: Blaster pistol
APPEARANCES: VI

This flat, classic-style hair piece was first used for Han in 2004

Olive green and tan feature in the 2015 wave of Endor minifigures rather than the previous sand green

Han's black vest is visible under his greatcoat

Long camouflage coat printing continues on Han's leg piece

One moon, two moods
This side of Han's head shows how he feels when he is faced with destroying the Death Star; the other side is his expression when the Death Star explodes.

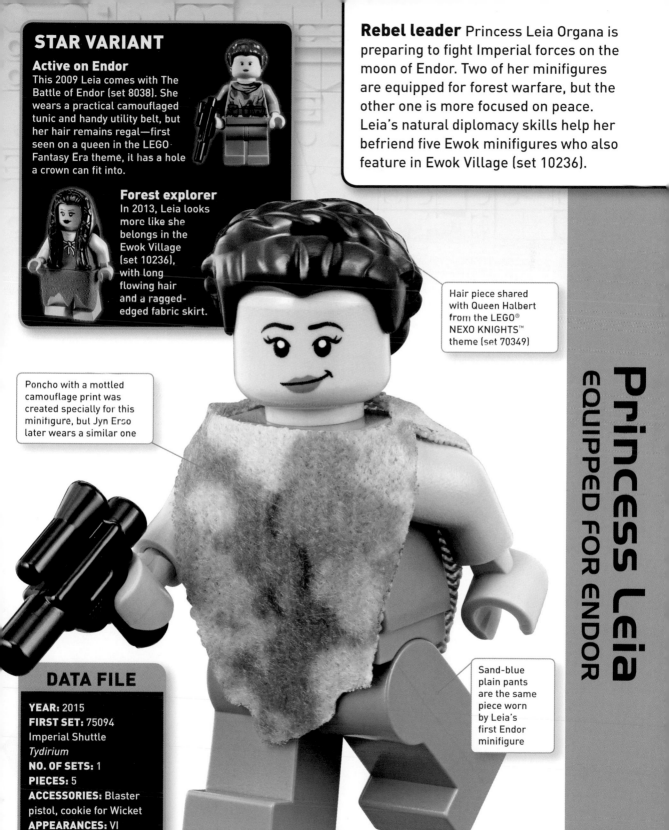

STAR VARIANT

Active on Endor

This 2009 Leia comes with The Battle of Endor (set 8038). She wears a practical camouflaged tunic and handy utility belt, but her hair remains regal—first seen on a queen in the LEGO Fantasy Era theme, it has a hole a crown can fit into.

Forest explorer

In 2013, Leia looks more like she belongs in the Ewok Village (set 10236), with long flowing hair and a ragged-edged fabric skirt.

Rebel leader Princess Leia Organa is preparing to fight Imperial forces on the moon of Endor. Two of her minifigures are equipped for forest warfare, but the other one is more focused on peace. Leia's natural diplomacy skills help her befriend five Ewok minifigures who also feature in Ewok Village (set 10236).

Hair piece shared with Queen Halbert from the LEGO® NEXO KNIGHTS™ theme (set 70349)

Poncho with a mottled camouflage print was created specially for this minifigure, but Jyn Erso later wears a similar one

Sand-blue plain pants are the same piece worn by Leia's first Endor minifigure

Princess Leia
EQUIPPED FOR ENDOR

DATA FILE

YEAR: 2015
FIRST SET: 75094
Imperial Shuttle *Tydirium*
NO. OF SETS: 1
PIECES: 5
ACCESSORIES: Blaster pistol, cookie for Wicket
APPEARANCES: VI

The Imperial scout trooper is often sent on dangerous missions on his own. His minifigure wears a specialized scout helmet and white armor that is more lightweight than regular stormtrooper armor. He also carries a powerful blaster. Five variants of the scout trooper minifigure have appeared in nine LEGO sets since 1999.

STAR VARIANTS

Second scout
An Imperial scout trooper with dark bluish-gray torso printing appears in two sets (2009 and 2011). Under his helmet is a plain black head piece.

Battle scout
This scout trooper with a black head piece and printed face appears in a 2012 battle pack (set 9489). He teams up with a stormtrooper to take on two rebels.

Scout Trooper
LONE SENTRY

Black LEGO head piece is visible through the helmet, creating a visor effect

Black arms and leg pieces show the jumpsuit worn under the scout trooper's armor

Armored knee pads printed on black legs

Kashyyyk trooper
The scout trooper's helmet piece is used in sand-green for the 2005 Kashyyyk trooper minifigure in Clone Turbo Tank (set 7261). These troopers are based in the jungles of Kashyyyk, where they require camouflage.

Built-in comlink system can support long-distance communication

The scout trooper often undertakes long solo missions so he carries survival rations with him at all times

DATA FILE

YEAR: 2013
FIRST SET: 10236 Ewok Village
NO. OF SETS: 2
PIECES: 4
ACCESSORIES: Blaster pistol
APPEARANCES: Reb, VI, M

Visor head
The first scout trooper variant, released in 1999, has a yellow head printed with a black visor. The minifigure has appeared in three sets from 1999 to 2002.

Original Ewok
The first Wicket W. Warrick is all brown, with no printing on his head-and-torso piece. The variant appears exclusively in the 2002 set Ewok Attack (set 7139).

Hooded Ewok
This second variant of Wicket's minifigure has a new orange hood on a head-and-torso piece and a little printed detail. It appears in The Battle of Endor set (8038) in 2009.

Wicket Wystri Warrick is a wide-eyed Ewok, native to the emerald moon of Endor. He is a minifigure of firsts in two ways: he is the first Ewok to befriend Princess Leia in The Battle of Endor (set 8038), and one of the first Ewoks to appear in LEGO form. Wicket wears a distinctive orange hood that sets him apart from other Ewok minifigures.

DATA FILE

YEAR: 2013
FIRST SET: 10236
Ewok Village
NO. OF SETS: 2
PIECES: 3
ACCESSORIES: Spear
APPEARANCES: VI

LEGO Ewoks
Along with his fellow Ewok warrior Paploo, Wicket was one of the earliest LEGO Ewoks. Chief Chirpa followed in 2009, while Logray and Tokkat appeared in 2011.

Wicket's dark orange hood has stitching where he once tore it

Detailed face printing is first seen on the 2009 design

Unique head-and-torso sandwich-board piece has textured fur

Ewoks are small in stature, so Wicket has short, unposable LEGO legs

Wicket W. Warrick
EWOK WARRIOR

Deep in the forest of Endor's moon lives a tribe of small bearlike creatures called Ewoks. They may look cute and cuddly, but be warned: Ewoks can be very fierce and their primitive wooden weapons are very effective even against Imperial troopers. Six of Wicket's companions can be found in the LEGO *Star Wars* galaxy.

Brown LEGO spear for forest combat

DATA FILE
NAME: Teebo
YEAR: 2013
FIRST SET: 10236 Ewok Village
NO. OF SETS: 1
PIECES: 3
ACCESSORIES: Spear
APPEARANCES: VI

Gurreck beast skull displayed on headdress

DATA FILE
NAME: Paploo
YEAR: 2009
FIRST SET: 8038 The Battle of Endor
NO. OF SETS: 1
PIECES: 3
ACCESSORIES: Staff
APPEARANCES: VI

Paploo has a distinctive orange feather pattern on his tan hood

Stitched-up tear

Like his former mentor, Logray, Teebo carries medicines in his shoulder bag

Ewoks
TREETOP DWELLERS

Shaman headdress adorned with a churi bird skull and brown feathers

Logray is the only LEGO Ewok with striped fur

LEGO Ewoks' legs are unposable

Shaman medicine bag

Shaman spear
Logray carries a brown spear in LEGO *Star Wars*, but in Episode VI he carries a staff of power adorned with the bones and feathers of his defeated enemies.

DATA FILE
NAME: Logray
YEAR: 2011
FIRST SET: 7956 Ewok Attack
NO. OF SETS: 2
PIECES: 3
ACCESSORIES: Spear/staff
APPEARANCES: VI

Tokkat has a white feather on his hood

Coarse rope holds Tokkat's hood shut

DATA FILE

NAME: Tokkat
YEAR: 2011
FIRST SET: 7956
Ewok Attack
NO. OF SETS: 1
PIECES: 3
ACCESSORIES:
Bow and arrow
APPEARANCES: VI

Ewoks carry primitive tools like this bow and arrow

DATA FILE

NAME: Ewok warrior
YEAR: 2013
FIRST SET: 10236
Ewok Village
NO. OF SETS: 2
PIECES: 3
ACCESSORIES:
Bow and arrow
APPEARANCES: VI

The horns on Chief Chirpa's staff are also seen on helmets in the LEGO® Vikings theme

Furry head-and-hood piece extends down to cover a plain dark-tan torso piece

Ewoks keep their ears free from their hoods so they are able to hear well when out hunting

EGO inoculars iece

DATA FILE

NAME: Chief Chirpa
YEAR: 2009
FIRST SET: 8038
The Battle of Endor
NO. OF SETS: 2
PIECES: 3
ACCESSORIES: Staff
APPEARANCES: VI

Green hood helps minifigure blend into the trees

Hand-crafted bow and arrow for perfect aim

The rebel commandos
are on a mission to destroy the shield generator bunker! A pair of different minifigures is introduced together in 2009, 2012, 2013, and 2015. Each time, one has more facial hair than the other. They all wear sand-green fatigues until 2015 when they switch to olive green.

STAR VARIANTS
All kinds of commandos
The two 2009 commandos appear in The Battle of Endor (set 8038)—a bearded one with a backpack (*left*) and another who is frowning. A 2012 battle pack (set 9489) has two more variants—a commando with stubble (*right*) and one who has a tan vest instead of an ammunition belt.

Rebel Commando
CAMOUFLAGED WARRIOR

Christmas treat
A rebel commando is in the 2013 LEGO *Star Wars* Advent Calendar. He has the same head as Boromir from the LEGO *The Lord of the Rings* theme.

Ammunition belt

Peach-colored hands. Some earlier variants have gray hands

Utility belt

DATA FILE
YEAR: 2015
FIRST SET: 75094 Imperial Shuttle *Tydirium*
NO. OF SETS: 1
PIECES: 4
ACCESSORIES: Blaster
APPEARANCES: VI

STAR VARIANTS

First Order Officer
A red-and-black cloth pauldron sets apart the First Order Officer from his regular troops in Kylo Ren's Command Shuttle (set 75104).

Squad Trooper
The squad trooper is senior to most troopers, so he wears a cloth pauldron, but it doesn't stand out as much as the officer's red one.

The LEGO *Star Wars* galaxy has seen stormtroopers before, under the Empire, but these are new. They have new armor, a new sleeker look, and a new purpose—to enforce the tyranny of the First Order. To fulfill this mission, the rank-and-file stormtrooper minifigure appears in eight sets between 2015 and 2017.

Helmet history
The original 2015 helmet mold has a very rounded shape down the center of the face. It was revised in 2019 with a more pointed shape.

This torso also comes as a variant, printed with additional black ammo pouches, for the megablaster heavy assault stormtrooper

The original, rounded First Order helmet shape

Pouches for ammunition

DATA FILE

YEAR: 2015
FIRST SET: 75103
First Order Transporter
NO. OF SETS: 8
PIECES: 4
ACCESSORIES: Blaster/ blaster pistol/stud-shooter/ megablaster/riot shield and riot control baton
APPEARANCES: Res, VII, VIII, IX

Gloved hands carry a riot shield and baton in First Order Transport Speeder Battle Pack (set 75166)

First Order Stormtrooper
NEW GENERATION WARRIOR

There is a flaw with this stormtrooper and it is a big problem for the First Order. Above all, stormtroopers must follow orders without question. Despite intense training since birth, FN-2187 has started thinking for himself. He concludes that the First Order is bad and he must run away, but the punishment for desertion is severe.

Solo stormtrooper
Having abandoned the First Order army, Finn is all alone with only his blaster and does not know where to go. He is also all alone in Finn (FN-2187) (set 30605)—a polybag that came with the deluxe edition of the video game LEGO *Star Wars: The Force Awakens.*

Hair piece because FN-2187 has already abandoned his stormtrooper helmet

Sandstorm
The black-and-gray prints on FN-2187's armor is the same as other First Order stormtroopers, but he is the only First Order minifigure to have sand stains. Imperial sandtroopers also have them.

Head piece appears with Finn in five sets

First Order blaster is kept by FN-2187

Stormtrooper armor is dangerous to be seen in—FN-2187 should find something else to wear as soon as possible

FN-2187
RUNAWAY STORMTROOPER

DATA FILE

YEAR: 2016
FIRST SET: 30605
Finn (FN-2187)
NO. OF SETS: 1
PIECES: 4
ACCESSORIES:
Blaster pistol
APPEARANCES: VII

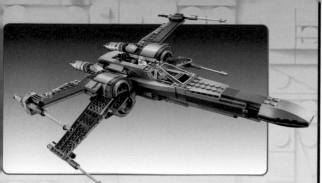

**Resistance
X-wing Starfighter
(set 75149)**
Hotshot pilot Poe Dameron
flies his blue X-wing to Jakku.
Unfortunately he is followed
there by the First Order. Can
he evade the flametrooper
that comes with the set?

Flying ace Poe Dameron considers
himself the best pilot in the Resistance.
There are variants of his minifigure wearing
his orange flight suit, but this Poe minifigure
is on Resistance business. He goes to Jakku
to meet with Lor San Tekka because he
believes that the devotee of the Jedi may
have useful information about how to find
Luke Skywalker.

DATA FILE

YEAR: 2016
FIRST SET: 75149
Resistance X-wing
Fighter
NO. OF SETS: 1
PIECES: 4
ACCESSORIES:
Blaster pistol, helmet
APPEARANCES: Res, VII

Torso is very similar
to Finn's minifigure
because they both
wear Poe's jacket.
The skin color and
undershirts are
different

Resistance pilot's
helmet, with a
built-in yellow visor,
can be swapped for
a hair piece that
comes with the set

Resistance flight
jacket

Lor San Tekka
This white-haired minifigure
appears only in this set with
Poe Dameron. He gives Poe
important information for
helping the Resistance.

Stormtroopers do not usually wear silver armor, but Captain Phasma is no ordinary stormtrooper. She commands all the First Order stormtroopers and personally oversees their training, seeking only the best soldiers. Phasma's minifigure has shiny gray pieces because, as she is the most senior trooper, her armor has a chromium coating.

STAR VARIANT

First Phasma

In 2015, Phasma's first minifigure leads troopers in First Order Transporter (set 75103). She has the First Order original helmet, which has a more rounded shape than her later 2019 helmet.

Removable helmet covers a plain black head piece

Ragged armorweave cape in First Order colors

Quicksilver baton
Two harpoon spike pieces fit onto each end of a LEGO lightsaber hilt to make Phasma's quicksilver baton. She uses the energy weapon in close-quarter combat.

Rare stormtrooper pieces in metallic gray

Captain Phasma
STORMTROOPER COMMANDER

DATA FILE

YEAR: 2018
FIRST SET: 75201 First Order AT-ST
NO. OF SETS: 1
PIECES: 5
ACCESSORIES: Silver blaster, quicksilver baton
APPEARANCES: Res, VII, VIII

TIE Silencer

Kylo has a fierce expression and flick-fire missiles as well as his lightsaber in A-Wing vs. TIE Silencer Microfighters (set 75196).

Red lightsaber . . . dark clothes . . . scarred face . . . Kylo Ren has the trappings of a Sith minifigure. Three of Kylo Ren's five minifigures wear his iconic helmet, inspired by the famous helmet of his grandfather, Darth Vader. Like his grandfather, Kylo is trained as a Jedi, but he struggles with his feelings and is finally won over by the dark side of the Force.

STAR VARIANTS

Silver-lined head
In Kylo Ren's Command Shuttle (set 75104) Kylo has a decorated head and a hood that can be swapped for his iconic helmet.

Mysterious mask
In 2016 in Battle on Takodana (set 75139) Kylo wears his matte-finish mask, but it can be swapped for a hair piece.

Unmasked
Kylo Ren's TIE Fighter (set 75179) introduces Kylo with a scarred face and a metallic-printed basketweave pattern on his long tunic.

DATA FILE

YEAR: 2018
FIRST SET: 75216 Snoke's Throne Room
NO. OF SETS: 2
PIECES: 4
ACCESSORIES: Red crossguard lightsaber
APPEARANCES: Res, VII, VIII, IX

Basketweave pattern covers the torso and continues onto the leg piece

Kylo Ren
MASTER OF THE KNIGHTS OF REN

Lightsaber hilt piece was first made in this shade of gray for Kylo Ren

Cross lightsaber blade is a single LEGO piece

These special stormtroopers can shoot streams of fire. First Order engineers latched onto this ancient Mandalorian idea that was further developed by the Republic's Clone Army. The result is the First Order flametrooper. Their visor shape is like a snowtrooper's, but the helmet shape is unique to flametroopers.

Flaming gun
The D-93w blaster can shoot flames up to 75 meters (245 feet). In a nod to this effect, transparent orange LEGO elements can be added to the end of the blaster.

Flametrooper
FIRE-POWERED STORMTROOPER

DATA FILE

YEAR: 2015
FIRST SET: 75103 First Order Transporter
NO. OF SETS: 4
PIECES: 5
ACCESSORIES: Flamethrower, backpack with fuel tanks
APPEARANCES: VII

Armor is reinforced so it can stand high temperatures

D-93 Incinerator flamethrower kit worn on back with round bricks for fuel tanks

D-93w flame projector gun is a LEGO rifle piece extended with a round brick

Black strip around right leg carries three capsules

Clever, loyal, and vital to the Resistance, BB-8 is a distinctive astromech droid in 11 sets, from an Encounter on Jakku (set 75148) to flying on the *Millennium Falcon* (set 75105) and confronting a First Order AT-ST (set 75201). But BB-8 is most at home helping Poe Dameron pilot his X-Wing Fighter (set 75102) and the Resistance X-Wing Fighter (set 75149).

BB-great

BB-8 was supersized in 2017 with a large-scale, 1,106-piece build in BB-8 (set 75187). His head turns and the hatch opens to reveal a movable welding torch. BB-8's minifigure also comes in the set.

Primary photoreceptor

Holoprojector can emit hologram messages

The four circular prints around the ball are all different

BB-8

ROLLING ASTROMECH DROID

DATA FILE

YEAR: 2015
FIRST SET: 75102 Poe's X-Wing Starfighter
NO. OF SETS: 11
PIECES: 2
ACCESSORIES: None except for Santa hat in 75184 LEGO *Star Wars* Advent Calendar
APPEARANCES: Res, VII, VIII, IX

Ball droid

The first spherical droid in the LEGO *Star Wars* galaxy, BB-8 is made from two custom-made molded pieces with never-before-seen prints.

The first Rey minifigure appears in six sets. Two are based on Jakku, where she scavenges whatever she can exchange for meager food rations. But one day, she meets a droid who turns her life upside down in Encounter on Jakku (set 75148). She flies on the *Millennium Falcon* (sets 75105 and 75192) and has a Duel on Starkiller Base (set 75236).

Desert explorer
For long days out in the harsh desert, Rey can switch to a head piece protected with tight wrappings. It reuses lenses from a stormtrooper helmet.

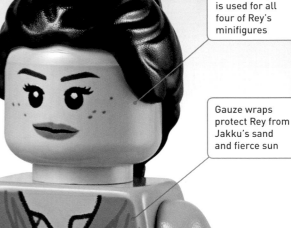

This double-sided head piece is used for all four of Rey's minifigures

Gauze wraps protect Rey from Jakku's sand and fierce sun

DATA FILE

YEAR: 2015
FIRST SET: 75099
Rey's Speeder
NO. OF SETS: 6
PIECES: 4
ACCESSORIES:
Quarterstaff, bag, helmet/silver blaster pistol/quarterstaff/blue lightsaber
APPEARANCES: VII

Leather straps for small satchel

Lightsaber is only with this Rey in Duel on Starkiller Base (set 75236)

Rey
DESERT SCAVENGER

Rey's Speeder (set 75099)
Rey zooms around the vast desert of Jakku on a speeder she cobbled together herself from spare parts and scrap.

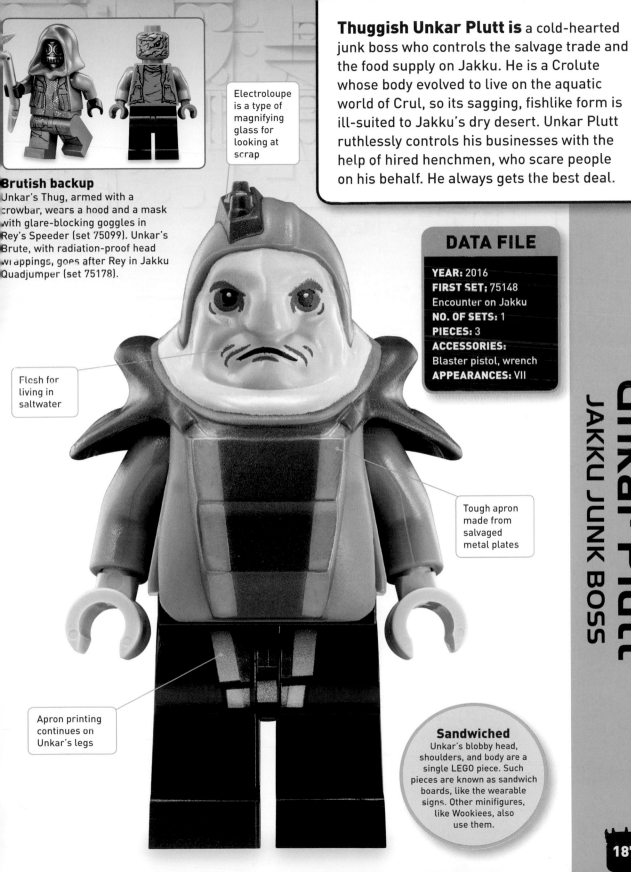

Thuggish Unkar Plutt is a cold-hearted junk boss who controls the salvage trade and the food supply on Jakku. He is a Crolute whose body evolved to live on the aquatic world of Crul, so its sagging, fishlike form is ill-suited to Jakku's dry desert. Unkar Plutt ruthlessly controls his businesses with the help of hired henchmen, who scare people on his behalf. He always gets the best deal.

Electroloupe is a type of magnifying glass for looking at scrap

Brutish backup
Unkar's Thug, armed with a crowbar, wears a hood and a mask with glare-blocking goggles in Rey's Speeder (set 75099). Unkar's Brute, with radiation-proof head wrappings, goes after Rey in Jakku Quadjumper (set 75178).

DATA FILE
YEAR: 2016
FIRST SET: 75148
Encounter on Jakku
NO. OF SETS: 1
PIECES: 3
ACCESSORIES:
Blaster pistol, wrench
APPEARANCES: VII

Flesh for living in saltwater

Unkar Plutt
JAKKU JUNK BOSS

Tough apron made from salvaged metal plates

Apron printing continues on Unkar's legs

Sandwiched
Unkar's blobby head, shoulders, and body are a single LEGO piece. Such pieces are known as sandwich boards, like the wearable signs. Other minifigures, like Wookiees, also use them.

Han Solo has gained a few wrinkles since his last minifigure. He is now a generation older, but he is no wiser—he still keeps getting himself into dangerous scrapes. His head from 2017 looks worried on one side and is snarling on the other. His 2015 minifigure has identical pieces, except he is smiling instead of snarling.

STAR VARIANT
Return of the rebel
In *Millennium Falcon* (set 75105), Han is reunited with his long-lost Corellian freighter, but there are two minifigures—Tasu Leech and a Kanjiklub gang member—who want to take it from him.

Millennium Falcon
(set 75192)
There have been 12 LEGO models of the *Millennium Falcon*. Some are small, microfighter versions, but this one from 2017 is the biggest yet with more than 7,500 pieces!

Old and gray
Now that Han is older, he has something in common with Luke's Uncle Owen and General Cracken—they all share the same gray hair piece.

Nerf-leather jacket

Black pants are worn by Han Solo for the first time on this minifigure

Han Solo
AGING HERO

Blaster pistol gives Han some protection when he does business with shady characters

DATA FILE

YEAR: 2017
FIRST SET: 75180 Rathtar Escape
NO. OF SETS: 2
PIECES: 4
ACCESSORIES: Blaster pistol
APPEARANCES: VII

STAR VARIANT

Resistance veteran

Now that Finn has become a key part of the Resistance, his jacket shows more signs of wear in Resistance Transport Pod (set 75176). He also has a new shirt, a belt, and a silver blaster.

Runaway stormtrooper Finn needs to get out of his telltale stormtrooper armor, and he needs to do it fast. This minifigure has the same head as Finn's stormtrooper minifigure, and it still wears the black body glove, but he has "borrowed" Poe Dameron's flight jacket to wear over the top of it. Fortunately, Poe is happy for Finn to keep it.

DATA FILE

YEAR: 2015
FIRST SET: 75105
Millennium Falcon
NO. OF SETS: 4
PIECES: 4
ACCESSORIES: Blaster/
Blaster, blue lightsaber
APPEARANCES: VII

Hair piece is worn by five Finn minifigures

Temperature-controlled body glove

Heavy-duty leather flight jacket issued by the Resistance

Finn
RESISTANCE FIGHTER

Lightsaber warrior

In the Battle on Takodana (set 75139), Finn finds a blue lightsaber. He's not a Jedi, but he wields it against his former fellow stormtroopers.

Bala-Tik works for the Guavian Death Gang. He is the front man of the group sent to get Han Solo to pay his debt to the gang—or face the consequences. Bala-Tik has worked with Han Solo before and he doesn't trust him. He boards Han's freighter with two security soldiers as backup: he knows Han will not pay up without a fight.

Dangerous freighter
The deadly rathtar was contained in its pen on Han's ship, but it has escaped. Bala-Tik should beware boarding people's ships without their permission.

DATA FILE

YEAR: 2017
FIRST SET: 75180
Rathtar Escape
NO. OF SETS: 1
PIECES: 4
ACCESSORIES: Stud-shooter
APPEARANCES: VII

Terrified face has seen the rathtar—the other side looks confident and fierce

Long coat has an armored lining—Bala-Tik trusts no one

Gray print on dark gray pieces creates a mottled metallic look

Bala-Tik
GUAVIAN DEATH GANG

Percussive cannon
Bala-Tik and his Guavian henchmen carry LEGO handheld stud-shooters with a twist. They are souped up with faucet pieces.

Ravenous rathtar

The security soldiers meet more than they expected on Han's ship: two deadly rathtars. The set comes with both a red version and a black one. Each is covered with posable claws, tentacles, and suckers. They can hold a minifigure in their grotesque mouths, caught in place with their terrible teeth.

Faceless, bright-red, and dangerous, these security guards work for the criminal Guavian Death Gang. Two of their minifigures follow Bala-Tik into Rathtar Escape (set 75180) as his firepowered backup. They are soldiers whose bodies have been upgraded with cybernetic technology so they are all stronger and more aggressive than a normal human soldier could be.

Helmet with a plain face plate is completely without expression

Black ring is a sensor system used for communicating with other security soldiers

Faceless head

The head and neck piece is mostly black with a red front covering, but it is all a single piece that does not come apart.

Armored plates on shoulders and chest

DATA FILE

YEAR: 2017
FIRST SET: 75180
Rathtar Escape
NO. OF SETS: 2
PIECES: 3
ACCESSORIES:
Stud-shooter
APPEARANCES: Res, VII

Tube delivers chemicals into body to increase soldier's abilities

Maz Kanata's personality is larger than life, but her minifigure is smaller than most because she has short legs. Her alien head and eccentric clothes make her one of a kind. Once a successful pirate, Maz still lives an unconventional life doing whatever she likes. She never trained as a Jedi, but she has some Force abilities.

Ancient castle
Maz has a flamboyant personality and turns a blind eye to illegal activity. Her castle on Takodana is a safe haven for many exotic characters—until Finn's arrival brings the First Order.

Cap print continues on the back of the single-mold head

Goggles give Maz sight beyond any normal glasses

Wrinkled skin is hundreds of years old

Handmade vest knitted by Maz

Short leg piece in this dark shade of red is also used for the Cloud-Rider Weazel

Maz Kanata
FORCE SENSITIVE

DATA FILE

YEAR: 2016
FIRST SET: 75139
Battle on Takodana
NO. OF SETS: 1
PIECES: 3
ACCESSORIES: None
APPEARANCES: VII, VIII, IX

No minifigure wears a First Order uniform as severely as General Armitage Hux. He longs to destroy the Resistance and he seeks power wherever he can get it. He is very jealous of the power that Snoke gives to Kylo Ren because he wants it all. The general is still young and he lacks experience, but he makes up for it with cruelty. This makes him very ruthless and dangerous.

First Order Heavy Scout Walker (set 75177)

Hux commands a First Order gunner and flametrooper against a Resistance trooper with this "crawling" walker.

Dark-orange hair piece with a left part is shared with five young Obi-Wan Kenobi minifigures

Great General

There are many types of First Order uniforms in the LEGO *Star Wars* galaxy. General Hux has a printed greatcoat over his uniform, unlike the minifigures he commands.

Wide collar with a triangular lapel and high-collared shirt

Rectangular brushed-metal silver-printed belt buckle

DATA FILE

YEAR: 2017
FIRST SET: 75177 First Order Heavy Scout Walker
NO. OF SETS: 1
PIECES: 4
ACCESSORIES: Blaster pistol
APPEARANCES: Res, VII, VIII, IX

Aboard Snoke's flagship, the *Supremacy*, there are many officers of different ranks. They are trained from birth to live and breathe the First Order. This officer is relatively junior, but he still looks troubled by the responsibility on his minifigure-sized shoulders. It is never safe when Snoke himself is on board your ship.

First Order Star Destroyer (set 75190)
The lieutenant—the most junior officer rank—serves in this set of the *Supremacy*, which has more than 1,400 pieces.

First Order badge in colors for a lieutenant

Tall upright brim goes all the way around the back of the cap

Tired, overworked eyes

STAR VARIANTS

General
The unnamed First Order General (set 5004406) from 2016 wears black, but like the other officers, he has a troubled expression. Printed on his left arm is a rank sash.

Major/Colonel
In the First Order Transport Speeder Battle Pack (set 75166), the officer minifigure wears the First Order uniform and command cap in dark blue.

DATA FILE

YEAR: 2017
FIRST SET: 75190 First Order Star Destroyer
NO. OF SETS: 1
PIECES: 4
ACCESSORIES: Blaster pistol
APPEARANCES: VII, VIII, IX

STAR VARIANTS

Fleet gunner
This 2015 fully masked minifigure controls the heavy guns onboard the large First Order ships. It comes in five sets, but it has a surprise under its mask—different colored heads.

Crew member
This 2016 crew member is from the First Order Battle Pack (set 75132). His cap's brim protects his neck rather than it being folded up.

First Order crew members carry out a range of tasks in the First Order fleet, and each role has its own twist on the standard military uniform. They are lower ranked than the First Order officers. Stationed aboard the *Supremacy*, this minifigure is a shuttle pilot. The arrival of these First Order minifigures in the LEGO *Star Wars* galaxy has brought a new selection of LEGO helmets.

Transport Corps flight helmet has a large, flared brim at the back worn only by this minifigure

Head with comms set is shared with five Imperial minifigures—and even two Rebel Alliance ones

Double crew
The fleet gunner has two variants. They are identical except their heads have different colors and expressions. One of each comes with Kylo Ren's Command Shuttle (set 75104).

Torso is shared with the fleet gunner and 2016 crew member

Fingertips of black gloves contain clearance for using certain touch screens

DATA FILE
YEAR: 2017
FIRST SET: 75190
First Order Star Destroyer
NO. OF SETS: 2
PIECES: 4
ACCESSORIES: Blaster pistol/stud-shooter
APPEARANCES: VII, VIII, IX

195

Much of the galaxy is frozen, so snowtroopers are vital for military control. The First Order has borrowed from Imperial technology and built upon it. Most First Order snowtrooper minifigures have a black neck brace for their backpacks—an environmental unit that keeps them warm. Their armor has an icephobic coating to stop frost.

First Order Snowspeeder (set 75126)
Atop this microfighter-scaled vehicle sits a snowtrooper. He is ready to attack with his blaster and a mounted rotating stud-shooter. Watch out, X-wings!

STAR VARIANTS

Snow officer
Just like stormtroopers, snowtrooper officers wear red-and-black shoulder pauldrons. This minifigure also has a blaster with a white lightsaber hilt attachment.

Traveling light
The 2017 LEGO *Star Wars* Advent Calendar (set 75184) features a snowtrooper just like the original, except without the backpack.

Cozy trooper
For extra warmth, one snowtrooper has an insulated cloth kama in First Order Snowspeeder (set 75100) and Defense of Crait (set 75202).

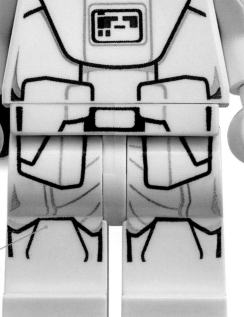

Thin, wide visor is new—Imperial snowtroopers have a lens for each eye

Unit insignia is printed in the center of the chest plate

Kneepad shape makes legs more flexible than regular stormtroopers

DATA FILE
YEAR: 2016
FIRST SET: 75126 First Order Snowspeeder
NO. OF SETS: 1
PIECES: 5
ACCESSORIES: Blaster, backpack
APPEARANCES: VII, VIII, IX

Fiercely determined and with a strong sense of right and wrong, Leia Organa masterminded the Resistance against the First Order. Since her last minifigure, princess-turned-military-strategist Leia has served the Rebellion and created the Resistance. She has been honored with the title of General. Two minifigures capture this older Leia, with her decades of experience.

Older hair
General Leia's two minifigures are the only ones to wear this braided hair piece in sand yellow. A brown version of the same piece is worn by a younger Leia in six sets.

This head piece is unique to this minifigure

Red TIE Interceptor
In 2019, General Leia appears in Major Vonreg's TIE Fighter (set 75240) as part of a new subtheme based on the animated television series *Star Wars: Resistance*.

Ornate silver buckle on what is otherwise a plain, practical outfit with no rank of status

These sand-green pants are also worn by Onaconda Farr, the Endor rebel trooper, and the Gamorrean guard

General Leia
LEADER OF THE RESISTANCE

DATA FILE

YEAR: 2019
FIRST SET: 75240 Major Vonreg's TIE Fighter
NO. OF SETS: 1
PIECES: 4
ACCESSORIES: Blaster pistol
APPEARANCES: Res, VII, VIII, IX

Admiral Ackbar's exploits

against the Empire are legendary and now, after six decades of military experience, he is a key figure in the Resistance. Age has not affected the Mon Calamari too much since his last minifigure. His skin has become more mottled over the years, but his head mold has stayed the same.

To Takodana!
Admiral Ackbar, Leia Organa, and two Resistance troopers fly in the Resistance Troop Transporter (set 75140) which has dual spring-loaded shooters.

Head mold, with a high cartilage dome and a gular sac with feeler tendrils, is common to all Mon Calamari minifigures

Admiral Ackbar
DEFENDER OF THE NEW REPUBLIC

DATA FILE
YEAR: 2016
FIRST SET: 75140
Resistance Troop Transporter
NO. OF SETS: 1
PIECES: 3
ACCESSORIES:
Blaster pistol, mug
APPEARANCES: VII, VIII

Resistance uniform with a tan tunic and simple belt

Blue-and-silver Admiral's rank badge

Squidlike minifigures
Admiral Ackbar's variants are two of four Mon Calamari in the LEGO *Star Wars* galaxy. Alongside his young and old versions, is an unnamed Mon Calamari officer and Admiral Raddus.

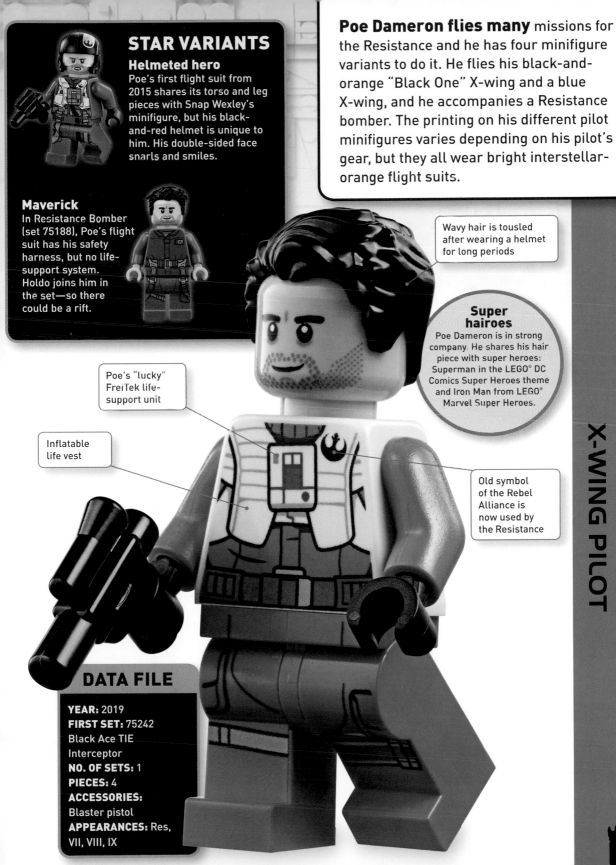

STAR VARIANTS

Helmeted hero
Poe's first flight suit from 2015 shares its torso and leg pieces with Snap Wexley's minifigure, but his black-and-red helmet is unique to him. His double-sided face snarls and smiles.

Maverick
In Resistance Bomber (set 75188), Poe's flight suit has his safety harness, but no life-support system. Holdo joins him in the set—so there could be a rift.

Poe Dameron flies many missions for the Resistance and he has four minifigure variants to do it. He flies his black-and-orange "Black One" X-wing and a blue X-wing, and he accompanies a Resistance bomber. The printing on his different pilot minifigures varies depending on his pilot's gear, but they all wear bright interstellar-orange flight suits.

Wavy hair is tousled after wearing a helmet for long periods

Super hairoes
Poe Dameron is in strong company. He shares his hair piece with super heroes: Superman in the LEGO® DC Comics Super Heroes theme and Iron Man from LEGO® Marvel Super Heroes.

Poe's "lucky" FreiTek life-support unit

Inflatable life vest

Old symbol of the Rebel Alliance is now used by the Resistance

Poe Dameron
X-WING PILOT

DATA FILE
YEAR: 2019
FIRST SET: 75242
Black Ace TIE Interceptor
NO. OF SETS: 1
PIECES: 4
ACCESSORIES: Blaster pistol
APPEARANCES: Res, VII, VIII, IX

Temmin Wexley, known as "Snap," is a pilot from the planet Akiva. Stationed at the D'Qar base, he flies a T-70 X-wing starfighter for the Resistance. Snap takes after his mother, who is also a pilot. She flew a Y-wing at the Battle of Endor for the rebels. Snap flies with Blue Squadron and is best at flying missions to gather information about the First Order.

STAR VARIANT
An unknown pilot
Countless X-wing fighters fight bravely and many do not survive. This minifigure could be any of the heroic pilots. He appears alongside the pilot, Poe, in Poe's X-Wing Fighter (set 75102).

Microfighter pilot
Snap Wexley comes with his microfighter blue-and-gray starfighter in Resistance X-Wing Fighter (set 75125). He flies it against the First Order and shoots the flick-fire missiles.

Helmet is exclusive to this set and has a built-in transparent-yellow visor

Bearded head piece is shared with the unnamed rebel trooper in Rebel Trooper Battle Pack (set 75164)

Torso and leg pieces are shared with the Resistance X-wing fighter and Poe Dameron

Printed tube for oxygen

Guidenhauser flight harness

DATA FILE
YEAR: 2016
FIRST SET: 75125
Resistance X-Wing Fighter
NO. OF SETS: 2
PIECES: 4
ACCESSORIES:
Blaster pistol
APPEARANCES: VII, IX

STAR VARIANTS

One, TIE, three

The original First Order TIE pilot (2015) has simpler line printing on its helmet.

Special forces

Two red stripes down the helmet mark the special forces TIE pilot from 2017. He flies in Kylo Ren's TIE Fighter (set 75179).

The First Order's TIE fighter pilots are an evolution of the Empire's earlier TIE pilots and so are their three minifigure variants. They still wear black with controls on the chest, but all the elements are new and the helmet has an updated design. Instead of a printed breathing hose, it is now molded to the helmet. The elite pilots fly the First Order's TIE Fighters.

Imperial-inspired breathing-tube connectors redesigned for the First Order

DATA FILE

YEAR: 2018
FIRST SET: 75194 First Order TIE Fighter Microfighter
NO. OF SETS: 1
PIECES: 4
ACCESSORIES: Blaster pistol
APPEARANCES: Res, VII, VIII, IX

Breathing tube touches the torso, but is not connected to it

Leg and torso pieces are common to all three variants of the First Order TIE pilot

First Order TIE Fighter Microfighter (set 75194)

It might be microfighter-scaled, but a TIE Fighter is still a daunting sight. This one has a rare transparent radar dish on the front—red for danger!

Luke Skywalker has not been seen for a long time until Rey tracks him down. His aged minifigure is found in Ahch-To Island Training (set 75200). Living alone, Luke has grown long hair and a ragged beard. His hair is a little duller in color, but it hasn't gone gray. Though his face is weathered, it still shows steely determination.

Pretty porg
Luke shares his island home with small seabirds who live on the cliffs. A new printed brick with a distinctive face tops this brick-built porg. One also comes in Porg (set 75230) and *Millennium Falcon* (set 75192).

Hair share
Luke's hair has faded over the decades, but the mold of his hair piece is brand new. It was made specially for him and was later used in dark brown for Sirius Black in the LEGO Harry Potter theme.

Troubled eyes, weighed down with responsibility

Remote hut
The desolate island of Ahch-To has a strong connection with the Force and the Jedi Order, so it's a good place for Luke to train Rey—if he's willing to.

Luke Skywalker
JEDI IN HIDING

Gray glove covers Luke's cybernetic hand

DATA FILE

YEAR: 2018
FIRST SET: 75200
Ahch-To Island Training
NO. OF SETS: 1
PIECES: 5
ACCESSORIES:
Staff
APPEARANCES: VII, VIII

Cape shelters Luke from the stormy island weather

On the attack
In 2017 Rey wears crossed wraps again, but now in gray. She battles a First Order Heavy Assault Walker (set 75189) and in Snoke's Throne Room (set 75216).

Rey swaps her desert clothes for more traditional Jedi wear when she travels to Ahch-To to seek out Luke Skywalker. On this desolate island, she braves the elements and Luke's hostility to explore the Force and hone her Jedi skills. Her minifigure carries the blue lightsaber that was made by Anakin and later passed from Obi-Wan Kenobi to Luke. She also has a training staff, which is a LEGO pole with a lightsaber hilt on each end.

Hair pulled back, ready for training

Unique torso is printed with a fitted tunic and a sleeveless jacket

Triple threat
Rey's signature three-knot hairstyle is captured in a LEGO mold that is unique to her minifigures.

Strap holds Rey's blaster

Reinforced fabric on knees

REY
JEDI IN TRAINING

DATA FILE

YEAR: 2018
FIRST SET: 75200
Ahch-To Island Training
NO. OF SETS: 1
PIECES: 4
ACCESSORIES:
Blue lightsaber, quarterstaff
APPEARANCES: VIII, IX

Once a wing commander, the legendary Resistance pilot Poe is demoted to captain after disobeying orders from his superiors. Now the Resistance is under attack again from the First Order on Crait giving Poe another chance to prove himself as a reliable soldier—and he has two minifigure variants equipped and ready to do it.

STAR VARIANT
Crait captain
Poe has a hair piece without the headset in 2017, but all his other pieces are the same. He battles the First Order Heavy Assault Walker (set 75189) on Crait with Rey and a Resistance trooper.

Stubbly double-sided head features on seven of Poe's minifigures

Ski speeder headset is molded to hair piece and appears only on this minifigure

Dark jacket is made from runyip leather

DATA FILE
YEAR: 2018
FIRST SET: 75202 Defense of Crait
NO. OF SETS: 1
PIECES: 4
ACCESSORIES: Blaster pistol
APPEARANCES: VIII

Glie-44 blaster pistol

Poe Dameron
RESISTANCE CAPTAIN

Defense of Crait (set 75202)
Poe flies the large Resistance Ski Speeder to make a counter-attack against the First Order. The longer he can keep the forces engaged and distracted, the better for the Resistance.

Tallissan "Tallie" Lintra is a lieutenant in the Resistance. She flies a RZ-2 A-wing intercepter and leads Blue Squadron in providing air cover while the Resistance try to flee their base on D'Qar before the First Order overruns it. Her minifigure has a double-sided head with a scared face and yellow visor on one side, and a serious expression with no visor on the other.

Air battle with Kylo Ren

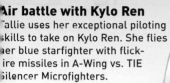

Tallie uses her exceptional piloting skills to take on Kylo Ren. She flies her blue starfighter with flick-fire missiles in A-Wing vs. TIE Silencer Microfighters.

Aurebesh lettering on Tallie's helmet refers to a common pilot's joke and reveals her sense of humor

Synthsilk scarf, tied in a knot, was given to Tallie by her father

DATA FILE

YEAR: 2018
FIRST SET: 75196
A-Wing vs. TIE Silencer Microfighters
NO. OF SETS: 1
PIECES: 4
ACCESSORIES:
Blaster pistol
APPEARANCES: VIII

FreiTek life-support system is printed on many minifigure torsos, but this one is unique to Tallie

Olive-green flight suit is worn only by this minifigure

Tallie Lintra
REBEL A-WING PILOT

A-wing colors

A-wing pilot minifigures with the Rebel Alliance usually wear bright-green flight suits. But years later, under the Resistance, Tallie wears one in olive green.

There's only one Amilyn Holdo. She brings a unique style and an independent spirit from her home planet Gatalenta. And her minifigure stands out, too, thanks to her purple hair and her decision not to wear a military uniform. A senior commander in the Resistance, she commands forces against the First Order with skill and personal sacrifice.

Purple hair
Holdo's hair piece was created in 2015 and has been seen in seven colors, but never in lavender until now. The only other LEGO figures to have lavender hair are in the LEGO® Elves theme.

Vice Admiral Holdo
HONORABLE LEADER

DATA FILE

YEAR: 2017
FIRST SET: 75188
Resistance Bomber
NO. OF SETS: 1
PIECES: 4
ACCESSORIES:
Blaster pistol
APPEARANCES: VIII

Dyed lavender hair is an example of Holdo's independent style

Draped clothing is typical of Gatalentan fashion

Defender-5 sporting blaster

MG-100 StarFortress
Vice Admiral Holdo fights alongside Poe Dameron, gunner Paige, a bomber pilot, and a bombardier called Nix Jerd in Resistance Bomber (set 75188).

Resistance Transport Pod (set 75176)
Rose zooms off on a near-impossible mission with Finn. She flies their pod so skilfully that they are able to pass without being detected by other ships.

Unique hair piece with flipped-up ends

Rose's technician uniform blends in aboard the *Raddus*, but she is noticed because of her courage and her sense of right and wrong. Her minifigure expresses the determination she has to stop the First Order after they took over her home planet, Hays Minor. She helps the Resistance with her engineering skills, but then a more dramatic role comes her way.

DATA FILE

YEAR: 2017
FIRST SET: 75176 Resistance Transport Pod
NO. OF SETS: 2
PIECES: 4
ACCESSORIES: Blaster pistol, electro-shock pod/blaster pistol
APPEARANCES: VIII

Brown top under overalls also has a hood, which is printed on the back of the torso

Rose's ID badge

Tool belt with self-coded data spikes

Controls are built into the outside of Rose's pocket

Aurebesh
The symbols on Rose's technician's suit are written in the language of Aurebesh. The larger letters translate into "GLD" (Ground Logistics Division)— the branch of the Resistance for which Rose works.

No place or information is off limits to DJ. He is a master of cryptography—the science of locking things away behind complicated computer security systems. DJ can break into any computer, and he uses this skill to steal and con people out of money. He agrees to help Rose and Finn from the Resistance—for a price.

On show
DJ does not want to attract the attention of the authorities, but he does like to be recognized for his skills, so it is hard to say how he would feel about being on display. His minifigure comes with a display stand with a connector for joining to stands with other minifigures in the series.

DJ's motto
It is appropriate that DJ's minifigure appears in a set on his own. His motto is "Don't Join." He is suspicious of any cause or organization or even of any other person. He prefers to work alone.

Scar on cheek from working in a dangerous underground world of criminals

Printing of holster crosses two separate LEGO pieces

Decorated lapels stand out against his otherwise plain clothes

Long coat made from kodyok-leather

DJ
CODE-BREAKING GENIUS

DATA FILE
YEAR: 2018
FIRST SET: 40298 DJ
NO. OF SETS: 1
PIECES: 4
ACCESSORIES: None
APPEARANCES: VIII

Unlikely rescue

Rose and Finn are caught by Captain Phasma. A First Order AT-ST approaches them, but instead of attacking, it comes to their aid—because it is piloted by their astromech, BB-8!

Normally Rose spends her days in mechanic's overalls, keeping the Resistance fleet going, but now she is on a mission with the Resistance hero, Finn. To turn off the First Order tracker that is monitoring the Resistance fleet, Rose and Finn must board Supreme Leader Snoke's personal ship, the *Supremacy*. Rose dresses as a First Order major so she can walk freely around the ship.

Hair is molded to the crested command cap

Face has the same expression as Rose's other minifigure, even though she is in disguise

DATA FILE

YEAR: 2018
FIRST SET: 75201
First Order AT-ST
NO. OF SETS: 1
PIECES: 4
ACCESSORIES:
Blaster pistol
APPEARANCES: VIII

Dark-blue uniform for a major

ROSE TICO
FIRST ORDER DISGUISE

Out of character

Rose's outfit has a very different look from her previous minifigure's. Her torso is printed with a very neat, fitted uniform, unlike her usual baggy, comfortable overalls.

Plain dark-blue legs appear in more than 300 LEGO sets

Not long after getting rid of his stormtrooper armor, the Resistance hero Finn is back in a First Order uniform. He has not changed sides again, though—he is posing as an Imperial captain in order to sneak aboard the First Order ship the *Supremacy*. This minifigure blends Finn's head with parts of First Order minifigures so he really looks the part.

First Order AT-ST (set 75201)
Aboard the *Supremacy*, Finn and Rose are captured and have to fight their way out. Finn commandeers this AT-ST walker. It is only partially built, but is good enough to help them with their escape.

First Order insignia worn on all First Order officers' caps

Blank data cylinders

Z6 riot baton
Armed with a riot baton, Finn duels with his old boss, Captain Phasma. She has never forgotten his betrayal, which she took personally.

Same torso (and hat and legs) as the officer in First Order Star Destroyer (set 75190)

DATA FILE
YEAR: 2018
FIRST SET: 75201 First Order AT-ST
NO. OF SETS: 1
PIECES: 4
ACCESSORIES: Blaster pistol, Z6 riot control baton
APPEARANCES: VIII

These troopers are tasked with stopping treason against the First Order. Unlike other stormtrooper variants, these troopers are not from a specialist unit. Instead, they are randomly selected to deal with anyone that dares to be disloyal to the First Order. Their specially marked armor—and extreme loyalty to the First Order—sets them apart from other stormtroopers.

Black mark of execution trooper on a regular stormtrooper helmet

Laser ax
Execution troopers have high-tech weaponry. Laser axes have rippling blue energy ribbons—recreated in a special transparent element first made for LEGO® Galaxy Squad.

This is the only stormtrooper variant to have black arms

First Order Specialists Battle Pack (set 75197)
The First Order has other methods for delivering justice, too. Also in the set is a rotating turret for a laser cannon with a spring-loaded shooter and gunner's seat.

Leg piece is shared with First Order stormtroopers

Executioner Trooper
DISPENSERS OF JUSTICE

DATA FILE

YEAR: 2018
FIRST SET: 75197
First Order Specialists
Battle Pack
NO. OF SETS: 1
PIECES: 4
ACCESSORIES: Laser ax, stud-shooter
APPEARANCES: Res, VIII

Behold the power behind the First Order: Supreme Leader Snoke! This cruel man is trying to seize control of the whole galaxy. His badly formed body is created as a minifigure for the first time in 2017. Snoke likes privacy so he is found in only two LEGO sets, where he stays in his throne room and aboard his personal ship, the *Supremacy*.

Snoke's Throne Room (set 75216)
Snoke swivels in his imposing throne. The floor tips with a mechanism to flip Rey across the room as if with a Force push. Snoke can also use a Force pull mechanism to summon Rey closer.

Supreme Leader Snoke
FIRST ORDER MASTERMIND

DATA FILE

YEAR: 2017
FIRST SET: 75190 First Order Star Destroyer
NO. OF SETS: 2
PIECES: 3
ACCESSORIES: None
APPEARANCES: VIII

Cold and deadly blue eyes

Extensive scarring and twisted expression make it hard to identify Snoke's species

Bathrobe-style outfit is made from very fine gold fabric

Gold printing on top of a pearl-gold base creates a shimmery effect

First Order Star Destroyer (set 75190)
Aboard his huge ship, Snoke travels in his working elevator up to his command center, where he holds high-level meetings via hologram.

Training session
Two guards practice their moves in Elite Praetorian Guard Battle Pack (set 75225). Each stands on a spinning disk and grips an electro-staff. All the guards use high-tech, electrified versions of classic melee weapons.

These minifigures, dressed head-to-toe in bright red, look similar to the Emperor's royal guards. They are the elite Praetorian guard—bodyguards who protect Supreme Leader Snoke. They stand at attention in Snoke's throne room, ready to leap into action. Typically eight guards stand by Snoke, and a total of eight minifigures come in three LEGO sets, in three variants.

Under the helmet is a plain red head piece

Segmented armored shoulder pauldrons sit between the head and the torso

STAR VARIANTS

Round helmet
Alongside the two guards with flared helmets in the battle pack, is one with a more rounded helmet. It is the same in every other way.

Throne attendant
Two skirted guards stand at attention in Snoke's Throne Room (set 75216). Black prints run down the backs of their skirts.

Long armorweave skirt sections protect legs

DATA FILE

YEAR: 2019
FIRST SET: 75225 Elite Praetorian Guard Battle Pack
NO. OF SETS: 1
PIECES: 5
ACCESSORIES: Electro-staff
APPEARANCES: VIII

This BB-series astromech droid rolls on the same type of body as BB-8, but BB-9E is not benign toward anyone in the Resistance. BB-series droids tend to be kind, but BB-9E is mean because of the way he is treated by the First Order. Nevertheless, he is loyal to the First Order and enjoys telling tales on its enemies.

Kylo Ren's TIE Fighter (set 75179)
BB-9E uses his flying skills to assist Kylo Ren in his sleek prototype TIE Silencer, which is armed with two spring-loaded shooters.

75190-1: First Order Star Destroyer
Aboard Snoke's flagship, the *Supremacy*, BB-9E catches Finn and Rose, who have infiltrated the ship, and he enjoys reporting them to the high command.

Head piece is the shape of the bottom section of a cone, rather than a dome like BB-8's

Red photoreceptor

Body uses the same mold as BB-8

Round grilles give ventilation

Base can attach to any LEGO brick

DATA FILE
YEAR: 2017
FIRST SET: 75179 Kylo Ren's TIE Fighter
NO. OF SETS: 2
PIECES: 2
ACCESSORIES: None
APPEARANCES: Res, VIII

Resistance trooper

Representing Ematt's improvized ground forces on Crait is an unnamed Resistance trooper. He has a peach-colored face under a transparent-yellow visor, stubble, and ammunition pouches strapped to his torso. His new green helmet has a removable chin guard.

General Caluan Ematt finds himself fighting against the odds, in charge of the Resistance troops in the Defense of Crait (set 75202). He has always been a soldier, first fighting with the Rebel Alliance from its early days and now with the Resistance. He and his troops must hold off the First Order for as long as possible to give the Resistance time to escape.

DATA FILE

YEAR: 2018
FIRST SET: 75202
Defense of Crait
NO. OF SETS: 1
PIECES: 4
ACCESSORIES:
Blaster rifle, electrobinoculars
APPEARANCES:
VII, VIII

Defense of Crait (set 75202)
Troops are limited, so the General himself is down in the trenches carved into the crystalline rock of Crait. He stands on the gun emplacement, controlling the stud-shooter on the rotating turret.

Digital electrobinoculars reduce the glare on Crait's salt flats

Waterproof and insulated jacket in olive green

Harness with pouches of ammunition is worn slung over Ematt's shoulder

White hair
Ematt is the only LEGO *Star Wars* minifigure to have this hair in white. It is used in dark orange for Obi-Wan Kenobi and in black for Ezra Bridger, a child Boba Fett, Kylo Ren, and Baze Malbus.

Drawing on the technology of the Empire, the First Order has built a large fleet of armored walkers that use brute force as well as firepower. One is the heavy assault walker, which is piloted by a specialist trooper. His gray coloring is similar to the Imperial AT-AT pilot minifigure, but he has the updated and unmistakable look of the First Order.

Micro-scale
The minifigure driver can turn his hand to piloting both the huge walker, with more than 1,300 pieces, and this tiny one from Ski Speeder vs. First Order Walker Microfighters (set 75195).

Heavy Assault Walker (set 75189)
The huge, armored walker stomps its way across the planet of Crait to crush the Resistance. One walker driver minifigure pilots it, supported by a stormtrooper.

Distinctive gray flash

Helmet shape is the same as the First Order snowtrooper, whereas AT-AT pilots have stormtooper shaped helmets

Gray jumpsuit is not seen on any other First Order trooper

DATA FILE
YEAR: 2017
FIRST SET: 75189
First Order Heavy Assault Walker
NO. OF SETS: 2
PIECES: 4
ACCESSORIES: Blaster pistol
APPEARANCES: VIII

Back in action
Like old pals Lando and Chewbacca, this brick-built Corellian freighter is a little worse for wear, but it can still complete the Kessel Run in 12 parsecs . . . probably. One thing is certain, these two minifigures still know how to pilot the iconic ship in *Millennium Falcon* (set 75257).

In his younger days, Lando Calrissian fought against the Empire. Although he does not battle against the First Order on the frontlines, Lando fights for what is right. Lando's distinguished new minifigure is ready to help the Resistance stop the First Order in any way he can—even if that means jumping back into the pilot seat of his late best friend Han Solo's *Millennium Falcon*.

High collar
Lando's minifigure wears a new cape in *Millennium Falcon* (set 75257). The high collar is similar to that on the short cape that young Lando wears in Kessel Run *Millennium Falcon* (set 75212). However, this new cape is longer.

New hairpiece for Lando with a swept-back look

This is the first Lando minifigure to show flecks of gray in his printed mustache

Cape consists of two pieces—a collar and the cape itself. Each fastens to the minifigure's neck separately

Trellgar silk dress shirt

Charging holster for Lando's blaster

Lando Calrissian
RESISTANCE ALLY

DATA FILE

YEAR: 2019
FIRST SET: 75257
Millennium Falcon
NO. OF SETS: 1
PIECES: 6
ACCESSORIES: Blaster, cane, communicator
EPISODE: IX

After Luke Skywalker becomes one with the Force, General Leia Organa takes over Rey's Jedi training. When the Resistance learns of a First Order threat, Leia gives Rey permission to look for clues on the planet Pasaana in order to stop the First Order. Rey's minifigure is dressed for desert conditions with all-new torso and leg printings.

Transport speeder
Rey and astromech droid BB-8 speed around Pasaana on this skimmer. Can they outrun the First Order treadspeeder that comes with this set?

Printing shows Rey's freckles

Bindings keep out sun and sand on the desert world of Pasaana

Rey
JEDI STUDENT

DATA FILE

YEAR: 2019
FIRST SET: 75250
Pasaana Speeder Chase
NO. OF SETS: 1
PIECES: 4
ACCESSORIES: Blue lightsaber
APPEARANCES: IX

Furrowed brow
Rey's double-sided head appears with all of her minifigures to date. The printed wrinkle between her eyebrows shows that she is often in worrying situations.

Capelet printing extends to legs

New printing shows Rey's cropped pants

After the death of Supreme Leader Snoke, Snoke's apprentice, Kylo Ren, becomes the Supreme Leader of the First Order. Completely loyal to the dark side of the Force, Ren will stop at nothing to maintain absolute power. His minifigure in Kylo Ren's Shuttle (set 75256) demands allegiance with his restored Knights of Ren helmet and impressive black cloak.

Command shuttle

Supreme Leader Kylo Ren travels around the galaxy in his trusted shuttle. In Kylo Ren's Shuttle (set 75256), he can scare off Resistance fighters with spring-loaded shooters.

Hard hat

In *Star Wars: The Last Jedi*, Kylo Ren breaks his helmet after becoming angry. Although it has been repaired, the helmet doesn't look quite the same. Printing shows where the minifigure's helmet is rejoined.

Mark showing where helmet has been repaired

Cloak also appears with Kylo Ren's minifigure in set 75179

Lightsaber blade can be removed from the hilt

DATA FILE

YEAR: 2019
FIRST SET: 75256 Kylo Ren's Shuttle
NO. OF SETS: 1
PIECES: 5
ACCESSORIES: Red crossguard lightsaber
APPEARANCES: IX

KYLO REN SUPREME LEADER

The First Order has an army of soldiers that draw power from a dark and ancient legacy: the Sith. Although Sith is in their name, this group of elite soldiers has no dark side Force powers. Sith troopers are specially trained in secret. They are equipped with high-tech armor and weapons to help the First Order in its quest to control the galaxy.

Sith soldiers
These Sith troopers appear in 2012 and 2013 sets based on characters from the video game *Star Wars: The Old Republic*. According to legend, these faceless troopers protected the Sith Empire rather than the First Order like the Sith trooper below.

DATA FILE

YEAR: 2019
FIRST SET: 75256 Kylo Ren's Shuttle
NO. OF SETS: 1
PIECES: 4
ACCESSORIES: Modified blaster rifle
APPEARANCES: IX

Sith Trooper
CRIMSON WARRIOR

T-shaped visor looks similar to a clone trooper's

Wireless data antenna

Sloped helmet deflects blaster bolts

High-resolution electroscope

Power cell ammunition

High-tech
Sith troopers carry ST-W48 blasters. These high-tech weapons include many functions. This LEGO blaster rifle comes with a removable red bar so the Sith trooper can modify his blaster as needed.

Resistance Y-Wing Starfighter (set 75249)

Poe is an excellent X-wing pilot. He learned to fly with a band of pirates known as the Spice Runners. In this set, Poe's old Spice Runner friend Zorii Bliss zooms back into his life in a modified BTA-NR2 Y-wing starfighter.

The most daring pilot in the Resistance, Poe Dameron, is on a new mission. His previous minifigures have been seen wearing his signature flight gear—his black leather jacket or the orange Resistance pilot jumpsuit. In Resistance Y-Wing Starfighter (set 75249), Poe's minifigure dons a new outfit that lets him get to work outside of his usual X-wing pilot seat.

DATA FILE

YEAR: 2019
FIRST SET: 75249 Resistance Y-Wing Starfighter
NO. OF SETS: 1
PIECES: 4
ACCESSORIES: Silver blaster pistol, satchel
APPEARANCES: IX

Removable satchel not molded to torso

Breathable micromesh shirt for adventuring outside of an X-wing

Runyip-leather pilot gloves

Glie-44 blaster pistol

Leather straps hold equipment such as his blaster pistol

Poe Dameron
DARING ADVENTURER

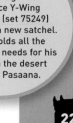

Brand new bag
Poe's minifigure in Resistance Y-Wing Starfighter (set 75249) comes with a new satchel. The bag holds all the supplies Poe needs for his mission on the desert planet of Pasaana.

Index of Minifigures

Senior Editor Tori Kosara
Senior Designer Lauren Adams
Pre-Production Producer Marc Staples
Senior Producer Lloyd Roberston
Managing Editor Paula Regan
Design Manager Jo Connor
Art Director Lisa Lanzarini
Publisher Julie Ferris

Additional text by Hannah Dolan, Clare Hibbert, Tori Kosara, Shari Last, and Victoria Taylor
Designed for DK by Lisa Sodeau
Additional minifigures photographed by Gary Ombler

Dorling Kindersley would like to thank Randi Sørensen, Heidi K. Jensen, Paul Hansford, and Martin Leighton Lindhardt at the LEGO Group; Troy Alders, Chelsea Alon, Leland Chee, Jennifer Heddle, Pablo Hidalgo, and Michael Siglain at Lucasfilm; Nicole Reynolds at DK for editorial assistance, and Megan Douglass for proofreading.

First edition published in the United States in 2011 by DK Publishing
Revised edition published in the United States in 2015 by DK Publishing.

This new edition published in the United States in 2020
by DK Publishing
1745 Broadway, 20th Floor, New York NY 10019

Manufactured by Dorling Kindersley
One Embassy Gardens, 8 Viaduct Gardens, London, SW11 7BW
under license from the LEGO Group.

Published in Great Britain by
Dorling Kindersley Limited.

A catalog record for this book is available from the Library of Congress.

ISBN 978-1-4654-8956-2
978-1-4654-9164-0 (library edition)

Printed and bound in China

www.dk.com

MIX
Paper | Supporting responsible forestry
FSC™ C018179

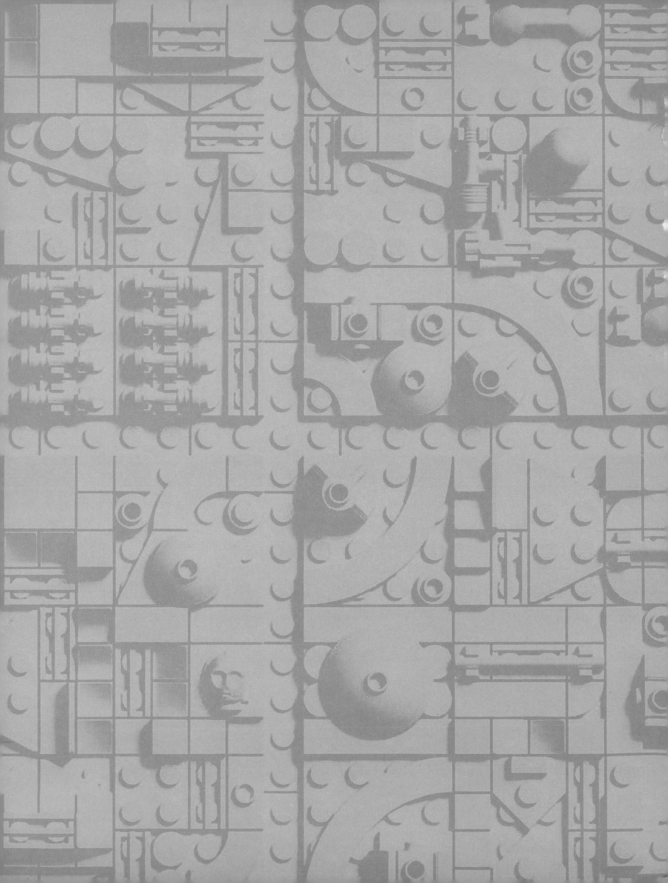